# In the Light of

# MADNESS

## Hemmie Martin

Winter Goose Publishing
2701 Del Paso Road, 130-92
Sacramento, CA 95835

www.wintergoosepublishing.com
Contact Information: info@wintergoosepublishing.com

In the Light of Madness

COPYRIGHT © 2013 by Hemmie Martin

First Edition, November 2013

Paperback ISBN: 978-0-9894792-9-5

Cover Art by Winter Goose Publishing
Typeset by Odyssey Books

Published in the United States of America

Also Available By Hemmie Martin:

*The Divine Pumpkin*
*Attic of the Mind*

*To Andy*
*With best wishes*
*Hemmie*

*To DI Andy Yeats, of the Metropolitan Police Service
for his unwavering enthusiasm and patience in answering
all my police and crime related questions*

*I thank you deeply*

# Chapter One

Gravestones jutted out of the ground like candles on a birthday cake. They marked an occasion in a person's life, but were ultimately forgotten once the ceremony was over.

"What have we got, Boss?" DS Jacob Lennox asked, stepping inside the newly erected white tent to stand next to DI Eva Wednesday.

"A boy, early- to mid-teens. At first sight seems to have no visible injuries and no obvious cause of death. Edmond will tell us more just as soon as he gets here and does a preliminary assessment."

Looking down at the boy, it occurred to Wednesday that she was old enough to be his mother. The thought sent a frisson down her spine as she tucked a loose strand of chestnut hair behind her ear.

"Who called it in?" Lennox asked, noticing his new boss had an ethereal quality about her in the white-paper forensic suit.

"An anonymous male from the payphone in the market square."

There was no ID on the victim, but a young lad had been reported missing earlier that evening by an anxious father, and the victim appeared to match the description.

Through the gloom, Wednesday saw a bald man of stocky build, wearing a tweed jacket with leather elbow patches bend down to pass beneath the crime scene tape. There was something reassuring about the pathologist Edmond Carter; rather like a favourite uncle who always had intriguing stories to tell, and who could make a grazed knee feel better. Following him was the forensic photographer, Marcus Drake. Marcus was slim with a thin face; his jet black hair spiked up with a heavy use of wax.

Wednesday and Lennox stood back whilst Edmond snapped on some latex gloves and set to work. Marcus took a couple of scene shots, sending pin-pricks of dazzling light orbiting around their eyes.

"Was he suffocated?" she asked Edmond as he shuffled around the body.

"In the first instance I'd say that's a strong possibility. I'll check for fibres in the cavities back at the lab. No obvious external injuries except for bruising around the mouth and nose." He let out an audible sigh and stood up to let Marcus document the victim *in situ*.

"Time of death?"

"I don't think rigor mortis is going to be a reliable concept if the body's been out for hours in this cold. I'll have to do a battery of assessments and tests; you know, post mortem, blah de blah." Edmond often interjected his sentences with the word *blah*. Wednesday believed it was because he could not be bothered to converse with the living; preferring the frozen silence of the dead.

"I know you people don't like to be pushed, but an approximate time would give us a vital start," said Lennox, his voice resonating powerful calmness.

Edmond raised his bushy eyebrows that compensated for his bald head. "My preliminary estimate on liver temperature would be between seven and eleven p.m."

"I'll get a family liaison officer to meet us at the parents' house," Wednesday said, putting a call through to the station.

"You'll have to direct me; I'm still not used to the scenic borders of Cambridge," Lennox said.

Wednesday glanced back to see the boy's lifeless form being placed in a body bag, whilst Lennox remotely unlocked his black Ford Mondeo and climbed into the driver's seat.

The interior of his car was pristine, with the faint smell of leather lingering in the air. She knew he smoked but clearly not in his car. A pity, she thought to herself, as she really wanted one before talking to the family.

Lennox pressed his fingers into the steering wheel as he drove along a narrow hedge-lined lane to the neighbouring village of Lavendly

They pulled up outside a tiny cottage, illuminated in every window, and found the family liaison officer was waiting for them.

Knocking on the front door, Wednesday inhaled deeply, letting the air drift slowly out through her nostrils. A tall man with a pallid, drawn face answered the door; his expression fell further at the sight of them. He was a mirror image of the dead boy.

"Mr James Dolby? I'm Detective Inspector Wednesday, this is Detective Sergeant Lennox, and this is the family liaison officer, DC Janice Parker. May we come in please?" she said, trying not to let her voice betray her inner emotions.

As they stepped inside, a frantic woman appeared behind James Dolby, shrieking for her son. He ushered them in quickly before catching his wife in his arms. He had anticipated the hopelessness they brought with them.

The couple were older than Wednesday had imagined, and the house had a musty smell, reminiscent of her grandmother's house.

Inside the slightly antiquated, but nevertheless comfortable lounge, was a wood burning stove harbouring the remnants of glowing embers. Motes of dust caught the light and danced around like a parade of fairies. A row of Toby jugs hung on the chimney breast, and a large ceramic figurine of a spaniel sat on the hearth.

James Dolby guided his wife, Emily, to the sofa where she grabbed a cushion and clutched it tightly over her abdomen.

"You've come about Tom, haven't you?" he asked as he looked anxiously towards his wife.

"Yes. I'm afraid we've found a body matching your son's description. May we sit down?"

The man extended his arm towards the chairs, but remained standing. Wednesday noticed a photograph of a boy dressed in Markham Hall school uniform on the mantelpiece, and she was in no doubt that the dead boy was their son.

"Is he going to be okay?" asked Emily meekly, clearly not registering Wednesday's words. Her wide eyes betrayed her.

"I'm sorry, the young boy matching Tom's description was found dead in the cemetery in Barksbury."

Emily covered her face with the cushion to muffle her wailing. Her chest heaved violently as her husband sat down, placing a protective arm around her shoulder and drawing her into him. Fat drops of salty tears dribbled silently down his ashen cheeks.

Wednesday watched the scene unfold, digging her nails into her palms. She sensed Lennox watching her out of the corner of his eye.

"Our boy, our dear little boy," whispered James Dolby.

"May we offer you our sincere condolences," Wednesday spoke with genuine feeling.

"You found him in a graveyard? How did he die?" James asked, dabbing his face with a crisp white handkerchief.

"We're working on it, sir. We're still gathering evidence," replied Wednesday, who was beginning to wonder if Lennox was ever going to join in.

In a telepathic triumph, Lennox let his deep, soothing tone waft into the atmosphere.

"We know this is a very difficult time for you both to answer questions, but we need to move as fast as possible. The first few hours are vital. We'll need to see his bedroom, if you don't mind."

Lennox nodded to the family liaison officer as she entered with a tray of tea for the parents. Wednesday retrieved her notebook from her bag and tapped her front teeth with a pen until both parents had sipped the proverbial hot sweet tea.

"Do you know where Tom was last night, and with whom?" she asked.

They looked at one another with penetrating eyes.

"He just said he was meeting up with Darren and that he wouldn't be back late." James's voice was quiet, requiring Wednesday to sit forward in her seat.

"Are you sure it's him, you might be mistaken," blurted out Emily with a glimmer of hope in her eyes.

"We'll require a formal identification of the body, but it doesn't have to be you, it could be another relative." Wednesday waited for the words to register in Emily Dolby's mind before continuing. "We'll also need Darren's address."

James Dolby rose and picked up the address book, flicking through the pages then handing it to Wednesday.

"Could you tell us what kind of boy Tom was?" asked Janice Parker.

The parents looked at one another, then Emily finally spoke.

"He was quiet and kind. He was never in any trouble, you know. He didn't drink, smoke, or do drugs." Her face shone as she talked about him. She sipped some more tea from the cup she was nursing in her hands.

Wednesday thought how often she had heard bereaved parents say similar things about their child; almost chapter and verse. All that was missing was the silent Amen.

"He was a bit of a loner, except for seeing Darren. They'd been sort of friends since primary school." Emily drifted off momentarily, clearly remembering the past and savouring the closeness of Tom's spirit in the room. Parker placed her hand on top of Emily's clenched fist, encouraging her to talk.

"We weren't keen on him being friends with Darren; he has an unsavoury home life." She blew her nose before continuing. "His brother's in prison for assault, and the stepdad can be a nasty piece of work, too."

"Was Tom bullied at school?"

"Not that we know of."

Wednesday and Lennox quietly excused themselves to take a look at Tom's room, leaving the couple in the capable hands of Parker.

His room was what they expected for a sixteen-year-old boy; black bedding and furniture. Scattered on the floor was an assortment of socks, trainers, and crumpled up computer magazines.

"We'll take the laptop for technical support to have a look at. We might get some clues from his MSN pages, or whatever it is they're into these days," said Lennox.

He was methodical in his examination, but Wednesday could not help feeling overwhelmed with the poignant sadness of the room that would never be used again by the boy.

"Finished?" he questioned as he observed her rigid stillness.

"I've got a couple of notebooks from his bedside table which might prove useful," she replied, slipping them into an evidence bag.

Returning to the lounge, they found the group sitting in solitary contemplation. Lennox gave James Dolby an evidence slip for the laptop and notebooks before making eye contact with Parker so she knew what he was going to say.

"We'll need someone to identify the body now," he asked, rising up and down on the balls of his feet.

"I'd like to go now," answered James Dolby in an almost inaudible tone.

"I need to go too," implored his wife, displaying her tear streaked face for all to see.

"Okay, Janice will take you and we'll meet you there."

Wednesday and Lennox sat quietly in his car for a few seconds before he started up the engine.

"They seem like a normal functioning family," she ventured as he reversed the car.

"Perhaps substitute normal for dull. It was hardly an inspiring environment for a teenager," he replied, driving off to follow the patrol car. He noticed curtains twitching as they headed off down the road.

Wednesday wondered what he would make of her family home, with its eclectic mix of hand-thrown pottery and hand-painted canvases. If he saw that, would he perhaps expect her to wear tie-dyed maxi dresses with coloured braids in her hair, rather like her own mother, who was far from dull in so many ways.

Twenty minutes later, they arrived at the police station in Cambridge. Sending Lennox to the incident room, Wednesday played with the packet of cigarettes in her pocket before following the shuffling parents towards the mortuary.

The parents' anguish clung to the air as they stood behind the large glass window overlooking the stark white room. A metal gurney where the body lay stood in the middle, covered by a crisp green sheet.

Wednesday gave the nod to the mortuary assistant who peeled back the sheet to reveal the peaceful looking boy.

"He . . . He looks asleep," whispered Emily Dolby.

"Is this your son?" Wednesday asked gently.

"That's our boy," replied James in a breaking voice. "How did he die?"

"We're trying to determine that, sir."

"Did he suffer?"

"There are no visible wounds or abrasions. The pathologist's report will tell us more. I'm sorry I can't be more precise."

"Who would do that to our son?" he said, looking directly at Wednesday with his sunken eyes; his skin translucent.

"We don't know yet. I am truly sorry for you both," she said, placing a hand on Emily Dolby's arm in a symbolic gesture.

"I want to kiss him goodbye," she said, turning around to face Wednesday. "I have to say goodbye to my baby."

Wednesday could feel the sensation of tears welling behind her eyes. Her throat constricted as she escorted the pair into the room. She then moved to stand with the technician close to the wall, leaving a respectable distance between themselves and the parents, in order to give some semblance of privacy for their last family moment. Wednesday found the montage painful to witness.

Slowly, the parents drew away from their only child; their arms outstretched in a vain attempt to magically make him rise up from the table.

Janice Parker escorted them out of the room to the sound of Emily Dolby sobbing into her hands, whilst James Dolby looked like a walking spirit roaming the dark arena called limbo. Wednesday asked for the parents to be escorted home and for Parker to remain with them if they so desired. The parents nodded dolefully and moved stiffly down the corridor. As they reached the door, James turned around.

"You will catch them won't you, DI Wednesday? I couldn't go on living knowing that justice wasn't done for my boy."

"We will do our upmost, I can assure you, Mr Dolby," she replied softly, as she handed him a card. "If you think of anything else, please contact me on this number, anytime." A smile felt inappropriate so she inclined her head as they moved away.

She noticed how tired and old the pair suddenly looked as they drifted through the doorway, a cloud of sorrow hanging over them.

With a deflated heart, she went to the Incident Room to hook up with Lennox.

# Chapter Two

It was the early hours of the morning, and they knew that Darren's parents were not going to appreciate the untimely call. However, they needed to get as much information from Darren about Tom's last whereabouts as soon as possible.

The address was in the same village as the Dolby's but at the opposite end. The not-so-affluent end. Lennox pulled up outside the house that was in complete darkness.

Wednesday felt emotionally weary and did not relish breaking the news to a young person that his friend, perhaps his only friend, was dead.

They walked up the front garden which was crowded with overgrown shrubs. Lennox tripped on a raised slab on the pathway.

"Bloody hell," he snapped under his breath.

Wednesday sensed fatigue was unravelling his composure. He rang the doorbell several times before a light came on. They were both poised with their IDs on view in the hopes of placating the occupants.

The door was wrenched open and a towering man with the stature to match that of Lennox, stood before them in baggy boxer shorts and an off-white vest. A snarl ripped across his face and his eyes darted between the pair. Lennox explained the reason for their visit so he reluctantly let them in.

"Judith," he hollered up the stairs, "it's the police. They want to talk to your Darren."

The three of them stood in the cramped and cluttered hallway listening to the creaking floorboards above, accompanied by swearing as a door opened.

Wrapped in a grubby towelling bathrobe, Darren's mum sauntered heavily down the stairs bringing with her the unmistakable stench of cheap wine.

"He's not in his room," she said, slurring her words as she clung to the banister.

"Are you Darren's mother?" Wednesday enquired.

"Yep, I'm Judith Wright. This here is Des, Darren's stepdad."

"If Darren's not in his room then where is he?" Lennox asked, wondering why parents allowed their teenagers to roam freely without knowing their whereabouts.

"No idea. I thought he was in bed," she said before licking her dry lips with a furry tongue.

Wednesday and Jacob eyed one another, then she took the lead.

"This is very important, Mrs Wright. It's imperative that we find Darren, can you think of anywhere he might be?"

Judith shuffled on her feet, then crouched down to sit on a step, allowing the dressing gown to reveal a blotchy pink, dimpled thigh.

"He's probably round that Tom's house. His mum is a stuck up old cow, always looking down on us. Beats me why the boys are friends."

Wednesday bit her bottom lip, allowing her time to compose her words before answering.

"I'm afraid Tom has been found dead. So you can see why we urgently need to speak to your son. Can you contact him on his mobile?" She rolled on the balls of her feet in order to alleviate the cramps in her calves.

"What's the stupid bugger done now?" bellowed Des, lighting a semi-smoked roll-up which he held between his grubby-nailed fat fingers. He inhaled and then blew the smoke out so it swirled around the naked light bulb suspended from the ceiling.

"Have you any idea where your son and Tom were supposed to be or who they were meeting?" Terseness reverberated through Lennox's voice.

"His mobile's switched off," Judith uttered.

The Wrights looked at the detectives with their dulled eyes.

"God knows then. Anyway, isn't it your job to go looking for him, that's what you lot do all the time, isn't it?" Des spoke, smoke seeping from between his lips.

Wednesday could sense Lennox's hairs on his neck bristle, so she interjected. "May we take a look at Darren's bedroom? We might find some clues to his whereabouts."

"Suit yourselves," replied Judith, standing up and brushing past Wednesday as she headed for the kitchen.

Before they moved upstairs, Lennox asked the pair about their whereabouts that evening.

"Why, are we suspects?" replied Des with a semi-smirk on his lips.

Lennox just stared at him until he told the detectives he'd got paid for a labouring job, so they were celebrating with a fish supper and some alcohol at home.

Des led the way, mounting the stairs two at a time. On arriving on the landing all the doors were open so it was obvious which room was Darren's. Wednesday wrinkle up her nose at the distinct smell of urine on entering the room.

"Bunk beds," said Lennox. "Probably for the brother in prison." He gave a guttural snort after his comment.

The bedroom was unkempt and filthy like the rest of the house. It was, indeed, making them wonder what Tom and Darren actually had in common. It certainly wasn't their family background or lifestyle.

Tucked into the corner of the room was a piece of furniture that resembled a desk, piled with scrap paper and a laptop. Lennox picked it up and tucked it under his arm.

"Anything else of interest?" he asked

"Not that I can see under this jumble. I just want to get out of here," she said in a hushed tone. "I'm beginning to itch."

They took one final look around the sorry state of Darren's bedroom before heading downstairs.

"You can't fucking take that," exclaimed Des as he pointed a sausage-like finger at the laptop.

"I'm afraid we can, there may be information pertaining to Darren's whereabouts and who he was meeting. You'll get it back. For now I'll give you an evidence receipt." Lennox raised his six-foot-two frame to dominate Des, whose veins were throbbing in his temples and neck.

"His dad got it for him. You lose or damage it and you get another," piped up Judith into the glass tumbler, making her voice echo.

"If Darren returns or contacts you, please get in touch with us straight away," said Lennox, handing a card to the puffy faced mother. He avoided eye contact with the stepdad. "It would be helpful if we could have a recent photo of Darren for the officers who'll be looking for him."

Judith Wright lumbered off towards the kitchen and returned with the latest school photo of him. Wednesday noticed how Darren's face did not have the innocent appeal of Tom's.

She strode after Lennox as he gunned towards the car, avoiding slamming the car door as he had done. Nicotine cravings were ravaging her mind, so when Lennox reached for a packet of cigarettes in his glove compartment, a sense of relief washed over her. He brandished the packet in front of her, not knowing whether she smoked or not.

"I don't normally smoke in the car, but needs must," he said as he flicked the lighter and lit the cigarette. He turned the engine on and sped towards the station. "It beggars belief. One family is torn apart by grief for their dead son, and the other family show no bloody concern for their missing son who could also be dead."

He wound down his window to allow the noxious fumes to escape. Wednesday mirrored his actions, inhaling the smoke with grateful, guilty pleasure, whilst reflecting on the night's events so far.

"We might as well get a few hours sleep before visiting the school tomorrow morning," she said, flicking the cigarette butt out of the window without thinking, before they entered the station car park.

She levered herself out of his car, every muscle in her body crying out for bed. Her brain, however, was re-examining the interviews.

She walked towards the cream convertible VW Beetle she had bought herself as a gift when she became a detective inspector. As she turned on the purring engine, she pushed in a classical CD and let Beethoven's piano concerto accompany her home. Tomorrow would hopefully bring more clues and not just more unanswered questions.

# Chapter Three

Wednesday opened the front door and crept in quietly so as not to wake her half-sister, Scarlett. They shared the three bedded, detached Georgian property on the outskirts of the city of Cambridge. The house belonged to Wednesday. Scarlett was her lodger.

She removed her shoes and padded along the parquet floor to the kitchen. The room was swathed in comforting warmth thanks to the Aga that sat in a recess. A large scrubbed pine table and chairs, and a carver chair at the head of the table sat proudly in the centre of the room.

Wednesday poured herself a bourbon and lit a longed for peaceful cigarette. Grotesque images of the past few hours played in her head, and her heart felt loaded with the parents' pain. She knew she was too sensitive for the job at times. But she didn't want to change the essence of her being.

Wednesday was up and out before Scarlett had risen, which was not unusual. Breakfast was brief before climbing into her car. She relished being enclosed in her own private space, but the journey was not long enough to either unwind from a hellish shift or prepare for the next onslaught.

She pulled into her space and noticed that Lennox was already there. She had heard he sometimes slept in his office in his previous post, so it puzzled her how he remained so immaculately presentable. Perhaps his recent divorce suited him, she thought as she mounted the stone steps into the station.

She had never worked on a case with him before but she understood that he was quietly persistent and methodical, whereas she tended to be more organic; less regimented and meticulous, but got results all the same.

She arrived in the Incident Room in time to hear DCI Hunter announce that he was calling a briefing in two minutes. Suzy Simmons tapped Wednesday gently on the arm and asked her if she wanted a coffee.

"Yes please. Milk no sugar," she replied with a nod as she took her notebook out in time to hear Hunter clapping his hands to bring the room to his attention.

On the incident board behind him were pictures of the dead boy, Tom Dolby, and the missing boy, Darren Giles. The stare of youthful innocence penetrated the room. The murder of children always rocked the team hard.

"Right, preliminary findings indicate that Tom Dolby was asphyxiated, most likely smothered by some form of clothing. It stands to reason that he may have been drugged as there's no evidence of a struggle. No DNA under the fingernails or defensive wounds on the hands. We're waiting for toxicology. For now we have bugger all to go on." He took a sip of strong black coffee whilst the room remained tacit and focused.

"SOCO are at the cemetery now and a fingertip search is underway. Wednesday and Lennox will go to the school where both boys went. Arlow and Damlish can head up the team to search for the missing boy, Darren Giles, and I'll prepare a statement with the chief press officer for the media. Right, let's get to it, we need a lead."

The Incident Room erupted into a hive of activity, each officer keen to find the breakthrough needed in the first forty-eight hours. All keen to impress Hunter.

"Shall I drive?" Wednesday asked.

"Mind if I do? I think more clearly when I drive."

Walking in his wake, she was slightly overpowered by his musk aftershave. She hoped her own perfume was masking her cigarette stench just as successfully.

Markham Hall School was nestled in an expanse of neatly trimmed grass, with wooded areas to either side. It was an imposing building with the semblance of a fortress. It used to be an all boys grammar school, but it was now a mixed comprehensive, much to the annoyance of the elders in the town and surrounding villages.

Clusters of students dribbled their way to the main entrance, unaware of the devastating news they would soon be privy to.

"Would you take this interview, Boss," Lennox announced as he pulled into a parking space. "You've got the air of an all girls grammar school about you."

"Is it that obvious?" she replied, blushing slightly.

He remained mute, rubbing his hand through his spiky hair, making the ends stand to attention. Surreptitiously he checked himself in the rear-view mirror before getting out of the car.

Being in plain clothes meant the students were not fazed by their arrival. If anything, the pair looked more like a visitation from OFSTED. Entering the double doors, they were jostled by a few boisterous lads playing rugby with someone's rucksack. Wednesday heard Lennox mutter something under his breath.

"We're looking for the headmaster," announced Lennox to the woman sitting behind the reception hatch. She peered over the glasses on the tip of her nose. Her white hair clung to her scalp in tight curls.

"Is he expecting you?"

They retrieved their ID cards from their pockets and flashed them at the unflappable woman.

"I see," she said, still unmoved. "I'll phone through."

Within seconds, a suave man of slim build with slicked back hair arrived.

"I'm the headmaster, Stewart Cleveland. How can I be of assistance?"

"Could we have a word in your office, Mr Cleveland?"

With a shrug of his shoulders and a raise of eyebrows, Stewart Cleveland guided them down a corridor.

The opulence was apparent as soon as they stepped through the heavily studded door. A large walnut desk housed a laptop and a set of Montblanc pens. His chair, which looked rather like a throne, was made of green leather and swivelled around so he could survey every angle of the room. Tennis courts could be seen through the leaded windows behind his desk.

"I'm sorry to inform you that one of your students was found dead last night. His name was Tom Dolby."

"Dead? How?"

"We're not sure exactly. And Darren Giles is missing."

Cleveland's face visibly drained. "Good God, I've never had this happen before."

"We'd like to know more about them; their friends, teachers, any problems at school."

Cleveland swivelled towards his computer and pounded on the keyboard.

"Not much to say really. Tom was a bright lad who was heading towards uni. Generally quiet with no behavioural problems reported. Darren was the exact opposite." He swivelled around again so he was facing them once more, cupping his hands together and resting them on the leather-bound blotter on his desk.

Wednesday scanned the plethora of silver framed certificates hanging on the wall, all embossed with his name.

"Perhaps their form tutor would be able to tell us more," she suggested.

"Indeed, that'll be Colin Pollock. I'll take you to him." Cleveland stood up and ushered them out of his office.

They followed him down a corridor lined with framed photos of sports teams, music and drama clubs. The air was stale and reminded Lennox of his own miserable school days. The hairs on the back of his neck bristled with the memories.

Cleveland showed them into a classroom where Colin Pollock sat at the front of the class at a desk on a plinth, marking papers.

"Colin, this is . . ." he waved his hands about as he struggled to remember their names, so Wednesday took over.

"DI Wednesday and DS Lennox. We're investigating the death of Tom Dolby, and the disappearance of Darren Giles."

Colin Pollock stopped writing and looked over to them in numbed silence.

"Good God . . ."

"In order for us to thoroughly investigate the issues, we need to know more about them. Who were their friends and who were their enemies?" Wednesday asked, gripping her notebook.

Colin cleared his throat and loosened the knot in his tie.

"Tom was quiet but he had a good sense of humour if you spoke to him on a one to one." He rose from his chair and walked over to Tom's desk. "He sat here, next to Dylan Frost. They spoke to one another, but I'm not sure you'd call it a friendship. Maybe just a convenience as they sat together." A thin line of sweat sparkled on Colin's top lip.

"Did he ever mention if he was being bullied?"

"No, not that I know of," he said, bowing is head and shoving his hands in his trouser pockets.

There was a knock at the door and a few faces peered through the glass panelled door.

"It's time for registration, can they come in?" he asked.

Wednesday nodded. "We'll need to speak to his friends and class-mates, then see his locker, so we'll need to use your office," she said, turning towards Cleveland.

He made an audible sigh before ushering them out of the room as the students stood back, wide-eyed and chewing gum; a rebellious move in front of the head had it been a normal day.

One by one, the students entered Cleveland's office looking fearful, anxious, or arrogant. Lennox particularly despised the last trait as he was getting enough of that from his own two sons. They remained stunned or silent when they were informed of Tom Dolby's demise.

Dylan Frost entered looking the picture of calm.

"What was Tom like to talk to?" Wednesday asked, pen poised before her lips like a cigarette.

"All right I suppose," he replied, cocking his head at her.

"What did you talk about?"

"Football mostly."

Wednesday could sense Lennox's irritability at having to sit through yet another dead-end interview. She was finding it difficult to imagine him as a father.

"Did you ever meet up with him out of school?"

"Not likely," he said rather abruptly before blushing wildly. Wednesday sat back and studied him carefully.

"Is there something you want to tell us, but aren't sure how we'll react? We're not here to judge you. We want to find the person who did this to your friend."

"He wasn't my friend. He was a geek with old people as parents. He was a loser and I only spoke to him because we sat together in form." Dylan slouched down in the chair as soon as he had finished spouting the words, scuffing the toe of his shoe into the deep pile carpet.

"Is that what everyone thought about him?"

"Yep."

"What about Darren Giles? They were friends weren't they?"

"I dunno. Darren was a loser too; I mean have you seen his parents? They're like gypos," he replied, standing up swiftly, ready to go.

Wednesday could not deny that Dylan's description of Darren's parent's hit close to the mark. But she still flinched at his words.

"If you think of anything else, no matter how insignificant you think it may be, call me," she said as she handed him her card, which he promptly shoved into his blazer pocket.

They watched the boy swagger out, leaving the door swinging wide open behind him.

"Arrogant arse," Lennox muttered.

"Not all kids are like him."

"I know that, but I fear my two are going to turn into his type." He looked down at his shoes and pursed his lips.

By the time they had interviewed the entire twenty-nine surly or overly animated students in Colin Pollock's form, they were exhausted and no closer to discovering more about the two boys, except that they appeared to be misfits and not well liked.

"I think we need to re-visit Tom's parents. They may be more emotionally stable to talk now," Lennox said.

Somehow, Wednesday doubted that. The Dolby's may not welcome the police's presence in their home, as that would make their nightmare real.

Stewart Cleveland gave them a frosty look when Lennox announced he could have his office back after showing them the inside of both boys' lockers. They followed him towards the cloakroom area where he opened them.

Tom's locker contained a pack of football stickers, a local map, a French dictionary and a packet of cheese and onion crisps. They bagged the contents and then moved onto Darren's locker. There they found a smelly sports kit, some school books, and an appointment card to meet the school counsellor at the end of the week. Again, the contents were bagged to take back to the station. After giving Stewart Cleveland an evidence slip, they returned to the car.

Lennox leant forward and delved into the glove box to retrieve a packet of cigarettes. He helped himself to one and then indicated to Wednesday to help herself. She frequently toyed with the notion of quitting, but as Lennox smoked, she thought it would be near impossible.

"We need to concentrate our focus on Tom Dolby. The Giles boy smacks of a runaway teen from a hellish home." Lennox did not look at her as he spoke.

"I hear what you're saying, but I sense a link. A boy goes missing the same night his friend is found murdered." Wednesday twirled strands of hair around her finger whilst she savoured the smoke.

Lennox inhaled deep into his lungs and then breathed the smoke out through the crack of the open window. "We've got to call in to see the reverend at the church first then we'll go back to the Dolby's. No point in putting it off. By the way, did you get anything from Tom's notebooks?"

"I haven't had time to check them. I'll glance at them now."

She thumbed through the dog-eared pages. Page after page she read scribbled ramblings about "eternal light," and saw drawings of eyes placed all over the pages. She came across one page that had the word "hate" scrawled all over it. He had pressed so hard with the pencil that the word was indented on the following four pages. The other notebook contained nothing but a list of songs and a few mathematical problems that were scribbled out.

"For a young person with a seemingly normal home life, he was certainly full of anger about something."

"Maybe the parents weren't telling us everything about their little angel."

"Sometimes, there's never enough truth," Wednesday replied as she closed the notebooks.

# Chapter Four

Reverend George Olong placed the receiver back in the cradle before heaving a sigh. His mop of curly grey-flecked hair bounced around as he made his way to his study, where his wife, Vera, was placing a tray of mid-morning tea and biscuits on his desk.

"Something wrong?" she asked as she saw his face drain of colour.

"That was the police. Young Tom Dolby was found dead in the cemetery late last night. They're crawling all over the grounds right now."

He put two lumps of sugar in his teacup and slowly stirred the steaming liquid. He breathed out heavily through his flaring nostrils.

"I'll need to visit the Dolbys and go to Markham Hall to counsel the students. This will rock the community." Absentmindedly, he munched on a digestive biscuit whilst words of condolences and soothing phrases swarmed around his mind. He didn't notice his wife leave the room.

He was composing a speech for the Dolbys when the doorbell rang. He heard Vera's footsteps heading for the front door. Hearing voices he braced himself for the visitors he sensed were heading his way.

"George, this is DI Wednesday and DS Lennox."

George stood up and proffered his hand. "You've come about young Tom, I presume," he said as he waved his arm to encourage the pair to sit. "Can we offer you a tea or coffee?"

The pair declined.

"We're sorry about the disruption to the church grounds. Give it a couple more hours and you'll be able to enter the church again," Lennox said as he sat back in the chair.

"Were you both here last night?" queried Wednesday.

"We're both out on Wednesday evenings. I teach Lay preachers in the next village, and Vera leads choir practice in the village hall. We both get in around ten."

"So neither of you heard nor saw anything out of the ordinary last night?"

The reverend and his wife looked at one another before shaking their heads in unison.

"It's common knowledge that the vicarage is empty on a Wednesday evening. Besides, with the tall hedge between us and the church, we can't see what goes on there." Vera's voice wasn't as soft as Wednesday had expected, even though the job had taught her never to expect or assume anything.

"Did you know Tom Dolby well?"

"Indeed we did. He attended church most Sundays with his parents. They'll be devastated," he shook his head slowly.

"Did he seem troubled lately? Or changed in any way that concerned you?"

Both George and Vera shook their heads symbiotically.

"He seemed interested in a group I was trying to set up for the local young people."

"Group?" reiterated Lennox showing too much cynicism in his voice which the reverend picked up on.

Red faced, he continued the conversation. "Yes, there's not much for the young to do around here, unless they train into Cambridge. Anyway, I'm trying to start up a rambling club. The church has even paid for a hut that's nicely nestled in the woodland area."

Wednesday and Lennox eyed one another.

"Could you tell us precisely where the hut is?" Wednesday asked, monitoring her tone of voice and pacing the urgency.

"I can do better than that, I'll take you there. George should really visit the Dolbys," Vera offered, as she mimed to her husband that he should get going.

"One last thing before we go," asked Lennox, reluctant to be pushed around by Vera. "Do you know Darren Giles? He appears to have gone missing."

Vera put both hands to her face as she took a sharp intake of breath.

"Murder and now a missing boy. All this will destroy the sense of security amongst the parishioners," she uttered.

Neither of them had any information about Darren Giles, so Wednesday placed her card on his desk before following them outside.

The vicarage garden had a semi-wilderness about it. Clearly money was not squandered on hiring a regular gardener. They walked along the narrow pavement, passing the cemetery where the white tent and crime scene tape still remained, incongruously. Rows of officers were on their knees undertaking a fingertip search of the area.

"Is that where he was found?" Vera asked in a hushed tone before putting her hand to her mouth. Wednesday nodded and placed her hand under Vera's elbow to guide her past the macabre scene.

After walking through dense woodland for ten minutes, they arrived at a small clearing where the newly erected hut stood.

"My husband is devoted to the parish. This rambling club idea was intended to give the young people something constructive to do, whilst getting them interested in nature," she said as she opened the unlocked door and stepped inside.

Inside, the hut smelt of new wood, and the windows still had protective tape on them. Their footsteps and voices echoed in the sparse space where only a rectangular table stood, surrounded by eight chairs.

"Has this place been used yet?"

"The club hasn't officially started, but it's not for the want of trying on his behalf," she said as she glanced around. "He mentions it every Sunday in church and advertises it in the fortnightly parish magazine." She stood by the window and gazed at trees. "I think it's a waste of time, but George has always loved working with young people."

Wednesday said nothing whilst taking notes.

"Tom and Darren showed interest in the club, so George brought them to see this," said Vera as she waved her arm around the space.

"When was that?"

Vera suddenly seemed hesitant. "I don't know. You'd have to ask him."

"We will," replied Lennox.

Whilst searching around the hut, Wednesday spied a cocktail stick on the floor which she picked up and put in an evidence pouch.

"What was that?" asked Vera.

"Looks like a cocktail stick. It's probably nothing," she replied, putting it in her bag.

Reverend George Olong drove his burgundy Volvo estate to the Dolby's home. It was his first experience of dealing with a murdered adolescent and fear was pounding in his ears.

James Dolby opened the door, his face speckled with stubble and his hair desperately in need of a brush. George sensed the oppressive and airless atmosphere as soon as he stepped inside.

Dolby led him to the kitchen where he switched on the kettle in an automatic action.

"I'll make it," said George, wishing to feel useful in some way as he suspected that spiritually, James Dolby was beyond help at that moment in time.

"My wife's in bed. The doctor gave her a sedative."

George nodded. "And how are you holding up?"

"I'm living in a nightmare that I'll only wake up from when Tom walks through the front door."

George nodded again as he poured two cups of tea.

"The whole community feels your suffering, and God is reaching out to embrace your pain—"

"Don't talk to me of God. What God would allow such an atrocity to occur? I am too full of pain and anger to accept God's so-called love."

George did not blame him and knew that part of his role was to mop up the out-pouring of grief. God would have to take a backseat for a while.

The next time George looked at the clock on the buttercup yellow wall, he saw that he had been there for an hour and a half. The kitchen table was covered in photograph albums and school certificates, mapping out the short life of a much loved son.

He was contemplating an appropriate way to depart when the doorbell rang. James Dolby eased himself out of the chair and shuffled to the door; he'd aged twenty years over night, thought George.

Wednesday and Lennox were standing at the door. Dolby stood to one side to let them in just as George was heading out.

"I should leave you to get on. I'll call you tomorrow," he said as he squeezed passed the detectives, nodding at them as a parting gesture.

The detectives could see the remnants of Tom's life littered across the kitchen table, but there was no time for sentimentality.

"Were you aware that Tom wanted to join a rambling club the reverend was trying to set up?" asked Lennox, glancing at Tom's school photos.

"Yes," he nodded. "The reverend had a keen interest in Tom as he thought he was a good example to other boys with his good manners and all that."

"Did the reverend see much of Tom then?"

James frowned at Lennox. "Not sure what you're getting at."

"We're just trying to piece together Tom's habits and the people he interacted with. We're building a profile of him."

Dolby's shoulders drooped and his head dropped forward as though his neck could no longer support it. "He attended church with us every Sunday. He also spent time at that Darren's house much to Emily's disapproval, and he saw the reverend occasionally about church matters or the rambling club. Tom liked to be helpful to others."

"Church matters. What would they be exactly?"

"The reverend wanted Tom to be an altar boy, but he was worried that word would get out, and that he'd be bullied at school for it."

"I see," said Lennox, brushing his hand over the top of his head, intertwining his hair through his fingers.

"Mr Dolby, I read your son's notebooks and he seemed to be quite an angry boy." Wednesday looked directly at him and tilted her head. "Do you have any idea what that was about?"

"Just teenage angst, I imagine. I don't know what he had to be angry about."

The nineteen fifties style home for starters, thought Lennox to himself. Wednesday seemed to hear his words and chastised him with her eyes.

"Did you or your wife have many arguments with Tom?" she asked.

"No more than any other parent I shouldn't think. Why, are you accusing me or my wife of killing our son?" His voice vibrated with an undertone of anger.

Wednesday stuck her hands out with the palms down, indicating the need for calm. "Mr Dolby, we sometimes have to ask painful and difficult questions, it's part of our job. I'm sorry if I've offended you."

Dolby slumped into a kitchen chair and buried his head in his hands. "I just want this intense pain to go away. I feel so powerless."

Lennox tapped his foot lightly. "Mr Dolby, can you think of any incident where Tom complained of being bullied, harassed, or frightened by someone in or out of school?"

Dolby shook his head, and spoke into his hands, muffling his words. "Although my wife doesn't want to admit it, he had changed somewhat. He was less . . ." he searched for the right word. "He was less affectionate towards us."

Lennox thought the word "affectionate" was an odd way to describe a teenage boy. Even his parents, who were both psychologists, never referred to teenage boys in such terms. He remembered many intellectual arguments between his parents. His mother took a systemic viewpoint, whereas his father preferred the Jungian standpoint.

"Would you like the FLO, Janice, to come and stay with you? She would be someone to talk to whilst your wife is sedated."

Dolby shook his head slowly. Lennox tried to hide his disappointment. Parker may have got more information out of him.

The detectives showed themselves out and headed back to the car.

They had only reached the end of the road when a call for assistance came in from DS Arlow. They were in a potentially volatile situation with an aggressive Des Wright. Wednesday radioed in that they were close by and on their way. Lennox put his foot down.

# Chapter Five

Approaching the front door, they heard Des Wright's enraged voice bellowing at the officers. Lennox decided that knocking first was not a prerequisite, so they marched straight in to find the commotion coming from the kitchen. The sound of splintering wood ripped through the air.

Both Wednesday and Lennox braced themselves. To Wednesday's surprise, Lennox's voice became the dominate force in the house.

"Mr Wright, what exactly is going on here?"

"What the fuck? How many more of you are needed to take me away?" His face was puce and spittle gathered at the corners of his mouth.

"I'd rather not waste my time taking you anywhere, unless you've hurt an officer," Lennox replied in an even tone as he glanced around to check on his colleagues. Everyone appeared fine albeit on high alert. Stillness descended on the group while an electric tension coursed through the air. Broken pieces of chair lay scattered around the floor.

"These fuckers think I've done something to Darren," he blasted, pointing at Arlow and Damlish with a nicotine stained finger. "Just because I said I didn't care for him much and because of these bruises," he pointed to under his chin and his hands, "which I got outside the bloody pub." His face glistened and his eyes darted from one officer to another.

Wednesday and Lennox noticed green and blue tinged marks on his arms, too. They could see his jaw muscles twitching but at least the glare in his eyes was subsiding.

Wednesday turned her attention to Judith Wright who was sitting impassively at the chipped Formica table, hands trembling and the broken thread veins on her cheeks and nose glowing brightly.

"We're doing everything we can to find your son," said Wednesday, sitting down next to Judith. "You must be feeling very anxious."

"She don't feel nothing. Alcohol has dulled her senses," interjected Des without a nuance of compassion. Judith looked up at him with her bloodshot eyes, but said nothing.

Lennox advised Des that he could either finish answering the questions there, or he could do it at the police station. He said it in such a way that Des knew he had no choice.

Wednesday noticed holes and dents in the walls and doors. If she was not mistaken, they were battle scars of domestic violence. She felt a rage brewing in her gut. "Would you like us to move to another room whilst they talk to your husband?"

"I ain't got nothing to say to you. Just 'coz you have a posh suit and hair trussed up like a ballet dancer doesn't mean you're better than me."

Wednesday was stunned by Judith's ascorbic words whilst subconsciously touching the loose tendrils around her face; she wondered whether Judith was masking her fear of Des behind a barrage of insults. Before she had the chance to process her thoughts, Des began shouting again.

"There's fucking four of you here. Who's looking for Darren?"

Lennox tapped his fingers on the table and took a deep breath before addressing the irate man. "Mr Wright, I must ask you to stop swearing at us or you'll be arrested. Now there's a team out searching for Darren with sniffer dogs. He hasn't been forgotten about."

Des leant against the wall and stared out of the window, the redness in his face fading.

"Now so far, nothing has been found untoward on his laptop and I understand his mobile is switched off," said Arlow, visibly more in control of his emotions. The dark circles of being a first-time father hung heavily below his eyes.

The detectives finished their interview, collating names, dates, and times relating to Darren. Judith Wright watched their every move with her bloodshot eyes.

Back at the station, the phones were incessantly ringing with people reporting sightings of Darren, all of which had to be sifted through by the indexers, Suzy Simmons and Audrey Smith. Thus far, none of the sightings had resulted in a positive outcome.

DCI Hunter was sitting in his office, rubbing the back of his neck when he saw Wednesday and Lennox return. He beckoned them into his office with a wave of his hand.

"Bring me up to speed," he said, tension cramping his neck and shoulder muscles.

Wednesday took out her notebook. "Forensics' preliminary report indicates that Tom Dolby was asphyxiated by smothering. They'll give us fibre clues later. No signs of sexual assault." She looked up to see that Hunter was still listening. "Tom's mother is sedated and his father is distraught. No obvious evidence of foul play in the home . . ."

"That's as may be, but we need to bear in mind that the victim often knows their killer. We must consider that someone placed an anonymous phone call and laid the body down with care," interjected Hunter, drumming his fingers on his desk. "Someone close to him."

Lennox ran his hand over his hedgehog-like hair. "We've just come from Darren Giles's home. The stepdad was getting wound up by the journalists outside his house. He has a temper and fresh bruising on his neck, arms, and hands."

"So why hasn't he been brought in?" Hunter's tone was not easy on the ear.

Wednesday could feel her neck going red and instinctively put her hand to her throat. Out of the corner of her eye she saw Lennox remaining cool and collected in the face of adversity.

"There's insufficient evidence that he's done anything wrong, sir. And besides, Darren fits the profile of a runaway." Lennox's voice sounded composed as he spoke.

Wednesday fidgeted in her chair which caught Hunter's attention.

"Did you have something to add?" he asked her.

"Only that Reverend Olong seems to be keen on setting up a club for the local youths. And he apparently had a special interest in Tom."

Hunter's brow furrowed. "You're not pointing down the route of child abuse and the clergy are you?"

"Not particularly, especially with no signs of sexual assault. I was just highlighting facts. Also, there may be a case of domestic violence at the Wright's, but I need to see whether previous reports have been logged." Wednesday sat back in her chair and began tapping her hand on her knee.

"So the only thing linking these two boys together is some semblance of friendship, the same school, and an interest in joining a rambling group. That's not much to go on."

The room fell silent until Hunter slapped his palm on the table and announced he wanted them to dig deeper at the school. The detectives rose and left Hunter as he began to make a phone call. Lennox followed Wednesday to her cluttered office, which he found visually uncomfortable.

"Are you always that nervous in front of Hunter?" he asked.

Wednesday brushed back strands of hair that had worked their way loose from the bun. "I didn't know that I was."

"Oh come on; blushing, red neck, foot tapping. Need I go on?"

"That won't be necessary thanks. I'll phone the school and let them know we're coming." She picked up the receiver and dialled, ignoring Lennox and hoping he would leave the room. As he reached the door, he turned.

"He's married, but not happily according to rumours." He grinned and ducked as she threw a pencil at him.

After speaking to the belligerent school secretary, Wednesday wondered whether she was going to like working alongside Lennox. "Only time will tell," she muttered to herself as she grabbed a chocolate bar from her desk drawer and went off in search of him.

"He's having a cigarette break in the courtyard," Simmons said as she saw Wednesday scanning the room. With a nod of acknowledgement, she descended the stairs and exited through the rear door that led onto a very uninspiring courtyard, enclosed by the brick walls of the station. A few scattered pots filled with last year's dead summer plants were no cause for celebration, and a tiny over-head piece of plastic sheeting protruding from the wall provided minimum shelter.

She retrieved a cigarette from the packet, lit it, and then sauntered towards Lennox who was perched on the only bench. He was gazing up at the thick cloud that had formed a mantle above his head.

"You've calmed down I see," he said, looking at her with an unmistakeable twinkle in his hazel eyes.

"Just because I'm single, doesn't mean I fancy every man I come into contact with," she snapped—more than she intended to—before inhaling deeply on the cigarette.

Lennox made a humming sound and flicked some ash onto the ground. "So no light banter between us then?"

"You don't do light banter. You like to embarrass a colleague you hardly know. We're also on a case that's depressing and going nowhere."

Lennox sucked in air through his teeth but remained mute, which piqued Wednesday more.

"Anyway, I don't think you'd like it if I assumed that just because you're divorced means you see every woman as a potential date."

"Actually, I wouldn't mind that. And potentially they are, don't you think?"

Wednesday got up sharply and stubbed her cigarette out into the wall mounted ashtray. "We should be going. I'm driving."

She did not see Lennox smiling behind her as she marched to the car park.

"Nice car. Very you," he said as he climbed into the passenger seat of her cream VW Beetle convertible.

"Thanks, I think," she replied, setting her car in motion.

The journey to Markham Hall was conducted in stony silence. Lennox planned the imminent interviews by flicking through his notebook and Wednesday gripped the steering wheel, focusing on the road.

As they drove up the gravel driveway, to the left they saw a group of boys playing rugby, and to the right a group of girls playing Lacrosse.

As their windows were wound down slightly, they could hear the male sports teacher hollering abuse at the sportingly challenged youths.

"He's got a voice that carries," commented Lennox.

They made their way into the building, where the receptionist waved a bony hand in the direction of Stuart Cleveland's office.

"Detectives, to what do I owe this pleasure?"

"There's no pleasure in our visit, Mr Cleveland. As you are aware, one of your students has been murdered and another one is still missing," Wednesday informed him. "We think it would be useful to address the whole school, including the teachers, about the boys. It might jog someone's memory. Any small detail they might have thought inconsequential could open up the enquiry."

"It's not very convenient right now," he replied, looking down his arched nose. "We could arrange it for tomorrow?"

"No, Mr Cleveland, this is too serious to put off. For all we know, the same fate that happened to Tom may be awaiting Darren."

Cleveland inhaled deeply before phoning through to his secretary to round up all the students and teachers into the main hall. The detectives heard the woman's irritated tone on the other end which only seemed to exasperate Cleveland more.

It took twenty-five minutes for the hall to fill with curious and excitable students, followed by harassed teachers. In the far corner of the hall, Wednesday spotted Reverend Olong trying to merge into the shadows.

Wednesday relaxed when Lennox said he would address the gathering after noticing her twisting her hair tightly around her middle finger. She admired Lennox's composure for public speaking.

Most of the students had heard the news already, but Lennox was careful to remind them that they should all be cautious when out. He made a strong request for information regarding the two boys.

After his speech, they watched the subdued students file out, followed by pale-faced teachers. His words seemed to have had the desired effect in reaching the teenage brains. They now hoped someone would come forward with a snippet of information that would prove to be a lead they required.

Wednesday scanned the room to see that the reverend had already disappeared. Never mind, she thought to herself, he will save for another time.

They sat in the only available room, the nurse's room, awaiting any students who would hopefully have something to impart.

The nurse had been amenable in relinquishing her work space, and had even made them a mug of instant coffee which they gratefully sipped.

Just as they began wondering if they were wasting their time, there was a tentative knock at the door and a teacher entered the room. He stood before them in black chinos and a beige roll-neck jumper. Thick round-rimmed glasses framed his treacle-coloured eyes.

"I'm not sure if I'm wasting your time," he began.

"We'll be the judge of that, Mr?" Wednesday said.

"Mr Cannon. Harvey Cannon. I'm a French teacher."

His name duly noted down, she waited for him to continue.

"I know that Tom Dolby had been experiencing some difficulty in PE lessons with Mr Gould. Saying it aloud sounds a bit foolish and melodramatic now," he said faintly.

"Could you expand on that, Mr Cannon?" Lennox said, wishing to move things along.

"Well, Mr Gould seemed to dislike Tom. Perhaps because he was slightly overweight. Anyway, sometimes he would make Tom do PE in just his boxer shorts merely to show the other boys what their bodies would be like if they didn't exercise."

"Were Mr Gould's actions reported to the head?"

"I had a quiet word with Tom, but he insisted I didn't report it to the head nor his parents, come to that."

Harvey Cannon looked at the detectives briefly then scratched his chin. "I'm only telling you this as I believe Mr Gould to be a bully and I felt you should be aware of the matter. What you do with the info is up to you. Just leave my name out of it."

"Indeed," Lennox finally said, tipping back in his chair so he was looking down his nose at the teacher.

An awkward hush enveloped the group until Wednesday thanked him for taking the time to come and see them. He nodded in her direction, pointedly avoiding eye contact with Lennox before walking out into the bustling corridor.

"Well Hunter's going to be ecstatic. This was a bloody waste of time. All we got was some in-house gossip from some flaky teacher." He shoved a pencil in between his lips.

"We can't disregard any info given to us at this stage. I mean, if this Gould is a bully, who knows what he could do if he lost control? We'll talk to him."

"How come this Gould's temper is worse than that of Des Wright?"

Wednesday tapped her foot rapidly on the floor. "I haven't ruled him out for Darren's disappearance, but I can't see his motive to murder Tom."

"Let's suppose Darren caught Des suffocating Tom during a moment of rage. Darren was then either killed at the same time and his body hidden, or Darren did a runner through sheer terror." Lennox lolled backwards and rested his head in his hands.

"I can't think in this room that stinks of vomit and antiseptic," she replied, shoving her notebook in her bag. "Let's go and find Mr Gould."

They found him in the staff room drinking from a bottle of water and reading a newspaper.

"Mr Gould, DI Wednesday and DS Lennox. We'd like a word about Tom Dolby."

He looked at them briefly before returning to the paper, saying he had no information for them.

"We were rather interested in your attitude towards Tom during your PE sessions."

"Who's complained?"

"Were you not always professional?"

"I used him to show the other lads what they'd be like without sport and exercise in their life. He was the kind of boy to run away from the rugby ball, not towards it. I didn't beat him or even touch him. Every student will vouch for that."

"We'd still like your personal details to keep on record whilst this investigation is ongoing."

He begrudgingly relinquished his details before flexing his biceps and getting up.

"Just because I used him as an example, doesn't mean I killed him."

Lennox nodded, feeling the pressure of getting nowhere fast crushing his torso.

"There must be something or someone we've overlooked," he said as they stepped outside into the crisp autumnal day. He turned his collar up and headed towards Wednesday's car.

She drove them back to the station to the melodic strains of JS Bach. Lennox was right, she mused, we are missing something.

# Chapter Six

Pulling into the station car park, they saw Arlow and Damlish escorting a bloody-nosed Des Wright inside.

"Now what's happened?" she asked Lennox who was already half way out of the car before she had pulled on the hand brake.

She hurried behind him, almost receiving the main door in her face.

"Manners," she snarled, even though she knew he could not hear her.

Des Wright's raised voice was heard emitting from the interview room; every expletive ripped through the flimsy walls.

"What's going on?" Lennox asked a passing officer in the Incident Room.

"He assaulted a journalist outside his house, so the DCI wanted him dragged in here."

Lennox raised his eyebrows before moving towards his office. Wednesday caught Suzy and Audrey performing a mock swoon. *God, they all fancy him.*

Hunter rapped on Wednesday's door before marching straight in. He stood over her desk as she was about to write up her report.

"You've heard Arlow and Damlish are about to interview Des Wright, I suppose?"

"Yes Guv. Apart from the assault, have we got much to go on?"

"You're not convinced about his involvement in all this, are you?"

Wednesday shuffled around in her chair. "I'm more convinced about him being a violent man towards his wife and possibly to Darren."

"So in your mind, Darren's a runaway?"

"It seems too coincidental that something happened to both boys on the same night, unless of course, Darren was actually involved in Tom's murder?"

"All this supposition is getting us nowhere. I want you to accompany me to see Judith Wright whilst she's on her own; we might get more out of her without her husband around. See you in five," and with that, he left her office leaving a subtle scent of musk in the air.

Wednesday put her cold hands to her burning cheeks as Lennox's words trundled through her mind. Gathering her things together, she took another chocolate bar from her desk drawer, guessing that a more substantial snack looked unlikely for the next few hours.

Following Hunter out of the Incident Room, she deliberately avoided eye contact with Lennox, even though she could sense his mocking eyes boring into her.

Hunter rang the doorbell a couple of times before a shadow moved towards them through the bubble-glass panel. Judith Wright opened the door, reeking of alcohol.

"You brought my Des home?"

Hunter introduced himself and reminded her of Wednesday before saying it was her they had come to see. Judith passed a derogatory glance in Wednesday's direction and then stood back to let them in. Wednesday noted that she did not ask if they had found her son.

They followed Judith into the kitchen where an open bottle of cheap German white wine stood on the table next to a mug with a chipped rim. Judith picked it up and took a swig.

"We're still looking for Darren and we wondered if you'd had any more thoughts about his possible whereabouts," Hunter said.

Judith looked at him with a vacant stare.

"Perhaps without your husband around, you could speak more freely about your concerns," said Wednesday, trying to appeal to Judith on a woman-to-woman level.

"Are you married?" Judith slurred.

"No, I'm not."

"Well then, what d'you know about anything? I can speak freely in front of my Des. I've just got nothing to say to you."

"You don't seem overly concerned about your son's welfare. Has he run away before?" continued Wednesday, undeterred.

"No he hasn't. This isn't some kind of shit-hole he hates, you know. You're all the same, just because we ain't educated like you, you think I'm a crap mum . . ." She stopped mid-flow to take another sip, visibly shaking as she did so.

"I'm sorry if we've given you that impression. We need to find out as much as we can about the background and home life of a possible run-away. Have you any family close by that he may have gone to?" Hunter spoke calmly, giving her constant eye contact.

"No. Now when are you bringing my Des back?"

Wednesday decided to pursue her preferred line of enquiry.

"Mrs Wright, please don't take offence, but I've noticed some signs of violence around the house. Is your husband aggressive towards you?"

Judith laughed manically, lolling her head backwards so the fillings in her back teeth were displayed.

"For the police, you have very little idea about the goings on in life. No wonder you can't find Darren." Her eyes began watering with the mirth that had taken hold of her, and only after taking a sip of drink did she calm down.

"Are you saying, Mrs Wright," said Hunter, "that the violence in this household stems from Darren?"

Wednesday and Hunter eyed one another as Judith let out another stream of cackling sounds. Wednesday could see that he was not amused, and for a man of a mere five-foot-seven, the power of his voice was imposing.

"Mrs Wright, I'm unaware of anything to laugh about. Your son is missing; his best friend has been murdered; your husband has been arrested and you are clearly drunk during the day. What may I ask is so funny?"

His words reverberated around the unkempt room, and for the first time during their visit, Judith Wright sat in shocked silence as his words penetrated her alcoholic smog.

"Now think hard if you will. Where was Darren going that night?

Perhaps he left some clues you didn't pick up on straight away." Hunter's stare brought a flush of colour to her insipid cheeks.

"He spends quite a lot of time at that Tom's house, and sometimes they're here, cooped up in Darren's bedroom. Des thought it was a bit un-natural like. He wondered if they were queer. He could've been with Tom last night . . ." she faltered as the words finally reached her addled brain. "Hell, you think my Darren killed that lad don't you?"

She became agitated and aggressive, forcing Hunter to rise from his chair, informing her that if she did not calm down, they would have to continue the interview at the station.

"We're looking for Darren as we're concerned about his welfare. We're not hunting him as a potential murderer," interjected Wednesday. "Was your husband ever violent towards Darren?"

"I keep telling you, I don't know where Darren is. And no, my Des was never violent towards him. He may not amount to much, but he ain't that bad."

Real emotion appeared to be surfacing, and Wednesday felt a pang of pity for the woman and her sad dysfunctional life.

"What about drugs or alcohol? Where you aware of Darren using any substances?"

Judith's gaze dropped to the floor, clasping her trembling hands in her lap.

"I know he's partial to taking a few cans of beer each week from Des's stash. I think he and Tom drank it in the woods. I don't know about drugs."

Hunter rolled his eyes. "Mrs Wright, how would you feel about doing an appeal on local TV for the safe return of your son?"

Wednesday gave him a sideways glance, wondering how they were going to dry her out enough to give a coherent interview.

"I'll have to have my Des with me. I ain't doing it alone."

"That shouldn't be a problem. I'll need to arrange it and then an officer will bring you to the station. DI Wednesday will tell you what it entails." He finished speaking and rose to leave.

They left Judith clutching her mug of drink and staring at the floor. Her belligerent demeanour had diminished, and she looked a pitiful sight.

Wednesday followed Hunter down the path as he tripped over the same loose slab that Lennox previously had. Wednesday smiled to herself.

Des Wright had calmed down in the interview room. Damlish had got him a cup of tea, and Arlow was looking over the notes he had already taken when Des was highly agitated.

"Mr Wright, would it be fair to say you have a temper which you can't always control."

Des looked him directly in the eye. "And what if I have?"

"Well, your stepson is missing and we might be wondering whether you have anything to do with his disappearance. So, instead of seeing us as the enemy, clarify things for us."

Des puffed out his chest as his jaw muscles pulsated rapidly.

"I keep telling you people that I don't know where the little sod is. I don't know and I don't really care." His voice sounded strained and his eyes crackled with fire.

Arlow straightened up in his chair. "Your words are telling us one thing, but your nonverbal is saying something else."

"What the fuck is 'nonverbal'?"

"Nonverbal communication is your body language. You seem nervous and it looks like you're hiding something. You're not telling us the truth. It would be better for you to come clean now, it would look better in court."

Des Wright's ability to remain calm expired. He stood up, grabbed hold of the table then tipped it up with such force that the officers barely had the time to get out of the way. Arlow pressed the panic button on the wall, and within seconds four more officers entered the room and had Des Wright on the floor in a control and restraint hold.

But Des Wright was strong, and as he undulated on the floor, the officers looked like they were riding a bucking bull. Hunter bounded into the room and bellowed out for order. Des's aggression subsided as he remained on the floor panting and exhausted, but still angry.

"Mr Wright, you're in serious trouble. Now sit down and calm down, otherwise you'll be put into a cell until you do." Hunter's voice was full of power that transgressed Des's fury and permeated every pore of his sweaty body.

He was hoisted up and shoved back down into his chair by two officers. Their hands remained clamped onto his shoulders in readiness for any further outburst.

"Now, Mr Wright, what exactly is going on here?" Hunter said.

"They won't believe me; they won't believe that I've got nothing to do with Darren being gone."

"Maybe your demeanour is suspicious, Mr Wright. We are concerned for Darren's welfare and perhaps the officers don't think you are worried at all."

Des let out a deep sigh, putting his hands on the table, palms up so they looked like slabs of fatty ham.

"I don't know where he is. He uses the house like a hotel, comes in for food and then buggers off out. Judith is usually too drunk to notice and I don't much care." Des then looked Hunter square in the face. "You may think I'm an uncaring bastard and because of that I would harm him, but that's not true. You've no proof so you can't keep me here."

Hunter knew he was right. They had no evidence to link him to the disappearance. Hunter felt frustrated, and the pressure from his boss was weighing on his shoulders. He decided to leave his detectives to finish the interview as he was running low on patience and ideas.

Marching back to his office, he demanded that Wednesday join him straight away.

"Right Wednesday, I want you and Lennox down at the forensic labs, we need leads and we need them fast. Des Wright isn't letting up; he's hiding something so we'll have to keep an eye on him."

"You want surveillance on him?"

"Maybe not around the clock, but a patrol car up and down his street enough times to unnerve him. He needs to know he's not off the hook."

Wednesday nodded then turned to leave; she really wanted to get home a bit earlier to see Scarlett.

"Oh and Wednesday," he said as she was almost out the door. "Get some bloody leads. The press will castigate us if we don't push on. And make sure the Wrights are ready for their TV appeal."

She left his office knowing that access to her private life would be once again delayed. She strutted over to Lennox's desk and found him stuffing a chunk of fruit cake in his mouth. She informed him of Hunter's orders as he stood up and brushed crumbs from his trousers before descending into the bowels of the building.

Wednesday always found the descent into the laboratories and mortuary sinister, as the stench of death pervaded the corridor and every corner of every room. In her dreams she sometimes saw her own body on a gurney.

The sight of Edmond Carter in the mortuary always appeased her rising fears. His kindly smile made her feel alive instead of a body of evidence lying on a slab.

A laboratory assistant wheeled out the metal gurney with Tom's body shrouded in a green sheet. As Edmond pulled back the sheet, she felt a shiver run down her spine; the sight of a young person in that situation was distressing.

"What have you got for us, Edmond?" she asked, willing him to have a bounty of leads for her to take to Hunter.

"Still early days, Detectives. Toxicology will still take a few more days. From the absence of markings around the neck, and the bizarre contusions on his upper torso, I'd say we're looking at intense pressure being applied to his thorax."

The stillness of Tom's pale body, illuminated under the glowing, clinical lighting, made Wednesday's own chest feel tight. Her deep sigh did not go unnoticed by Lennox, but Edmond was in full throttle and was busy focusing on the evidence before him.

"There are other obvious signs that go with asphyxia. His face is swollen, and you may notice how his head, neck, lips, and fingers are visibly blue, due to cyanosis."

Wednesday watched Edmond's hands as they lay on the dead flesh, rather like a butcher's hand ready to carve up a carcass.

"And if you look closely, you can observe tiny petechiae in the whites of his eyes, on the outer eye-lids, and around the lips."

"Petechiae?" queried Lennox.

"Ruptured blood vessels due to applied pressure to the area."

Edmond then moved Tom's arm and lifted it up.

"Now, we thought the lad didn't resist. However, we found fibres under his fingernails and inside his nasal passages. I've sent them to be analysed. In his struggle, his front teeth made an imprinted contusion on the inside of his lips."

"This is all fascinating, Edmond. But are there any clues as to the identity of the assailant. You said sexual assault wasn't the motive?" interrupted Lennox, as he rocked back and forth on the balls of his feet.

"No signs. If there had been we may have retrieved some DNA to give us a lead."

Edmond covered Tom's body up again and signalled for the assistant to take him away.

Wednesday thanked him before they left the room. "Let's go and see if Alex Green can offer us anything."

They walked further down the corridor towards the room where forensic scientist Alex Green was hunched over a microscope. Wednesday tapped on the door and smiled as Alex looked towards them.

"I didn't think it would take you long to be beating down the door."

"Alex, I'd like to introduce Jacob Lennox, my new DS."

Alex gave Lennox a guarded look before summarising his findings, which revolved mainly around the fibres and some fine splinters found on the back of Tom's jumper and jeans.

"You're looking for a wool blanket in a green and red colour-way, possibly a travel blanket. We're putting it through the system to find the make."

"And what about the splinters?"

"Again, we're trying to identify the type of wood. However, it all takes time as you well know."

"Unfortunately the DCI and press don't agree. Not with a child murderer on the loose."

Alex shrugged his shoulders and intimated he was going as fast as he could. "I'll call you as soon as I have anything else." He let his eyes linger on Wednesday as she left with Lennox.

"A bloody green and red travel blanket. Is that all we've got to go on?"

"It's still early days, Lennox. Anyway, we've got to get the Wrights ready for their TV appeal, which means keeping the mother away from alcohol for a few hours. God help us."

"What about an appeal from the Dolbys?"

"Too soon. The mother is medicated to the eyeballs. Their turn will come. Mr Dolby has written a statement for the press to be going on with," she replied as they entered the Incident Room.

She approached DS Maria Jones who headed up the Incident Room, to inform her of the latest from forensics and that they were heading for the Wright's home.

"Des Wright has been released, but he's still a bit agitated, so be careful," she warned.

"I'll drive," Wednesday said, grabbing her jacket.

"Okay, but can we forego the classical music."

"Heathen," she replied as she closed her office door.

They arrived to discover that Des Wright had already gone out. As Judith was the main parent they wanted to work with, Wednesday thought it made their life easier. She inhaled deeply on noticing Judith's glassy eyes.

"Mrs Wright, the appeal is going out at six thirty tonight, have you had any thoughts about what you want to say?" Wednesday used her gentle coaxing voice to appeal to Judith's softer side.

"I'll tell the silly bugger to get his arse straight back home. He's causing big problems for my Des."

Lennox rolled his eyes and folded his arms.

"That's not quite the appeal we had in mind," sighed Wednesday. "Perhaps you could write down something less confrontational. We want Darren to know he's not in trouble and is welcome home."

"He is in trouble, and I want him bloody home to stop the neighbours sneering at us."

"Then perhaps you need to show a softer side for the media. Let everyone see how much you love and miss your son."

Judith's face creased as she picked up her mug and took a large gulp.

"Perhaps I'll make some coffee," said Wednesday, stomping to the sink to fill up the kettle, aware of irritation trickling down her spine.

"I don't want a bloody coffee, and I don't want you in my house." Judith was on her feet, unsteady and swaying around. The thread veins on her face flushing vivid red.

"Mrs Wright, we know this is a highly emotive time for you, but the need for calm is paramount." Lennox's masculine tone instilled some calm to the atmosphere, although Judith's face was still knotted with anger.

Wednesday made the coffee and placed it in front of Judith. As she tried to remove the other mug, Judith's hand whipped out and gripped onto it tightly. Their eyes locked together.

Twenty frosty minutes later, the front door swung open and Des Wright marched in. Wednesday and Lennox braced themselves instinctively.

"I see you pigs can't get enough of me," he snapped as he reached for his tobacco pouch.

"We're holding a TV appeal this evening," replied Wednesday.

Des let out a staccato laugh which was instantly quelled by a glance from Judith.

"She wants you by her side," continued Wednesday. "Will you want to say a few words?"

"Not bloody likely."

Judith shot Des another heated glance after which he lit his roll-up and strutted out into the overgrown back garden.

"A car will collect you at five fifteen. We'll see you at the station," Wednesday said as she and Lennox left, leaving a mist of much needed sobriety hanging over the kitchen.

# Chapter Seven

"Canteen food doesn't match up to home cooked," lamented Wednesday.

"I don't really cook for myself. I mainly live off ready-made stuff."

Wednesday wrinkled up her nose. "Scarlett is a terrific cook when she has the time."

Lennox tilted his head before forking some more semi-congealed lasagne into his mouth. "What does she do?"

"She's a journalist on the local paper, *The Cambridge Times*."

"God, I deplore journalists. They're nothing but parasitic entities, feeding off the flesh of the dead."

"Sounds like I've hit a nerve."

Lennox sneered at her before wiping his mouth with a serviette.

"You'll get over the fact that she's a journalist soon enough. Most men she comes into contact with fall under her spell."

"I've heard the rumours of her beauty, but it couldn't detract me from the other stuff."

"What d'you have against journalists anyway?"

"They get in the way of a case, they sensationalise the felon and they often make us look like burkes."

Wednesday sipped her orange juice. She could not argue with him as she sometimes had similar complaints herself.

She decided to move the conversation away from her private life, as she always did with colleagues. But doing just that sometimes made her appear aloof, verging on conceited. However, she was not prepared to sacrifice her privacy to be a more affable colleague.

"I'm dreading the Wrights' appeal. I can't see that woman being up to it. Hunter will do his nut if she cocks it up, and he'll blame us," he said, spraying particles of congealed lasagne over the table.

Wednesday concurred, pushing her plate away. "I'm curious about the anger Tom displayed in his notebooks. There was never any mention at the school, or from his parents, come to that." She sat back and spread her fingers on the table.

"You know teenagers; they're full of angst and misery. They've got 'the whole world's against me' attitude."

"I'm sure there's more to it than that. I've got this gut feeling."

Lennox rolled his eyes. "Women's intuition, eh?"

She chose to ignore him.

They cleared their trays and headed for the Press Room, where they were to meet up with the Wrights and Parker. Wednesday had the sinking feeling it was going to be painful watching Judith slur her way through the appeal.

She caught sight of her reflection in a window, and saw strands of hair sprouting out from the bun, giving her a bohemian look. She hurriedly redid her hair as they walked towards the Press Room.

Parker was sitting with the Wrights at the long table. She had provided the pair with a cup of coffee at Wednesday's request. Even though they had had a period of sobriety, Judith still looked inebriated and Des looked bored.

Dave Arlow entered the room and positioned himself at Wednesday's side.

"Just to let you know, Des Wright's story about being in a brawl outside the pub hasn't been corroborated. The landlord wasn't aware of an affray in the car park, so we still don't know where his bruises came from."

Wednesday thanked him and drew a deep breath before addressing the couple. "Okay Mrs Wright, let's run through what you want to say before we start."

"I don't know whether someone has taken him, or whether he has run away, but he's got to come home."

"That's a good start, although perhaps address Darren directly when you look at the camera. Let's try that again."

"Darren, we want you home. You've caused enough trouble, so get yourself home, now."

Wednesday closed her eyes and dug her fingernails into the palms of her hands. She heard Lennox expel a long breath of air.

"Mrs Wright . . . Judith, we don't want Darren to think that he'll be in trouble when he returns home—"

"But he will be," she interrupted. "He'll be in serious shit. He ain't causing me and my Des all this hassle and getting away with it."

Judith became red in the face, whilst Des remained placidly by her side, disengaged from the proceedings. Lennox leant closely into Wednesday so she could feel his hot breath on her earlobe.

"If the unthinkable has happened, and Darren is involved in Tom's death, then after watching this pair, the public may feel poor parenting is a contributory factor."

"God preserve us from that route," she whispered back.

Wednesday bent over the table and wrote a more appropriate appeal on a scrap of paper. Judith read it then shoved the paper back to her.

"This don't sound like me, Darren would know these ain't my words."

"They sound . . . softer, shall we say?"

Judith rolled her eyes, but nevertheless, took the sheet of paper back and read silently whilst mouthing the words. After repeating the action a couple of times, she spoke the words aloud.

"If someone's got Darren, please send him home. We miss him. Please come home, Darren, you're not in trouble. We love you." She put the sheet down on the table. "Do I have to say that last bit?"

"I think it would sound better. It would also look better if you didn't read it."

Judith let out an audible sigh then stared at the paper in her trembling hands.

"I hope her shakes make her just look nervous to the viewers," said Wednesday, quietly.

"Not to those who know her. I'm not sure that Hunter has made the right call on this one."

"It wouldn't be right not to do this."

"But with this pair? You're bound to take Hunter's side, anyway."

The tweak of taunting in his voice riled her. Her cheeks stung with heat as she watched the unsympathetic pair before her.

The doors swung open and in strode the press officer, Dana Booth, followed by the local news crew and journalists. Wednesday saw Scarlett sashay in, her flame-red hair tumbling over her shoulders in pre-Raphaelite curls. They had an understanding not to acknowledge one another at the press meetings, Wednesday felt more comfortable that way.

Dana Booth walked up to Wednesday and gave her a faint smile. "I saw them earlier. Are they any better now?"

"As much as they can be," she replied with a shrug of her shoulders.

The room filled with a low buzz of chatter. The melange of cheap aftershaves and perfumes helped mask the smell of fear and alcoholic fumes radiating from the Wrights sitting at the front of the room. Behind them on a blue board, was a photograph of Darren, and the hotline number for the public to call with claims of sightings or snippets of information.

Noticing Judith Wright's increased tremors, she walked up to her and put a reassuring hand on her arm.

"I don't need pity from the likes of you," she said, whipping her arm away.

She was defensive and agitated, but there was no time to appease her as a hush fell over the room. Booth sat next to Judith Wright and opened proceedings by talking about the missing young person. She placed a gentle hand on Judith's arm, making her forehead crease like parchment paper.

"Darren," she began before glancing down at her note. "We want you to come home. You're not in trouble."

After the incessant clicking and flashes from the cameras, the room returned to stifling silence. Wednesday noticed there was no mention of loving or missing Darren by Judith. It was Hunter's turn to speak, giving the hotline number for the public to use. The press then began hurling questions towards him, and he batted them back saying it was still early days in the investigation.

In truth, the police hoped Darren would reappear in a couple of days, which was a possibility in the case with teenage runaways.

"Is there a connection with Darren and the death of the graveyard boy?" said a voice.

"I'm sorry but I'm unable to comment on another investigation." Booth stood up and led the Wrights away from the glare of the lights. Hunter followed closely behind.

Wednesday recognised Scarlett's voice as the one asking the last question. She could see her sitting next to a rotund reporter, wrinkling up her nose at being rebuffed. Scarlett was used to getting her own way.

Following her gaze, Lennox moved closer to her side. "Something troubling you?"

"No, not really."

The press were on their feet and shuffling out the door.

"That wouldn't happen to be your sister asking that question?"

"Half-sister. And yes that was her."

Lennox let out a low grunting sound and folded his arms. "She looks nothing like you."

"I know."

"I hope she's not going to cause us any trouble."

"No more than any other inquisitive reporter."

"What about insider information?"

Wednesday turned to face him. "That's a line we never cross," she hissed. "I'm going for a cigarette. Join me if you wish."

Lennox watched her strut out of the room with a subtle grin on his face. He liked working with her, even though he already hated her beautiful sister.

Wednesday felt a rush of cold air engulf her as she opened the door onto the courtyard. The harshness of the outdoor security light shone onto the barren space, making the area inhospitable. Igniting the lighter within her cupped hand, she welcomed the heat for the few seconds before her cigarette was lit.

When she heard the door opening behind her, she did not turn around. Instead, she walked over towards the bench and perched herself on the edge. Pulling her jacket tightly around her, she blew a cloud of dirty smoke into the icy air.

"Well, how do you think it went?" asked Lennox as he stood over her.

"Not sure that Judith looked genuinely concerned, and Des was a non-entity. We'll know more after the papers have gone out."

"Depends if the press write favourably."

"If by that you're inferring to what Scarlett may report, then I don't know. She doesn't consult me or ask for my permission before submitting an article."

"Perhaps she should."

"Oh that would go down well, wouldn't it?" Wednesday took a drag of her cigarette before continuing. "You know you haven't even met her yet. You might actually like her; most men do."

"So you keep saying. But I don't think I could ever like a journalist, I never trust them and neither should you. Living with her could compromise your cases."

"In what way exactly?"

"Oh work it out," he replied as he vigorously crushed his partially smoked cigarette under foot. "An alcohol-fuelled evening could loosen your lips, and hey presto . . ."

"You're very quick to judge people. Perhaps we should just write our reports then go home."

Sitting in her car, she pushed in the Vivaldi CD for the drive home; letting the images of the day slowly leach from her mind.

Pulling onto her drive, she saw lights glinting through the stained glass panel in the front door. Scarlett was in and most likely waiting to see her.

Opening the front door, she was greeted by the inviting smell of warming cookies. Scarlett's speciality usually reserved for when she wanted a favour. *Oh how Lennox would crow.*

"Just in time," said Scarlett, bending down to pull a tray of golden cookies from the Aga. "I'll make a pot of Earl Grey to go with these."

"This is a warm welcome. What's the catch?"

"Oh the cynicism. Can't I bake something just for my big sister?"

"No, as it either means you've got some relationship hiccup, or it's something to do with work. Which is it?"

Scarlett was unfretted by the comments. She plated up the warm cookies and brought the pot of tea to the table. Sitting opposite her, she bit into the doughy cookie, leaving crumbs in the corner of her mouth. Wednesday looked at her over the rim of her teacup and admired her Cupid's bow and high cheek bones.

"I bet I'm right that there's a link between the missing boy and the dead boy." Her eyes flashed with excitement.

"You know I can't discuss cases with you. House rules, remember."

"I know, but this is my first major case. This is my chance to show-case my talent. I won't mention you."

"You know that wouldn't make a difference, lots of people know we live together; they'd figure it out instantly."

Scarlett's shoulders drooped but her emerald eyes retained a sparkle. "Perhaps I could take a different angle? I could do an article on you. I could shadow you, that way I'd be open about my source."

"No, this case is complicated enough without you tagging along. Besides, my boss would never go for it."

Wednesday hated to be harsh with Scarlett, and it hurt her to see the disappointment in her perfect face. But rules were rules for a reason; she wanted to keep her personal and work life as separate as possible. Too much could go wrong.

# Chapter Eight

The doorbell rang as Wednesday bit into the last piece of toast with apricot conserve.

"I'll get it," Scarlett called out as she danced to the front door.

She found an immaculately dressed, tall man with sharp hazel eyes gazing at her from the doorstep.

"Detective Jacob Lennox, what a pleasure to meet you," she said as she extended a willowy arm. "I saw you in the press room yesterday," she added in response to his quizzical look.

"I've come to collect Eva, is she ready?"

Scarlett ushered him in and led him towards the kitchen. Wednesday recognised his voice and crammed the last morsel of toast in her mouth, rendering her unable to speak.

"Morning Eva, nice house."

She mumbled a response, spraying a few crumbs onto the Victorian pine table. Wiping crumbs off her chin she turned to observe the ritual that always occurred when any man met Scarlett. They became like courting pigeons, bobbing about and cocking their heads as they chased the semi-reluctant female.

"I'm Scarlett, by the way," she said.

"The journalist . . ." his voice was meaningfully derisory.

"Yes, and I understand you have an acute disliking of my profession. Perhaps I'll be able to persuade you to reconsider." She gazed at him from under her eyelashes then flicked her hair as she left, leaving him irritatingly wanting more.

"I didn't know you were calling," Wednesday said, interrupting his trance.

"I was driving near when the call came in about another body in the woods. I thought I'd save time and pick you up."

They jumped into his car and sped towards the crime scene. Scarlett occupied their minds in different ways, but neither brought her up for discussion.

He parked on the edge of the woodland where they saw flickering flashes of blue lights through the array of established and sapling trees.

Beneath their feet, a thick covering of autumnal leaves stuck to their boots with the morning dew. The air smelt musty, like an attic in an old house, and once again, Wednesday could sense the grim odour of death cloying the atmosphere.

Drawing nearer to the scene, they saw a young male officer bend over next to a rotund tree trunk and vomit onto an earthy mound. His pallid face turned towards them as they approached; his watery eyes full of revulsion and horror.

Edmond Carter and Marcus Drake were already at work on the grim task. Within seconds, Wednesday's and Lennox's eyes were drawn to the wretched scene before them.

Hanging from a solid gnarly tree branch was the semi-naked body of a teenage girl; her body a mass of cuts and bruises in what looked like whip- and baton-like markings. A deep gash had been sliced across her abdomen so some of her intestines were hanging out like Christmas garlands. Her mouth was bulging, clearly stuffed with something then sealed with black masking tape. Her protruding eyes screeched a silent scream of terror.

They stepped onto the plastic stepping-stones to preserve the scene. A harrowing look was etched on Edmond's grey face as he turned towards them.

"Nasty one, this," he said as he took a handkerchief from his pocket and wiped his brow and the top of his bald head. "With luck forensics may get prints from the black tape."

"Do we know who she is?" asked Wednesday, trying not to let the feeling of nausea take over her body.

"The dog walker who found her recognises her as Claudia Edwards. Poor girl attended the same school as her granddaughter; Markham

Hall. Apparently her parents are in London for a couple of days, we're trying to locate them through the Met."

Wednesday could see the dog walker talking to a constable just beyond the cordon. She wore a green Barbour wax jacket and matching hat, from under which her grey hair sprouted out erratically. Her rich black Labrador lay at her side with its chin on her muddy boots. She had a ruddy complexion, watery pale blue eyes, and looked in her early sixties. As the detectives approached, the constable took a step back.

"This is Mrs Rhodes who discovered the body."

Wednesday nodded and introduced herself and Lennox. "We understand you recognise the girl."

"Yes, from functions at the school. She was on speaking terms with my granddaughter. I wouldn't class them as close friends. I remember she always wore her school kilt rather too short. But you know the girls of today."

The woman's face had a frozen look of abhorrence etched on it as she answered the questions. She swayed from side to side and held her finger under her nose in an effort to filter out the stench.

"Do her parents go away often?" continued Wednesday.

"Yes, it's common knowledge. I believe they go to London for a long weekend about once a month." She shrugged her shoulders, until she caught sight of the pendulum body to the left of her once more, making her face turn ashen.

No matter how short her kilt was, she didn't deserve this, Wednesday thought to herself.

"Please leave your contact details with the officer as we may need to speak with you again," she said as she gently directed the woman further away from the scene.

"The common denominator appears to be the school, doesn't it?" Lennox said as he arrived next to her.

"It appears that way at the moment, but it's early days. The bodies, and lack of, seem to be mounting rapidly."

"Have you finished seeing the body *in situ?*" an officer asked.

"Most definitely," replied Lennox, rubbing his hand over the bristles on his head.

Wednesday turned her attention to Alex Green who was scrutinizing the ground.

"We've got some partial footprints in this mossy earth, but so far no evidence of tyre tracks. The victim either walked here or she was carried," he said, preparing to take a plaster cast of the various partial footprints.

A reflective and intense atmosphere shrouded the macabre scene, as two officers brought the dead girl down and placed her in a body bag. It began drizzling, so the team moved fast to preserve the scene as much as possible by bagging and tagging findings. The body bag was placed in the black van and driven away, leaving the shadow of a ghost hanging from the tree.

"Door to door enquiries are being organised; and I suppose this means another visit to that bloody school," Lennox said, rubbing his hands together to fight the cold.

Wednesday called the station to advise them that they were heading to Markham Hall. With a sinking feeling, she knew it was going to be another long day trying to piece together the story unfolding before them.

As Lennox pulled up outside the school, they were aware of a frisson of excitement coursing through the students who were hanging around the entrance. Their identity was no longer a secret so the students knew something else was going on.

The receptionist looked resigned and picked up the receiver as they approached.

"This really is bad timing, Detectives. I have a meeting in fifteen minutes," said Cleveland, looking rather unkempt.

"We apologise, sir, but this is important."

"Isn't it always," he mumbled as he led them to his office.

His desk was littered with papers, and peeking out from under a file was an electric shaver. Cleveland caught them looking at it.

"I got up a bit late this morning," he said, shoving the shaver into his top drawer.

"Another one of your students has been found dead this morning. Her name is Claudia Edwards," said Lennox.

Cleveland visibly shook and dropped into his leather chair, his sweaty palms gripping the arms.

"Now sir, we have two dead students and one missing, all from your school. There seems to be a disturbing pattern immerging, which all leads back to here. Do you have anything to say?"

He sat muted by his state of confusion and shock, his eyes focused on his hands. After a few minutes he replied. "This is a most unfortunate string of events. Any teenagers living locally will naturally attend this establishment. So it's no coincidence, it's just fact."

He pushed himself upright in his chair, suddenly pumped up by defiance. "I can assure you that there is nothing sinister going on at this school."

"Where were you last night?" asked Wednesday, undeterred.

"Me? I was at home all evening," he replied as his gaze drifted towards the window.

"Can anyone corroborate that?"

"No, I live alone. You can't possibly think I have anything to do with all this?"

"We have to keep an open mind. Nothing is ruled out during an investigation."

Cleveland ran his hand over his bristly chin, making a rasping noise.

Lennox spoke again. "Was Claudia in the same form as Tom and Darren?"

Cleveland checked his computer and nodded.

"So that would be Mr Pollock," said Wednesday, checking her notebook.

"I suppose you'll want to see him now?"

"That would be useful. It will also give you time to shave before your meeting," replied Lennox with an ill-hidden smirk on his face.

Walking out of the office, Wednesday dug her elbow into Lennox's ribs. "No need to antagonize him. I've got a feeling we're going to be spending quite a bit of time here."

"Well, I don't think he's as innocent as he proclaims to be."

They arrived at Mr Pollock's form room to find him once again hunched over his desk, sifting through a pile of papers. They tapped on the door.

"Is it important, I've got some marking to finish," he called out as he glanced in their direction.

"Someone else who was too busy last night to get things done," whispered Lennox, as he leant into her. He got a gentle waft of her vanilla and burnt sugar scent.

"I'm sorry, Mr Pollock. We've come with some more bad news. And we'd like to ask you a few questions," Wednesday said calmly.

Pollock hurriedly pushed the papers together and looked at them from underneath his bushy eyebrows. The corners of his mouth twitched as they approached him.

"Claudia Edwards was found dead this morning."

Pollock's eyes blinked rapidly. "I somehow knew something bad would happen to her one day."

They gazed at him and waited for him to expand on his statement.

"She was quite flirtatious with the boys, you know, wearing her kilt too short, flicking her hair over her shoulders and giggling at the stupid things boys said. I often thought she'd be the first in the class to get pregnant."

No chance of that now, thought Wednesday.

"Did she have a boyfriend?"

"She had a few on the go according to the gossip."

"We'll need their names and to talk to them."

"You can interview them in the room next door. That class is on a museum trip today."

Wednesday and Lennox watched the students file in and take their seats, still talking to one another and immune to their presence. As

Colin Pollock called out the names Ralph, Tony, and James, the rest of the class jeered and whistled as the three red faced boys rose up to join the detectives. Lennox fetched Cleveland to join them.

Wednesday and Lennox sat opposite the boys, the smell of tobacco seeping from their blazers. It was exactly that repulsive smell that made Wednesday desire to give up.

"We understand you're all friends of Claudia Edmonds," Lennox said.

The boys nodded whilst nudging one another and suppressing giggles. Cleveland glared at them from a corner of the room.

"When was the last time you saw her?"

"Yesterday, in class," replied the lanky blond boy, Ralph, who slouched in his seat at the end of the table.

"Did any of you see her last night?"

The boys scuffed their shoes on the floor, eyes firmly cast down. Lennox repeated the question and this time the boy with severe acne on his forehead replied.

"We were supposed to meet up with her last night, but . . ." he stopped as he was punched on the arm by the boy with the angular face.

"But what?" asked Lennox, staring at them.

"Why, what's she saying about us?"

Lennox fixed his stare on them. "This is serious. We can meet up with your parents at the station if you prefer."

The lanky boy swiftly sat upright with a look of panic on his face.

"We didn't see her in the end," he said in a shaky voice.

"Come on lads, give us the whole story. Did you go round for some fun, but she refused, is that it?"

"No," said Ralph, slamming his palms on the table and glaring at Lennox.

Cleveland growled Ralph's name but Wednesday raised her hand to him.

"Well then, tell us what happened."

James and Tony turned to Ralph and widened their eyes. Taking his cue, he inhaled deeply before speaking.

"Claudia said her parents were away, and that if we went around at seven, we could have some fun." The boy flushed before continuing. "Anyway, we were all there, ringing on the doorbell but she wasn't in."

"How did that make you feel?"

"Pissed off. She'd led us on all day at school and then backed down. Sign of a true bitch."

"Typical teasing cow," muttered Tony.

"Do you think she was in the house but not letting you in?"

"Of course she was. Where else would she be?"

"What makes you so sure if you didn't see her?"

"We don't know for sure. No lights were on, but we guessed she was hiding upstairs or something."

James yawned loudly and began shifting his feet around on the floor so that the soles of his shoes made squeaking sounds.

"How long did you wait outside for?"

"Dunno," he shrugged, "about ten minutes I suppose, then we went back to mine." Ralph shoved his hands in his trouser pockets.

"Can your parents verify that?"

"No, they weren't in. That's why we went back there. My dad has a stash of beer, so we had a bottle each and played on the Xbox."

Lenox sat back in his chair. "We'll need you to make statements at the station in the presence of your parents."

The boys looked at one another before James spoke.

"What, because we had a beer?" The three of them sniggered openly. "Our parents won't care about that." They slapped each other on the back.

"No boys," said Wednesday, standing up to stretch her legs. "It's more serious than that. Now if you're telling the truth, you have nothing to worry about."

A look of alarm spread across the boys' faces, and the acne on Tony's face flushed a violent puce. Ralph's face drained of colour as he wound his school tie around his fingers.

Lennox stood up to join Wednesday. "Leave your names, addresses, and phone numbers on that sheet, then you can go back to class."

As they were walking out of the school, Wednesday's mobile rang and she was informed that Claudia's parents had been informed of their daughter's death by the Met officers and they were now at home. The family liaison officer was already there.

"Let's smoke before this one," she said, sensing every muscle in her body tightening.

Lennox reached into his pocket and pulled out a battered packet of cigarettes, from which they both took one. "This is an unpleasant one," he said before lighting up.

Wednesday lit hers and took in a deep drag before answering. "The violence of her death will be impossible to conceal in this place. Gossip spreads like oil on water," she replied, letting the smoke swirl out of her mouth with every word.

They pulled up outside a sizable detached property, and saw Janice Parker's car outside. A black convertible BMW sat outside the garage.

The hefty brass lion-head door knocker made an impressive and apt sound of doom as Lennox swung it. Seconds later, a tall elegant man opened the door.

"You'd better come in," Greg Edwards said.

He led them into the lounge where a statuesque woman in grey cashmere stood with her arm draped across the black marble mantelpiece. She was the epitome of allure.

Mrs Lucinda Edwards looked right through them as though they were apparitions in a nightmare. But once Wednesday starting talking about the crime, she fainted. She crumpled onto the sheepskin rug, in almost slow motion. Tension and pain crackled through the air. The doctor was called out, and Greg Edwards poured himself a brandy. Parker went to the kitchen to make some tea whilst the claws of bereavement and death took a stranglehold on the house.

Lucinda Edwards was now lying on the sofa being attended to by her overly attentive doctor, who prescribed Valium to aid her through the shock.

"Would it be possible to talk to Mrs Edwards before she takes the medication, we know this is unspeakably hard, but we need to move fast," asked Wednesday.

The doctor looked towards his patient and she responded by nodding weakly.

"Do you often leave your daughter alone?" asked Wednesday.

Before Lucinda Edwards could speak, her husband answered.

"She is . . . was almost sixteen, there's no law against it." He stood rigidly in the bay window, warming his brandy before sipping it. His stance was defensive as he stared at Wednesday.

"That wasn't what I was insinuating, sir. We need to find out who else knew she spent time alone here."

"I don't know the answer to that. We go about once a month. Lucinda and I love the theatre and we have a flat in London."

"Did Claudia have a boyfriend?" she pointedly looked towards Lucinda.

"Certainly not, she was a serious student planning on becoming a lawyer. She didn't have the time for silly boys," replied the husband.

Wednesday looked towards Lucinda as he spoke. Big fat salty tears crawled down her cheeks, leaving behind muddy trails of mascara.

"She seemed quite popular with the boys at school," ventured Wednesday, all the while looking at Lucinda. She thought she caught a brief look of acknowledgement from her, whilst Greg Edwards protested at the degrading slurs against his daughter.

"None of the boys at that school were good enough for Claudia, none of them." He tipped the last of the brandy down his throat before pouring himself another.

Lucinda dabbed her face with a monogrammed handkerchief, then beckoned Wednesday towards her by waving the sodden cloth. Wednesday bent down to be as close as possible.

"Was she assaulted?" she whispered.

"We don't know presently. The pathologist is carrying out tests."

"I want to see my daughter now, my wife will remain here," demanded Edwards, looking directly at Lennox.

"Janice can stay with your wife, if she'd like."

Greg Edwards sat in wretched silence in the back of Lennox's car whilst Wednesday phoned ahead to advise Edmond Carter of their imminent arrival.

It felt all too familiar and all too soon for Wednesday. Watching the assistant wheel out the gurney on which lay the lifeless shell of another teenager, made her stomach churn. She observed Greg Edwards's impassive face as he viewed the body of his precious child. Some marks on her face were visible.

"I think it would be for the best if my wife wasn't told about the extent of injuries just yet, or ever." His voice cracked at the final words. He compensated for his perceived weakness by jutting out his chin and taking in a deep breath.

"We'll do our best, sir, but I can't guarantee it. I'll get someone to drive you home. We'll need to look over your daughter's bedroom tomorrow, but call me in the meantime if you have any questions." Wednesday handed him her card then led the subdued father to a waiting officer who took him back upstairs.

Wednesday then moved into the laboratory to speak with Edmond.

"What can you tell me?"

"It appears that the poor girl suffered a violent death looking at the extent of contusions on her body. When I removed the masking tape from over her mouth, I found a large piece of cloth, probably there to muffle her screams."

He paused to wipe his hand over his bald head that was glistening with perspiration. "The tape and cloth have gone for analysis. Maybe some latent fingerprints blah de blah."

Wednesday tried hard not to imagine the pain and fear the girl suffered, as her gaze hovered just above the body.

"There's one other thing," he said before clearing his throat. "I've deduced that she was hanged slowly whilst being beaten by some form of baton or stick. More than one person was hitting her; there are various pressures and force used with each weapon. She was alive when this was happening. Dead people don't bruise. Ghastly death."

Wednesday felt an icy frisson run down her neck and spine. "What killed her exactly?"

"I won't know for sure until I've finished the autopsy. There was a blow to her head, causing a fracture, but between that, the beating, the hanging, and the possibility of drugs; I'd be hazarding a guess at this point."

Wednesday stood back as the gurney was removed, and Edmond put his hand on her shoulder.

"This will send shock waves through the community when the gruesome demise of the girl is made public."

"I pity the mother. We'll keep most of the details private for now," she replied quietly.

She plodded her way up the stairs to find Dana Booth, the press officer, waiting for her.

"I'll need a breakdown on what I can give the press and what we're holding back," she said as Wednesday poured herself a tepid cup of strong coffee.

"No details of how she died, just that her body was found in the woods, and that any info would be appreciated."

Wednesday headed for her office, when Digby Hunter flung open his office door and summoned her and Lennox in.

"Please tell me you have some leads, I'm getting some serious pressure from above to get some results. Well?"

"We're working on the connection to all three kids, which is the school. The head, Cleveland, is hiding something but he's tight lipped, sir," Lennox answered.

"Then bring him in for questioning and break him. Take him out of his comfort zone."

"On what grounds, sir? It's only speculation."

"Surely you can come up with something? I know DI Wednesday can be innovative."

She reddened and wrinkled up her toes in her shoes. "Another connection could be the missing boy. If we find him we may have the missing link."

"I have a team working on reports of sightings, following leads, searching the surrounding area to his home. He may still just be a runaway teen for all we know."

As the detectives were about to leave, Hunter had one last thing to impart.

"I'm cancelling weekend leave, so I suggest you go home at the end of the day and get some rest. I'm calling a briefing at eight tomorrow morning. Let Jones know so she can organise the team."

"We might as well go and get Cleveland and try and break the bastard. Let's take a squad car to shake him up," said Lennox.

Driving up towards the imposing school building, they were spotted by students running cross country. They became instantly drawn to what was happening. Wednesday was aware of her thumping heart as she waited for Lennox to switch off the engine.

Lennox flashed his badge at the receptionist as they whizzed by without stopping. Cleveland was mortified by the abrupt nature with which he was whisked out of his office. He sat like a sulking teenager in the back of the squad car, allowing his heavy brooding to permeate the atmosphere. He was not going to make it easy.

"Do I need a lawyer?" he asked, as he was finally sitting on the hard chair in the Interview Room.

"Not unless you have something to confess. We just need you to answer some questions," replied Wednesday, seating herself opposite him. His presence made her feel as though a million ants were scampering over her flesh.

"Where were you last night, Mr Cleveland?" she began.

"At home alone."

"That seems to be your constant response. Don't you have a social life?"

"I object to your tone, Detective. I spend quite a lot of time at home, but I also have a social life. In fact, I'm meeting some friends at the pub tonight."

"Which pub would that be?"

"The Crow." He sat back in his chair and met with her eyes.

"Has it not occurred to you there may be something going on at your school that connects all these young people?"

"I have thought about it, yes. But I can't see what it is. There's nothing remarkable about any of them. Tom was bright but quiet, Darren doesn't have academic prowess, and Claudia . . . was . . . bright but audaciously flirtatious at times. No connections for me to see, but you're the detectives; it's your job to connect the dots."

"What about Mr Pollock? What's he like as a teacher?" Lennox asked.

"Nothing extraordinary. He seems popular with the students."

"Any particular reason to why that is?"

Cleveland shrugged his shoulders and began tapping his long fingers on the table.

"Do you ever socialise with your staff?" Wednesday asked.

"I don't like to generally, but I make an exception at Christmas."

"Were the three students involved in any after school activities?"

"I'd already checked that as I thought you might want to know, seeing as you're hell bent on implicating the school. The only semblance of activities would be field trips, but that would involve the whole class."

"What about any bullying element?"

"It's not a problem at Markham Hall."

"Come Mr Cleveland, bullying is a component in all schools to a certain extent." Wednesday felt her irritation rise in reaction to his supercilious nature.

"Naturally, if you put it like that. But it's not a major issue. I retain the discipline in the school and any form of bullying that occurs, I deal with rapidly."

"How exactly?"

"I involve the parents and I use detention. Look, I object to being questioned like this; you seem to be judging my role of head. These atrocities have nothing to do with me or the school. You're wasting your time with this."

"We frequently have to make seemingly unconnected interviews in a murder enquiry, sir; we're sorry you feel scrutinised."

"I feel hounded, that's what I feel. Now, am I free to go?"

"Yes, an officer will escort you back. Thank you for your cooperation."

As Cleveland left the room, Wednesday's eyes glided over Lennox's face as he stared into the middle distance.

"What are you thinking about?"

"Oh God, the very question women should never ask a bloke."

"I meant with regards to the case."

Lennox rubbed his hand over his spiky hair, and sucked in air rather loudly. "Cleveland is stalling, he knows something but he's not prepared to give it up just yet, although he's a weak man deep down."

Wednesday was just about to reply, when Jones walked into the room to inform them that the dead girl's father had come to see them. A few minutes later, Greg Edwards entered the room. His fine features looked haggard, but his eyes were alert.

"I want to know if the head, Mr Cleveland, has anything to do with my daughter's death."

"We're still making enquiries; no arrests have been made so far. We will inform you of any progress, sir."

"But you brought him in here. You must be suspicious."

"He is naturally part of the investigation, seeing as your daughter attended his school. May I ask how you know this?"

"I have my sources, DI Wednesday, which I'm not prepared to divulge. I never liked that man and you may have let him go too soon, mark my words."

"We had no reason to keep him any longer."

"You may think he's safe out in the community, but I for one will make sure his movements are monitored."

Wednesday took a deep breath. "Please be careful, there are laws against vigilantism and harassing people." Changing to a more tender tone, she continued. "I know you must be hurting deeply, but please let us deal with the investigation. We'll get there, it's still early days."

Edwards looked at Wednesday, words hanging from the tip of his tongue, but instead he just shook his head slightly then walked out.

"Fancy a smoke?" asked Wednesday, seeing the dark circles underneath Lennox's eyes setting in.

Outside, the rain was falling hard, so they huddled together under the insufficient shelter, whilst they simultaneously puffed on their cigarettes. Wednesday had grown accustomed to his aftershave which she now found comforting and subconsciously arousing.

"Would you like to go for a drink after work?" she asked.

Lennox took a couple of drags. "I suppose we could go to The Crow and do some background checks whilst we're there."

Wednesday's shoulders sagged. She knew he would never give her the look he had given Scarlett in the kitchen.

They returned inside with a fine covering of rain drops glistening on their clothes and hair, and found Maria Jones waiting for them.

"Reverend Olong is here to see you," she said, cocking her head in the direction of the seated man, who was staring intently at his clasped hands. He stood up as they approached.

"I'm sorry to bother you, but I wondered if I could hold a memorial service on Sunday, with respect to the recent atrocities. I want to pull the community together and support the suffering families."

"I don't see a problem with that," replied Wednesday.

The reverend gave them both a solemn nod before moving on.

"I imagine we've got a date in a church this Sunday then," sighed Lennox.

Wednesday blushed as she strode off to the toilet to apply some lipstick, and spray on more scent, before heading off to the pub with him.

# Chapter Nine

Wednesday and Lennox drove separately to The Crow. She followed behind smoking a cigarette and listening to Bach. After parking she gave a cursory check of her face and hair in the rear-view mirror before climbing out to join him.

There were only a handful of cars and motorbikes in the car park. The hanging baskets harboured tired looking plants, which aesthetically offered very little. The outside walls were painted a polluted shade of white, with charred black beams crisscrossing along the roof line.

Stepping inside, Wednesday still found it odd not to be greeted by the stale smell of tobacco smoke. It had instead been replaced by the odour of feet which rose up from the garishly patterned carpet.

It was an old fashioned pub with brass horseshoes nailed to the original beams. A welcoming log fire roared in the grand fireplace, over which hung a stuffed crow housed inside a glass showcase.

The other patrons compiled of four leather-clad aging bikers, an elderly couple, and a few suited men with slicked down hair. The female element was short in supply, except for Wednesday, the elderly woman, and the barmaid with the bleached blond crop. The latter wore a tight-fitting red t-shirt that clung to her diminutive torso, skinny black jeans, and battered cowboy boots. Her look was completed by a slash of deep red lipstick across her mouth.

Wednesday sensed a pinch of envy in her stomach as she observed Lennox studying the barmaid as he ordered the drinks.

"Is the landlord in?" he asked.

"Dick, you're wanted," she called out behind her.

From a room behind the solid oak bar, emerged a gargantuan man dressed all in black with an ostentatious pair of cowboy boots.

"Who wants me?"

"Dick Pennymore? DI Wednesday and DS Lennox. I wonder if we could ask you a few questions."

He looked to see if they had bought a drink before agreeing to Lennox's request.

"Do you know Stewart Cleveland?"

"I do as it happens. Why?"

"Is he a regular patron?"

"He's normally here every Friday and sometimes on a Wednesday."

"Was he here last night?"

"As it happens he was. What's all this about?" he said as he leant over the bar so Wednesday could feel his hot beery breath skimming across her face.

"We're just making enquiries. I assume you're aware of recent events."

"Too right I am. It's a bloody outrage. If you lot don't catch the guy soon, and we find the bastard, you won't find him alive."

Lennox decided it was pointless continuing the line of enquiry, or even setting the man straight about the law. Instead, he thanked Pennymore and then guided Wednesday towards the table for two in the bay window. He pulled out the chair for her to sit down.

"Quite the gentleman in private, aren't you."

"I'd like to think I'm the same at work, too."

Wednesday smiled and sipped her Diet Coke. "Seeing as we're working together, it would be nice to know a little more about you."

"What, on top of the office tittle tattle that you already know."

"You should know I never pay heed to that. Although I have noticed that quite a few female staff seem drawn to you."

"Is that so? Well, I have a news flash for them all; I don't do relationships in the workplace. In fact, I'm still a tad raw after the divorce."

"It's supposed to get easier as time passes."

"So I understand. However, every memory leaves a trace that's never extinguished."

"So, if anyone asks me, I'm to tell them it's a waste of time pursuing you."

"Pretty much."

"I noticed the barmaid bleeped on your radar."

"I said I was raw, not blind."

Wednesday prodded the ice cubes that were floating in her glass.

"There's not much to say about my life, so tell me about you," he asked.

"I'm not sure mine's any more interesting. I've never been married, I've no kids, my career is my boyfriend and I live with my half-sister; but you know that last one."

Lennox brushed his hand over his bristly hair. "Yes, the journalist. Do you share the same mother or father?"

"Mother. She divorced my dad when I was young and married Oliver. They had Scarlett. Things are a bit rocky at the moment."

"Sounds ominous."

"I'm probably just being overdramatic. I love Mum to pieces, and Oliver is good for her, but there's only so much giving a person can do. Marriage needs to be a mutually supportive union in my eyes."

She began twirling a strand of hair around her finger and gazed out the window, looking at the distorted view through the bull's eye in the pane. She wanted to keep talking, to open up her heart and let the emotions flood out over the table for him to mop up, thus relieving the pressure in her head. But she feared he would view her in a different light if he knew.

Outside the rain crashed down in sheets, so when the pub door opened a shower of rain followed the customers in. The first to enter was a group of scantily clad young women brandishing umbrellas, followed by a pair of workmen in fluorescent jackets. The last person to bluster in was Stewart Cleveland, who's normally slick appearance had been wrecked by the elements.

He marched straight up to Pennymore and began talking rapidly and gesticulating frantically. Pennymore pointed towards the detectives and Cleveland turned around to see them staring right at him.

Wednesday raised her glass in his direction, and his response was to storm out into the squally rain. They watched through the window as he turned his collar up before heading to his car.

"He appeared upset at seeing us here," Lennox said with amusement.

"I wonder what he was saying to Pennymore," Wednesday mused as she swirled the diminishing ice cubes in her glass.

"He won't tell us the truth, especially as he pointed us out to Cleveland. They're clearly more than mere acquaintances."

"Something to keep an eye on," she replied. "Would you like another drink?"

"If you're offering."

He watched her walk to the bar and he found himself wondering what she would look like with her hair down. He then let his eyes drift towards the dancing, hypnotic flames in the fireplace.

"May I ask why you are so raw after your divorce? I mean, if I'm being too nosey you can tell me to butt out," she said, placing a Coke in front of him.

"It's never easy when a divorce involves kids. My two boys seem to be getting along nicely with my ex's new boyfriend, and I can see myself falling through the cracks of a reconstituted family."

"So it's the relationship issues with your kids that's causing you pain."

"Truthfully, it's not just that. She left me because she said she couldn't compete with my job. I told her she didn't have to, but . . ." His voice trailed off and his eyes wandered back to the fire. His attention was drawn to the sparks spitting from the logs.

"Did you ever consider changing your career path?"

"I didn't want to. I like the buzz and adrenalin rush this job brings. I feel a compulsion to solve puzzles and to assign blame in the world of criminals."

"I hear what you're saying. However, you could end up a lonely old man if you live only for your career."

"And what about you then? When does work stop and your personal life begin?"

"I'm working on it," she replied quietly as her eyes were also drawn to the fire. "Why don't you come back to my place, we could both do with a wholesome meal. I could cook up a curry in no time."

Lennox raised his eyebrows and tapped the side of his glass with his fingertips. He answered "yes" quicker than he intended.

They noticed Dick Pennymore watch them leave before he disappeared into the back room. Wednesday did not notice Lennox giving a sly glance towards the barmaid.

Lennox sat at the kitchen table as Wednesday deftly chopped the vegetables and leftover roast chicken to put into the curry. Smooth classical music played softly in the background as the aroma of spices began melting into the air.

"How long do you think Scarlett will stay living with you?"

"Until she marries, I imagine."

"She's getting married?"

"Not yet," she replied, gripping the knife handle tightly. "She's currently single, but she attracts men easily so I imagine it will happen one day."

She poured them both a glass of wine and seated herself opposite him. In the centre of the table sat a cluster of large church-pillar candles, which gave a flattering glow over both their faces. It was not long before the pungent curry was ready to be served.

"What dark secrets do you conceal behind your placid facade?" he asked between mouthfuls of curry and basmati rice.

"What makes you think I have secrets?"

"Because everybody does to a greater or lesser extent."

"Well if I did, I'm not sure I'd tell you."

"Well you'd be wrong. We work closely together so we should trust and look out for one another."

Wednesday raised her eyebrows then picked up her wine glass.

"I've told you about my residual feelings after my divorce," he continued, looking at her with his sharp, hazel eyes.

"Okay," she said softly. "I do have something that lurks in the fleapit of my mind." She took another sip of wine to moisten her mouth. She was about to continue, when she heard the front door open.

"Something smells divine," Scarlett called out.

Her footsteps echoed like horses hooves on the floor. "Oh sorry, I didn't know we had company."

"We don't. I do. There's some curry left if you want some. I thought you were working late tonight."

Scarlett unravelled the multi-coloured knitted scarf from around her neck, and threw it over the counter. She helped herself to a bowl of curry and sat at the head of the table.

"So, Detective Sergeant Jacob Lennox, what's new?"

"Are you referring to the cases or my personal life?"

"Cynicism so late in the evening will give you indigestion."

"I'll cope," he replied as he scraped his fork across the plate. "I should be getting off home. We've an early start in the morning."

"Please don't go on my account, Jacob. I'm a good listener if you want to talk through pressing matters. A fresh pair of eyes and ears can do wonders."

Wednesday shot her a heated glance before escorting Lennox to the front door.

"Sorry about that."

"No worries. I'll see you at the briefing."

Wednesday watched him merge into the dark night and lingered there until his headlights vanished down the street.

"You're a dark horse," said Scarlett as Wednesday returned.

"Meaning what exactly?"

"Inviting Jacob over. I don't remember you doing that with other colleagues." Scarlett peered over the top of her wine glass with an impish glint in her green eyes. She couldn't fail to see the look of irritation etched across Wednesday's face.

"If you must know, weekend leave is cancelled and we've a heavy workload ahead. I thought a home cooked meal would be preferable to the crap he normally eats."

"He's single then."

"Divorced."

"So no emotions involved for you then?"

Wednesday shook her head and downed the dregs of her glass.

"Good," said Scarlett, as she got up from the table and danced towards her bedroom, leaving her empty plate and glass on the table.

Wednesday arrived early for the briefing, freshly showered and experiencing the adrenalin rush Lennox talked about.

Lennox walked into the Incident Room and gave her a nod of recognition before entering his office and closing the door. She wondered whether he regretted opening up to her over dinner.

She stood in front of the white board and examined the evidence. She was so transfixed by the photographs that she did not notice Hunter standing next to her.

"Share your thoughts, Wednesday?"

Her shoulders jerked as her cheeks donned a faint pinkish bloom. "I was speculating Darren's involvement in the death of the other two. Is he our murderer?"

"By all accounts he's not muscularly but rather fat. He'd need help to contain Tom, let alone hoist a sixteen-year-old girl up a tree." He looked directly at her and tilted his head, suggesting that she was a little off beam in his opinion. He moved to the desk at the front and clapped his hands to gain everyone's attention.

"Right everyone, let's focus. I want Arlow and Damlish to concentrate on the missing boy, Darren Giles; get more background on relatives and friends who live further away."

He took a sip of water before continuing. "Wednesday and Lennox, I want you to chase up forensics on Tom Dolby and Claudia Edwards. Whilst you're at it, visit the Edwards again; find out where she'd go and who she'd meet. Don't tell me a sixteen-year-old is that perfect. Visit the Dolbys too. Remember, parents always lie."

A murmur crackled across the room.

"Oh and I also want you two to attend the church service tomorrow, see who's there and who isn't. Talk to Reverend Olong as he might be able to give you more details about the congregation. Press him about the rambling club too."

Arlow smirked at Wednesday, knowing her immense dislike of any form of religion. He was about to walk over to her, when he was accosted by Jones who was busy organising everyone.

"Do you think Hunter has a penchant for worrying about the clergy and young boys?" said Lennox.

"That would be stereotyping all clergy by the acts of the clergy. Besides, I don't know what his thoughts are on that matter. I couldn't second guess Hunter's thoughts, and neither should you."

She knew she sounded clipped. But she also knew that if only he would mention last night, she would be in a smoother frame of mind. In order to initiate a firmer grip of her slipping emotions, she suggested they have a smoke on their way down to the forensic laboratories.

"You're a bit disengaged this morning," she said as she lit her cigarette.

"Sorry, I'm a tad preoccupied. I got home last night to a message on the ansaphone from my ex."

Wednesday waited to see if he'd say more whilst she blew grey fumes into the crisp morning air. She maintained visual contact in an effort to be empathic; remnants of her listening-skills training pulsating through her mind.

"Archie, my eldest, is in trouble at school for fighting, and Lucy is blaming me."

"How come?"

"Because I keep cancelling my weekends with them because of work. She says it's making him angry."

"I see, but it's not your fault."

"That means nothing to Lucy. Do you know, she actually said Brian, her new boyfriend, is more of a father than me?" He drew in a deep lungful of poisonous smoke then let it swirl out of his mouth as he continued speaking. "I suppose she's right, as always."

Wednesday flicked the ash from her cigarette whilst contemplating the most appropriate response from someone without children. "I'm sorry."

She wanted to touch his arm, being a tactile person, but she didn't want her gesture of compassion to be misread as an offer of sympathy sex.

"Anyway," she began, "what's your view on the Edwards?"

"Their alibi is solid. Neighbours in London confirmed their presence in their flat."

"I just can't make them out as individuals. The father appears to dominate his wife. I wonder what his relationship was like with his daughter?"

She turned towards Lennox and saw that he was staring into the middle distance once more, so she stubbed out her cigarette and told him they should get going.

As they were making their way down, Arlow caught up with them.

"We had an anonymous tip about the missing lad; he was spotted late last night near the church. They didn't realise who it was they'd seen until this morning. We're off there now."

His exhilaration was palpable, and Wednesday wished she was going with him instead of into the burrows of death with Lennox.

"I always think the labs are aptly located in the bowels of the building, don't you?" she asked Lennox as they descended.

"Never given it a second thought."

They found Edmond and Alex deep in conversation whilst periodically looking down a microscope.

"I wondered when we'd be seeing you again. Come and look at this, Wednesday." Alex beckoned her to look down the microscope.

"I'm not quite sure what I'm looking at."

"You're looking at green and blue fibres, but not just any fibres," interjected an animated Charlie. "We have now identified them as being manufactured in a Scottish wool mill. It's expensive and fairly exclusive." His face glowed with pride.

"So all we need to do now is search every car in the local vicinity for the matching blanket, do we?" Lennox's voice was flat with a tinge of exasperation.

"I don't tell you how to go about your job, Detective. Mine is to find the manner of death and the tools of the nasty trade; yours is to find the perpetrator."

Edmond rolled his eyes. "This is team work, gentlemen. Perhaps I should give you my recent findings. No damage was found on the larynx which isn't surprising, as the thyroid cartilage is pliable, not brittle in the young."

Edmond put on the latex gloves and opened the mouth to display more findings.

"It's obvious the poor lad took a while to die, as there are characteristic marks of congestion and petechiae on the face and on the inside of the mouth. There's also an imprint of his teeth on the inside of his lips."

He closed the mouth and drew back the green sheet to expose the boy's chest area.

"We noted these marks earlier when they were only faint. However, now I can tell you that they look like signs of over-zealous CPR; someone tried to resuscitate him."

A hush fell over the room as each person assimilated the words.

"Perhaps this was an accident?" said Wednesday.

"Possibly," replied Edmond. "But quite frankly, until you find the perpetrator, you won't know for sure."

"Any updates on the girl, Claudia Edwards?"

"Hair has been sent off for analysis, but fair hair holds less drug elements than dark hair, so don't hold your breath."

Wednesday and Lennox thanked them before returning upstairs and heading off to the Dolby's.

# Chapter Ten

James Dolby let them in and led them to the lounge, where the wood burning stove was already lit. It provided a welcoming hue, in contrast to the chilled aura surrounding the bereaved couple. No drinks were offered although none would have been accepted.

Emily Dolby sat in the fireside armchair like a lifeless ragdoll with dead button eyes; she barely acknowledged their presence. James looked at her coldly.

The detectives sat on the over-stuffed sofa whilst Wednesday explained the recent forensic findings. Emily Dolby visibly shuddered on hearing how her son died.

"Will his body be released soon?" asked James.

"All the forensic tests need to be completed before going to the corona, so I'm sorry, I can't give you an exact time," replied Wednesday as she deliberately turned towards Emily. "Will you be attending the church service tomorrow, Mrs Dolby?"

"My wife wants to, but I don't," interjected James rather briskly.

Wednesday continued looking at Emily. "Do you feel it will help you emotionally?"

Emily nodded, although her mouth remained grimly shut.

"I can't see how," James said. "How she can still believe in God after this. No God I know would allow this to happen, it's abhorrent."

He stood up swiftly and stormed out of the room. The next thing they heard was the kettle being switched on. Wednesday surreptitiously moved her eyes in the direction of the kitchen, so Lennox excused himself to join Dolby. Wednesday wasted no time.

"I couldn't help but notice some carved scratches and letters in the arms of the chair you're sitting in, as well as some dents in the doors. Did Tom do these?"

Emily shuffled forward and perched on the edge of her seat, her foot twitching rapidly. She looked towards the kitchen then back to Wednesday.

"He had the devil in him at times," she said in a hushed voice.

Wednesday beckoned her to continue whilst she began scribbling in her notebook.

"He would have terrible fights with his father, and he was often disrespectful towards me."

"What were the fights about?"

"Anything and everything. Times to be home by; where he could go and with whom."

Thus far, it all sounded like normal parent and teenager issues, but Wednesday felt there was more to it. "Would the fights get physical between Tom and his father?"

Again, Emily's gaze shifted to the kitchen then back to Wednesday.

"Only once, a couple of weeks ago. James slapped Tom and Tom retaliated by throwing the crystal fruit bowl, hence the dent in the door."

"What happened afterwards?"

"Tom stormed out and James shut himself away in his study."

"What did you do whilst all this was going on?"

Emily Dolby's shoulders sagged further as she recollected. "I tried to intervene at first, but James pushed me away. They couldn't hear me over their shouting."

"Where did Tom go?"

"I don't know, he never told us."

Wednesday was just about to ask more probing questions when Lennox and James re-entered the room, armed with a cup of tea for Emily which he put on the table next to her.

Wednesday opened up the conversation again by asking James what his relationship was like with his son. James looked intently at his wife before he asked why she needed to know.

"Your wife was telling me about the tension between you and Tom."

"We had our ups and downs." He took a sip of tea then sat back in the armchair. The glow from the fire highlighted the crevices etched around his eyes and his mouth. Emily's foot twitched more frantically and she had resorted to staring into her teacup; a self-imposed exile from the rest of the group.

"I'm not sure where this is leading, Detective. Are you implying that I had something to do with my son's murder?"

"I'm merely gathering background information to piece together Tom's movements and behaviour the last time you saw him."

"He'd been at school then he said he'd got some project to work on with that Giles boy. He went there and we never saw him again."

"That wasn't mentioned before," said Wednesday, flicking through her notes.

"Well excuse me for being distracted from the details by my son's death, Detective." His face flushed as he rose to his feet.

"No one is blaming you." Lennox spoke calmly, remaining seated.

"She does. She blames me," replied James, gesticulating in the direction of his wife. His eyes were bulging and he was sweating profusely.

Wednesday willed Emily to speak out to reassure her clearly distraught husband. Her silence had the disastrous affect of squeezing his heart until it pounded so hard it looked like he was on the verge of having a heart attack.

"Mrs Dolby, your husband looks unwell," prompted Wednesday.

Finally, Emily Dolby found the words to say. "No one is to blame. It was God's will. Tom wasn't right for this world."

"What the bloody hell are you babbling on about, woman?" James shouted as he paced up and down in front of the wood burner, holding a hand over his heart, as though preventing it from launching out of his chest.

"Please Mr and Mrs Dolby; this is a highly emotive time. You need to support one another, fighting is too destructive." Wednesday had risen to her feet and was guiding James back to his chair. He was compliant but shrugged his shoulders to rid himself of her touch.

Lennox proceeded to ask questions about Tom's life out of the home; steering the parents' thoughts to his last hours.

"That's where the blame lies," snapped James. "With Darren and his parents, that's where he went last. You had the stepfather in didn't you? You must think he's guilty of something."

Lennox's soothing tones went some way to pacify James, but tension still ripped through the air. Silent sounds of internal reflections dominated the room.

The parents had little to say about Tom's last hours, which made it all the more poignant. Wednesday and Lennox waited a few minutes before judging that it was appropriate to leave. As they closed the front door, the sound of raised voices rang in their ears.

"The death of a child can wreck a marriage," Lennox said as they walked to the car. Wednesday nodded, fumbling with the cigarette packet in her pocket.

With their nicotine levels topped up, they knocked on the Edwards' front door. As Greg Edwards opened the door, the smell of fresh coffee seeped out onto the porch. He directed them in and offered them a beverage.

Lucinda Edwards was draped over the chaise longue, appearing more waif-like than in their previous encounter. Her already fair hair was highlighted, and it gave the impression of a halo encircling her head. Wednesday was struck by her cheekbones which were more prominent in the morning light. Lucinda Edwards gave them a slow close and open of her eyelids as recognition of their presence.

Greg entered the room behind them with a silver tray laden with refreshments. He poured the freshly made coffee into the bone china cups and offered them cream and lumps of brown sugar.

"Did your daughter ever mention Tom Dolby or Darren Giles?" Lennox asked as he accepted a cup of coffee, savouring the rich aroma.

"That's the missing boy and the one found dead?" Greg said cautiously, his eyes skimming over his wife, checking her state of fragility.

"That's correct; we're looking to see if there's a correlation between all the cases."

"Claudia never spoke of any boys, and as I've said before, my daughter was only interested in her education."

Lennox nodded and drew breath to ask another question when the doorbell rang. Greg excused himself to answer the door, whilst his wife's eyes followed his every move.

"I think she was quite popular with the boys," she whispered, forcing the detectives to perch on the edge of their seats.

"Any boys in particular?" asked Wednesday, mirroring Lucinda's tone.

"I can't remember any names; she never spoke to me about them. I overheard things when she spoke on the phone, that's all." With a swift ballerina style swirl of her arm, she beckoned Wednesday closer.

"Can we keep this from Greg as it would upset him enormously? She was his perfect princess."

"That may not be possible, Mrs Edwards, as we need to conduct our investigations with clarity and openness."

Greg re-entered the room with an ostentatious bouquet of lilies and fern leaves.

"From the Women's Guild," he informed his wife.

She smiled weakly then asked him to put them in water. Resigned, he returned to the kitchen.

"I'm sure she met some of them after school," she whispered as she kept an eye on the door. "She'd tell me she was going to a girl friend's house, but if I phoned her on her mobile, she either didn't answer or bit my head off for checking up on her. I heard boys' voices in the background."

She took a bird sip of coffee before continuing. "I never mentioned it to her father."

"You never mentioned what?" Greg asked as he stood in the doorway.

Lucinda looked at Wednesday with her mellow eyes glistening.

"It appears that your daughter may have been friendly with a boy or boys, although we don't know who."

"What rot, where did you get that information from?"

Wednesday looked towards Lucinda before she recounted her words as he sat listening impassively. His head hung heavily as though his neck could no longer support it.

"Are you saying that she may have known her assailant?" he asked, fixing his gaze upon the Persian rug.

"There was no evidence of forced entry to your home, and her house keys were still in her pocket, so it's possible."

"And you knew about this?" he asked his wife.

"I only had my suspicions, dear, she wouldn't tell me anything."

Greg let out a deep sigh and picked up his coffee cup from the side table. He rotated the cup and watched the liquid swill around. "I suppose the next thing people will be saying is that she was a flirtatious trollop who deserved what she got."

"No sir, no one deserved what she got," replied Lennox, noticing Greg's eyes flicker.

"Was she . . . assaulted in a . . . sexual way?"

"It doesn't appear so."

"Thank God for small mercies." Greg bowed his head.

"Mrs Edwards, if any names come back to you, please do give us a call," said Wednesday handing over another card. She knew the first one invariably gets lost in the mêlée of the first hours of grief.

"One last thing before we go, are you attending the church service tomorrow?" Lennox checked.

The Edwards looked at one another, before replying that the reverend had called around to invite them, but they had yet to make a decision.

# Chapter Eleven

Wednesday sat at her kitchen table, nursing a mug of filter coffee. The steam drifted across her eyes, forming a mist to soften her view. After allowing her mind to wander aimlessly, she returned her focus to the sheets of paper spread out before her. It was customary for her to draw mind maps of a case in order to visualise the evidence and possible suspects.

"Still working the old fashioned way," Scarlett said, pouring herself a coffee.

Wednesday hummed a response and then looked up at her.

"You look over-dressed for a Sunday morning."

"I can't go to church in my PJs, now can I?"

Wednesday bit her lip and allowed her breath to seep slowly through her nostrils. "I don't need to ask *you* why a church service is on the agenda."

"And from your dour attire, I can see that you're breaking your athe-ist rule," replied Scarlett before lighting a cigarette and opening the back door.

"It's work related," said Wednesday, also lighting a cigarette.

"And the same goes for me. You can't stop me."

"No Scarlett, I can't stop you, but I can ask that you keep out of my hair and refrain from causing me any trouble."

"Okay sis. By the way, how's it going with the divine Jacob Lennox?"

Wednesday abstained from rising to Scarlett's bait; over the years she had learnt to master the skill. Blowing out smoke, she allowed a faint smile to grace her lips and brief flashes of Lennox to pass before her eyes. The sound of the doorbell intruded her thoughts. Scarlett flicked the half smoked cigarette onto the patio and went to answer it.

"Jacob Lennox, we were just talking about you," she announced, standing back to let him in.

Wednesday hurriedly gathered up the strewn paperwork and shoved it in a drawer.

"I thought we'd travel together to give us time to talk through our plan for today. Hunter wants us to check out people arriving so we need to go now."

"I couldn't cadge a lift could I?" asked Scarlett with hope in her voice.

"No. Lennox and I want to talk shop without the ear of the press looming over our shoulder."

Scarlett watched the pair leave before picking up her bag and keys. Marching outside she slammed the door for no one to hear.

Sitting in the passenger seat, Wednesday repeatedly brushed her hands over her black trousers to smooth them over her knees. His car smelt less of pristine leather and more like an overflowing ashtray.

"You seem on edge about something," he ventured.

"I detest churches. They conjure up tortured confusion in my mind."

"Hell, that's got to hurt."

She rolled her eyes. "I'm agnostic, but when I'm inside a consecrated building I feel both the presence of an omniscient power, and feelings of both hope and hopelessness."

"No wonder this case is gnawing away; you're far too sensitive."

She was about to bite back when she realised they were already there. Lennox parked a short distance away from the church so they could remain in the warmth whilst monitoring the arrival of the parishioners.

A gust of wind hurled autumnal leaves around the graveyard as though spirits were making their presence known. They watched Reverend Olong appear from the vicarage; the wind furling his black cassock around his ankles. He pulled the clothing tighter around his neck and walked towards the church with his head bowed down. Before he entered the graveyard, he gave them a quick wave in order to show he had seen them. Perhaps the people of God are indeed, all-seeing, thought Wednesday.

Small groups of people began arriving, but so far they were unfamiliar faces. Clusters of older people dressed in suitably mournful attire; black hats trimmed with black satin ribbon, and faces with the severity of the occasion drawn across their sagging flesh. The reverend stood by the arched doorway to meet and greet the arrivals.

Finally, recognizable faces began arriving. The first was Emily Dolby who appeared conspicuously alone, her face bearing a ghost-like image. She hesitated by the spot where her son was found, and after a few moments she reached the reverend at the door. He took her hand in both of his and could be seen offering words, no doubt, of peace and condolences to the grieving mother.

Next came a group of familiar faces from Markham Hall; a handful of irksome students interspersed by four members of staff. Stewart Cleveland headed up the group of students, with the receptionist keenly tagging alongside him. Wednesday could make out the boys who had gone to Claudia's house the night of her disappearance, and a couple of girls they had not as yet met. Following the group was Colin Pollock with his hands shoved deeply into the pockets of his chestnut tweed trousers.

"We need to think about going in ourselves," said Wednesday, putting on her leather gloves.

As they got out of the car, Greg and Lucinda Edwards pulled up behind them in their convertible BMW. Greg Edwards's face looked gaunt yet composed, whilst his wife's demeanour shrieked of fragility and numbness.

Wednesday and Lennox followed the Edwards into the church and sat on a pew at the back. The organist was playing sombre music which cast a weighted shroud onto the congregation. A tight sensation compressed Wednesday's lungs, and the giant wooden cross on the wall behind the altar loomed over her. Her skin prickled with sweat.

Just as Wednesday considered running from the scene, Reverend Olong stood up to address the throng. He gazed around then spoke. "How shallow has society become that we no longer value—"

He was interrupted by the church door as it swung open, allowing Judith and Des Wright to tumble in, along with some autumnal leaves caught up in the wind. He stopped talking as everyone turned around to look at them.

"What are you lot staring at?" slurred Judith Wright. "We ain't done nothing wrong and neither has my Darren."

Des Wright grabbed her by the elbow and led her to a space against the back wall. The reek of alcohol drifted around the congregation. Judith tried to hold her head high but it kept lolling forward as she kept drifting off to sleep.

Reverend Olong made a coughing sound to bring everyone's attention back to him.

"As I was saying, how shallow society has become, that we no longer value the community spirit that once bound us together. Don't look at your neighbour through guarded or mistrustful eyes, look at them with respect, honour, and love so we can live in harmonious peace. We need to cherish the children amongst us so they grow up knowing about the values of God and accord between brethren."

He paused to allow the words to filter into the congregation's thoughts and minds, and he took that moment to look towards his wife who sat at the end of the first pew. Wednesday could not see her face, but she noticed the reverend looked strained.

He continued with the service, and when the time came for the congregation to rise, Wednesday noticed that Greg Edwards remained seated, even though his wife was desperately tugging on his arm.

Wednesday could also clearly see Scarlett relishing the occasion as she kept jotting down words in her notebook. Trepidation about Scarlett's next article was rearing its ugly head.

"I'm surprised James Dolby hasn't accompanied his wife," whispered Lennox.

"I'm surprised any family member wishes to be here, it's so depressing. I wouldn't have thought this was helpful."

"Ah, but God can bring some semblance of peace to those that seek it."

"Are you a believer, Jacob Lennox?"

"Maybe I am and maybe I'm not. You can't deny that religion has lasted for thousands of years in various forms. That shows it has the ability to withstand a country full of cynics. There is some measure of meaning behind the prayers and the sermons."

"Religion has only created a powerful source for manipulative human beings to rule the weak of mind." Wednesday noticed her hissing was getting louder, and some people were turning around to look at her.

Reverend Olong mentioned in prayer the names of Tom Dolby and Claudia Edwards, who had both had their young lives cut short. He then mentioned the desire for the safe return of Darren Giles, and that was when the disquiet erupted with a low rumble from the congregation. Wednesday and Lennox watched as people whispered behind cupped hands, and turned around to look at the Wrights.

"You people think my Darren has done something to those two kids. It would be our fault wouldn't it, as we ain't as good as you lot." Judith was shaking from head to foot with her cheeks as rosy and shiny as gala apples. Des stood by her side with his arms folded across his paunch.

The detectives observed the spectacle then Lennox decided to stand up and motion to Judith to calm down. However, her voice had become shrill and her actions theatrical, so she did not notice his request.

In a stream of swear words, Judith fled the church, leaving a trailing stench of stale sweat and alcohol behind her. Wednesday moved to follow her out, when she saw Vera Olong stand up and make her way up the aisle. Her quickening steps echoed around the stone walls, as did the increased droning of voices from the parishioners.

Wednesday signalled for Lennox to remain inside whilst she followed the women outside. Reverend Olong appealed for calm, and with the wave of his hand, instructed the organist to commence playing the next hymn.

Stepping out of the dingy atmosphere, a ray of autumnal sun with remnants of warmth left in it, sliced through the clouds and touched her face. Wednesday squinted as she moved towards the pair. She could hear Judith's erratic speech, tempered by Vera's soothing tones. *She fulfils the duty of a vicar's wife well.*

"You've got a nerve, you owe me," said Judith as she lashed out and slapped Vera across the face.

"I owe you nothing; you live for alcohol, not for your son," replied Vera as she put her hand to her cheek. The crumpled lines on Vera's face erased as Wednesday caught her attention.

"Is everything all right here, ladies?"

"Yes, I'm trained to counsel those in emotional distress. We're fine I can assure you," replied Vera as she took her hand away from her face, revealing a red mark.

"How are you getting home?" Wednesday asked Judith, conscious of her alcohol consumption.

"With my Des of course; and no, I ain't driving. You coppers are all the same."

Wednesday let the sarcasm wash over her head, preferring to observe the two women. They both shifted around on their feet due to the cold breeze whipping around them.

"Any news on Darren's whereabouts, Detective?" Vera asked.

"I'm afraid not." Her eyes flicked briefly towards Judith then back to Vera. "Could I see you and your husband after the service?"

Vera nodded, turning to see people filing out of the church, shaking hands with the reverend as they left. Vera excused herself and went and stood at his side; she leaned in and whispered something in his ear.

Eve was about to speak to Judith when Des came marching over to where they were standing.

"Hope you're not bothering her," he said in a deep voice, towering above Wednesday.

Before she had time to reply, Des had put his arm around Judith's shoulders and guided her away. Wednesday watched as Judith shrugged her shoulders in order to release his grip on her. As the couple disappeared out of view, Wednesday strained to check she could not hear Judith's cries for help.

Lennox walked up behind her and tapped her on the shoulder.

"Time to talk to the Olongs, Boss?"

Wednesday turned to see Emily Dolby talking to the reverend, but as they approached, she finished her conversation quickly and walked straight past them with her head bowed low.

Reverend Olong smiled at the detectives. "Come to the vicarage, it's warmer than standing here. Could you take the detectives back, dear, whilst I just tidy up," he said to Vera as he headed back inside.

They followed Vera back and soon found themselves in a large farmhouse kitchen heated by a range. The walls were painted pea green with a mismatch of crockery displayed on a shabby welsh dresser. Vera made a pot of tea and put an assortment of plain biscuits on a chipped plate.

"This had taken its toll on George. He's never experienced such shocking acts of violence within a community. He's dealt with natural deaths within families, even of children, but never something like this." She shook her head slowly whilst she poured the tea and then placed the teacups in front of everyone.

Reverend Olong blustered into the kitchen, blowing warm air into his cupped hands.

"Did you notice anything unusual at the service, Reverend?" asked Wednesday.

George looked up at the ceiling. "I was very sorry to see Emily Dolby alone; I think James may be suffering a lapse in his faith. They're normally regular church goers. I was, however, surprised to see the Wrights as they rarely attend. Stress can make people behave in uncharacteristic ways, so I believe."

"We've received an anonymous tip that Darren Giles has been spotted around the church," began Wednesday before taking a sip of the overly milky tea.

"Really?" replied Reverend Olong.

"Yes, and in light of this, would you allow us to search the grounds and the church again, including the vicarage?"

Reverend Olong turned to his wife then back at Wednesday. "Will it cause much disruption?"

"We'll try and keep it to a minimum."

Reverend Olong nodded then turned away to look out the window. "Then I can only agree."

He excused himself as he had a sermon to write and felt Vera was more than capable of dealing with police matters.

Vera watched her husband amble out of the kitchen before turning to them.

"I do hope we're not going to experience the trouble we had in the last parish," she said quietly as she offered them more tea.

"What trouble would that be?" replied Lennox, declining a refill.

"It was nothing but malicious gossip, and although unfounded, the damage was done so we had to leave."

Lennox took out his notebook whilst Wednesday coaxed Vera to continue.

"George used to teach the choirboys in church, and one day a boy made an allegation about him. It caused quite a stir, as you can probably imagine. But when no proof was found, they moved us here. That's why I now run the choral sessions, so as not to leave us open to a repeat scenario."

Wednesday and Lennox looked at one another.

"I'm telling you this in confidence, mind, he gets really upset when he's reminded of that period."

"Where was your last parish?" Wednesday asked.

"Bethnal Green in London."

Wednesday excused herself and called the station, requesting sniffer dogs for the grounds. Whilst waiting for the support, the detectives decided to make a start, so they requested that Vera accompany them around the rambling vicarage.

The space inside was deceptive, with a large damp cellar providing pockets of rooms leading off from the main area, which housed boxes of church paraphernalia. The kitchen itself had a walk-in larder, with shelves full of tinned foods and homemade pickles and jam. There were nooks and crannies all over the house suitable for hiding purposes, although the spaces were generally crammed full of junk and books.

They moved to the upper floor and became privy to the night habits of the couple. Wednesday noticed that two of the four bedrooms appeared to be in use.

"Do you and the reverend sleep separately?" asked Wednesday.

"I'm not sure that is pertinent to the investigation, but yes we do. George sleeps facing the church and my room overlooks the garden."

The only place left to search was the loft. Wednesday followed Lennox up the ladder and was surprised by the sizable space they found themselves in. She could hear Vera climbing up the ladder behind her.

"Can you smell chips," Lennox said quietly, as he dusted a cobweb off his shoulder.

"Faintly. Perhaps you're feeling hungry and you're having an olfactory hallucination."

Lennox frowned and pressed forward through the large trunks and boxes. They weaved about in the loft, until suddenly they came across a disturbed pile of blankets and quilts. Wednesday bent down and moved the blankets using her pen. She prodded something hard, and when she pulled the blanket back, she saw a notebook. She picked it up and noticed Darren Giles's name scrawled across the cover.

"Take a look at this," she said, passing it to Lennox.

He flicked through the pages of mainly legible writing, with a scattering of crosses in red pen and the occasional tick. It was a history exercise book. Lennox turned towards Vera and showed her the book; her face showed no emotion.

"Any idea how this got here, Mrs Olong?"

"I've never seen it before. What is it?"

Wednesday told her whilst continuing to poke around the area to see if anything else belonged to the missing boy.

"This doesn't look good for you," said Wednesday. "If you have anything to say, now would be a good time."

"I have nothing to say. I never come up here."

"Are you implying that your husband may know something?"

"I'm implying nothing of the sort. I'm merely saying that I have nothing to say as I know nothing."

Nothing else was found. No evidence of food or drink and importantly, no blood that was visible to the naked eye. Wednesday phoned the station to request SOCO come and sweep the attic.

They descended the ladder and went to find Reverend Olong. Vera tapped on the study door then opened it slightly to request access. They found him hunched over the computer with his reading glasses settled halfway down his nose.

"Reverend Olong, we found a school book belonging to Darren Giles in your attic. Do you know how it got there?"

He swivelled round in his chair and removed his glasses that were sliding off his nose.

"A book you say. Why would that be up there?"

"We were hoping you could answer that. It looks like he may have been hiding up there. Do you think it would be possible for him to hide up there without either of you knowing?"

"I'm not sure, but this is a rambling old house that possesses many creaks and groans of its own. To be honest, I spend a lot of my time on parish work in here, which is the furthest away from the attic."

Vera stood quietly by her husband with her hand planted on his shoulder. "Detectives, we have nothing to hide. If young Darren chose to hide here, perhaps it was because he felt safe."

"If that was the case, Mrs Olong, then where is he now?"

Wednesday explained that forensic evidence would be gathered shortly and that they may be required to attend the station for an interview.

"Surely that wouldn't be necessary. You know gossip could do damage to my husband. We're happy in this village and we want to stay here."

"We'll be as discreet as possible, Mrs Olong."

The doorbell rang, announcing the arrival of SOCO. Vera Olong went to open the door, leaving her troubled husband with the detectives.

"I am truly unaware of how the book got here. There must be a logical explanation."

"Time is of the essence, Reverend, we need to find Darren. So I'll ask you again, do you know where he is?"

Reverend Olong shook his head and spread his hands out, palms up.

"We'd like you to remain here, and not venture to other villages, until further investigations have been carried out. If you do think of anything, please contact me," Wednesday said as she handed him her card.

The sound of sniffer dogs echoed from outside. With everything underway, they decided to go and look at the rambling club hut, to see whether there were any signs of Darren having been there.

"What do you make of our finding?" asked Lennox.

"It's a step closer to knowing that Darren hasn't gone far. We need to delve into the reverend's background now to see what that drags up."

The weak sun sliced through the semi-naked tree tops, dappling droplets of gold onto the mossy ground. Dogs barked in the distance intermingled with the occasional human shout.

Wednesday loved the sound of the red and orange leaves crunching under foot and it amused her to see Lennox kicking and scattering them around.

"There's still a child in you," she said with a little laugh.

"There's a child in everyone, only some people have disabled themso they are no longer fun."

They arrived at the hut, and took a look around the outside first, to look for any signs of disturbance.

"No signs of forced entry, let's take a look inside," said Lennox as he used the key the reverend had given him, having chosen to lock it following the crimes.

Inside looked the same as before and still smelt of newly sawn wood. The chairs looked as though they had been moved and so possibly used since their last visit.

"We need to check with the rev to see if his rambling group is underway," Lennox said. "Apart from that, I can't see anything else here, can you?"

Wednesday shook her head. "I can't help feeling that our answer lies in the vicarage. Perhaps the forensic guys will come up with something."

They walked back a different way towards the vicarage and found themselves at an arched gate set in a large evergreen hedge. The gate led into the back garden of the vicarage. Wandering in, they looked around when they saw Alex Green walking toward them.

"I've bagged samples to test for evidence, we should be able to get some skin cells or latent prints from the blankets and book. Have you guys found anything else?"

Although shaking their heads, they sensed they were getting closer to Darren Giles. They hoped he had the answer to the link between the two deaths. Wednesday willed the boy to sense they were getting closer to him. To save him or to save others.

# Chapter Twelve

Monday morning had the same inevitable lacklustre atmosphere like most Monday mornings, and the lack of major progress in the three cases was not helping the mood in the Major Crime Unit.

Wednesday was sketching a mind map after their visit to the vicarage yesterday, when her mobile rang. It was Scarlett.

"I couldn't wait until this evening to talk to you, sis. I received this bizarre letter this morning saying there are evil spirits in this village that are working their dark magic. What do think about that?"

Wednesday could hear Scarlett's voice buzzing with excitement, which was a worry in itself, never mind the anonymous letter.

"Scarlett, this is probably someone's idea of a joke. However, could you bring the letter and envelope to the station, and try not to handle it too much."

Scarlett mumbled something then put the receiver down, leaving Wednesday knowing that she was not happy with her lack of enthusiasm or intrigue about the matter.

There was a tap at her door before Alex Green poked his head around.

"Got some findings for you," he said, entering her office without waiting for her to speak.

"I found some small fragments of gravel at the dead girl's crime scene that I've managed to link to the school grounds. It could be the link you're looking for."

"Or it could just be from Claudia's shoes that she picked up whilst she was in school," she said as she looked at his youthful features and waited for him to look crestfallen.

"True, but she wasn't wearing school shoes and I couldn't find any trace evidence lodged in the soles of the shoes she was wearing, but I take your point."

"However, Cleveland doesn't have to know the full picture. Thanks Alex," she said, picking up the phone and dialling Lennox's number. "We need to visit Markham Hall to speak to Cleveland again."

They could detect a note of glee in the voice of the receptionist, Nina Prince, as she told them they had had a wasted journey, as Mr Cleveland had phoned in sick that morning. Undeterred, they decided to visit him at home.

The Victorian building converted into flats looked less ostentatious from the outside than Wednesday had expected. She ran her finger down the residents' names until she found Cleveland. She rang three times but there was no answer, so Lennox tried a new tactic and just leant on the buzzer without releasing it.

"What," came a wary voice over the intercom.

"Mr Cleveland, DI Wednesday and DS Lennox, we need to speak with you." Lennox's voice resonated with puissance.

"I'm sick, make an appointment with my secretary at the school."

"I'm afraid that won't be possible, this is a murder enquiry and unless you wish us to conduct the interview publically, I suggest you let us in."

There was a pause before the door buzzed and the lock was released.

"Nicely done, Lennox," she smiled.

The entrance hall was cluttered with bikes and piles of junk mail that no one had bothered to recycle. A row of four mailboxes were fastened to the peacock-blue wall.

Cleveland's flat was on the top floor, and as they reached his landing he was standing in the doorway waiting for them.

"I'm feeling rather persecuted, Detectives. I hope you have a damn good reason to cause this annoyance." He coughed and wiped his brow before allowing them to enter. He was dressed in jeans and a polo neck jumper underneath a tartan dressing gown.

The interior of his flat proved to be bland. The walls were painted magnolia on which hung prints of generic country scenes. The curtains were drawn which added to the dreariness. Cleveland had the expected book shelves containing text books and novels, but there appeared to be very little in the way of personal artefacts and photographs. Even his TV was rather small for the size of the room.

"You took awhile answering your door," remarked Lennox.

"I was in bed ill," he replied before coughing into a crumpled tissue.

"We found the same gravel from your school grounds next to Claudia's body."

He flung himself into a bucket armchair and allowed a smile to drift across his face.

"The gravel may be the same, but you can't say who got it there; it could have come from Claudia's shoes after all."

"She wasn't wearing school shoes, Mr Cleveland, so it's another piece of evidence that links the school to the crimes. I suggest if you have anything to say, no matter how trivial, you say it now."

"Or what, it'll look bad in court?"

"We're not trying to trick you, we have two dead students and a missing one all from your school; it doesn't look good now does it?"

"The word buzzing around the community is that Darren Giles is missing because he had something to do with the deaths," he said with a smug look on his face.

"You shouldn't listen to gossip. As a headmaster you should know that."

Cleveland began a violent coughing outburst making Wednesday discreetly cover her nose and mouth with her hand.

"We won't trouble you any longer; we can see you are suffering."

"No doubt I'll be seeing you again," he said, his voice muffled by the tissue.

"No doubt," replied Lennox, giving a mock salute.

They were about to drive off when they spotted Dick Pennymore getting out of his car and slamming the door. Lennox opened his window before lighting a cigarette.

They could see Pennymore ringing a doorbell several times before he stood back on the path and yelled.

"I know you're in there, Cleveland. Let me in right now."

It became obvious that Cleveland was not going to let him in, so Pennymore pressed the bell persistently before hammering on the door.

Wednesday and Lennox got out of their car and walked towards him.

"Is something wrong?"

"Detective Wednesday isn't it," he replied in a breathy voice, his face red and sweaty. "Nothing wrong, it's just his bar tab payment is long overdue, that's all."

"I see. You seem pretty angry about it."

"Well money's a bit tight for everyone at the moment, so I want what I'm owed."

"I suggest you might come back another time, he's unwell and clearly doesn't want any visitors."

He expelled a lung-full of air before stomping back to his car.


Wednesday sat in her office writing up the day's report, keen to get out of the station as soon as possible.

"Coming for a drink?" Lennox asked as he peered around her door.

"Sorry, I really must see Scarlett. Another time though."


Pulling into her driveway, Wednesday could see that Scarlett had left nearly every light on in the house. As she opened the front door she was greeted by the aroma of freshly brewed coffee.

"Is that a good idea?" Wednesday said as she nodded towards the coffee pot on the Aga.

"God yes, I'm on a roll, sis. I need to keep going. The editor has saved me the front cover for this piece on a cult in our midst, so I need to finish it and get it to him by one in the morning."

"What cult?"

"Children dying in the vicinity of a church always spells trouble and invariably spells cult."

Wednesday sighed. Living with someone who lived on an eternal rollercoaster, on a high for the majority of the time, followed by crushing lows without any explanation, was extremely tiring at times. Wednesday worried for Scarlett, and she worried for herself.

"I didn't have time to drop the letter at the station. I thought you could take it with you tomorrow," said Scarlett as she handed over the piece of paper.

Wednesday held it by the corners as she read it then placed it along with the envelope, into an evidence bag. She could see that Scarlett was far too busy to want to discuss anything further, so she poured herself a glass of wine and headed up for a soak in a deep bath.

As Wednesday lay staring at the ceiling, Lennox's and Scarlett's words intermingled in her foggy brain. Somehow she knew she should be worried about something, but her deadened mind was not receptive. The homely smell of freshly ground coffee floated around the air, and the fear of tomorrow filled her thoughts.

She could hear Scarlett moving around downstairs, clearly hyped-up. How on earth did she figure a cult would exist in rural Cambridgeshire?

Unwelcome thoughts about Lennox spun around her mind as she let the warm water lap over her shoulders.

# Chapter Thirteen

The indexers Suzy Simmons and Audrey Smith were busy talking about their Christmas plans by the coffee machine, when Wednesday walked up behind them.

"What's it like working with DD—the dishy detective?" Audrey asked.

"Is that what you two call Lennox?"

"Not just us, all of the women. Maria came up with it, but don't tell her we told you so. Anyway, how are you coping being around him so much?"

The pair grinned at her but before she had the chance to set them straight, Hunter entered the room clapping his hands. He stood by the white board with his arms folded, scanning the room.

"Arlow and Damlish have dug up more info on the Wrights. The neighbours heard frequent disturbances but never called the police. They said they were too afraid to get involved."

People murmured until he coughed.

"Wednesday and Lennox, I want you to find out more about Reverend Olong's interaction with the families. Damlish and Arlow can dig up the past issues in his previous parish, and carry out a visit if necessary. The trail for Darren went cold in the vicarage, but both Olongs deny any knowledge of his presence there." He took a sip of coffee before continuing.

"There is more to the vicarage than meets the eye; I want discreet surveillance to monitor who comes and goes." He turned towards the officers sitting on the edge of a table in the far corner.

"What has surveillance come up with at the Wright's?"

"Not much, Guv. She only seems to pop out occasionally to go to the local shop, and he has occasional labouring jobs," replied a young constable.

"Are they aware of your presence?"

"Yes, Guv, just as you wanted. Sometimes they give us two fingers to show us their displeasure."

Ripples of laughter swept across the room making the young constable go bright red. Hunter coughed pointedly.

"Jones will assign the other jobs. Get to it and get results."

Everyone moved into position whilst Maria Jones set about organising the staff.

"Wednesday, Lennox, my office, now," snapped Hunter.

They followed him in and shut the door behind them.

"I realise you may not be on board about pursuing the reverend due to the cliché factor, but I feel his movements are worth tracking. It may be too passé for you to take seriously, but I'm ordering you to take heed of him."

Wednesday's cheeks stung as though he had slapped her. They both nodded like obedient dogs on a car dashboard and returned to Wednesday's office to plan their movements. Lennox chewed on a pencil as he looked up the Edwards' phone number.

"Would you believe it, we've got to visit the Edwards first because they're going to their London flat for a few days. You'd think a holiday would be the last thing on their mind," he said, replacing the receiver.

"Maybe it's exactly because of what's on their minds that they want to get away. I can only imagine how they must feel. You can be a cold fish at times."

"And you can be too empathic."

The drive to the Edwards' house was conducted in flat silence. Pulling up outside the residence, they saw a few photographers hanging around.

"Like proverbial flies around shit," muttered Lennox to himself.

Having a half-sister in the press business did not help quash Wednesday's dislike of people who profited from other people's misery; although Scarlett would retort that the police did the same. Wednesday gave no eye contact to the watchful crowd as they walked up the path. Journalists called out questions to the pair, but Lennox just called back "no comment" before ringing on the doorbell.

"I hope you won't keep us long, Detectives," said Greg Edwards as he let them in through a half open door. "My wife is extremely fragile, and those hounds out there aren't helping."

"I'm sorry about that, we can move them on if you wish," replied Wednesday.

"No point in that now." He led them to the lounge where Lucinda was watering the houseplants. She turned around slightly as they entered and gave only a fleeting smile.

"What is it you said you wanted to talk about?" enquired Greg as he gestured to them to sit down.

"We were wondering whether Reverend Olong had been to see you recently," Wednesday asked.

"The reverend? He comes daily, as it happens. Why?"

"Has it been at your request?"

"No. But Lucinda has been a shell since . . . well since it happened, and I think his presence may be of some comfort to her."

"Is that correct, Mrs Edwards?"

She stopped watering. "I try to glean some semblance of peace and hope in this diabolical world. I wish to wash my soul of the anguish and grief that someone has smeared on it. Perhaps only God can help me now."

It was the first time they had really heard her speak. Her voice was as weak and as delicate as her feeble frame. Her whole being evoked pity and yet curiosity.

"Did you see much of the reverend before this tragedy?" Wednesday asked.

"Look, I'm not sure what this is all about. We're having a tough time here, and unless you think the reverend did it, I don't see the point in you questioning us like this." Greg had moved to stand next to his wife and put both hands on her shoulder. His face was contorted by unexpressed impotent rage.

"We often have to make linear enquiries in a case. We're sorry if we've caused you any distress."

"You didn't answer me when I asked whether you thought the reverend did it. Is he the murderer?"

Lucinda tilted her head towards her husband's face.

"We are just making enquiries. Please don't read too much into our conversations, we're looking at all those involved with the children in one way or another. We have your address and number for your London flat, so we'll get in touch if we have a lead."

Next, they drove to the Dolby's house, travelling in nicotine smog, both caught up in their fraught worlds.

James Dolby answered the door within seconds, as though he had been standing in the hallway waiting for them all morning.

"Any news?" he asked, forgetting to invite them in.

"Nothing new, sir, I'm afraid. May we come in?"

"Let them in, James," called his wife, who could be heard pottering in the kitchen.

James had the air of a man on the edge of a precipice, into which he was about to jump at any given moment. Emily Dolby, on the other hand, seemed more in control as she breezed in with a tray of tea. Without asking, she poured everyone a drink and passed the cups around.

"Have you seen much of the Reverend Olong lately?" Wednesday said as she put her cup down on the coffee table.

"Oh yes, he's been an enormous strength and solace for me," replied Emily.

"And you, Mr Dolby?" asked Wednesday, sensing a different response from him.

"The very mention of God is abhorrent at the moment. Emily still seems able to trust in the Lord and the reverend. I don't interfere with her needs."

"Perhaps you're both at different stages in your grief," said Lennox, placing his empty cup and saucer on the table. "You both normally attend church I understand, so the reverend was already involved with you all as a family, correct?"

"Indeed, and I'm sure my husband will return to the bosom of God once he has worked through the pact with the devil he's currently embraced." She looked directly at him.

He scowled back at her. "What are you blithering on about? How can God let this random act of violence rip our world apart?"

"You believe it was a random act, Mr Dolby?" interjected Wednesday.

"But of course. Who would wish our Tom dead? He'd harmed no one."

Wednesday noticed Emily look down at her shoes on hearing his words.

"Do you have the same thoughts, Mrs Dolby? Or is there something else you wish to say?"

"Of course she has the same bloody thoughts."

Emily's face dropped at her husband's outburst. She clambered to her feet, clutching a handkerchief to her mouth, and rushed from the room.

"I'll go and check she's okay," said Wednesday, instructing Lennox with a flick of her eyeballs to stay with the husband.

Wednesday heard muffled sobs emanating from behind the closed kitchen door, so she tapped on it lightly before walking in. Emily was standing with her back to the door so all Wednesday could see were her shoulders juddering with each mournful gasp.

"Perhaps you should sit down." Wednesday took her by the arm and placed her in a chair at the table.

"I'm sorry. My husband shouldn't speak as he does, not about a man of the cloth or the Creator himself."

Wednesday winced at the reverence Emily graced upon religion, and the awe she displayed regarding the reverend. She knew she had to respect an individual's right to choice, but it did not make hearing their choices any easier.

"You seemed a little uneasy when your husband mentioned Tom's innocent behaviour. Do you have a different take on things?"

Emily's puffy, blotchy face appeared from behind the tissue that was rendered useless by her copious tears.

"No child is always an angel; it's not realistic to expect that. I just wanted some help with his attitude."

"What kind of help?"

"Someone to listen to me. James never seemed to listen or to understand. I lacked the strength to cope at times."

"Did you find someone to listen to you?"

"God listened to me, but even He wasn't enough at times. I couldn't bring myself to talk to the reverend, I was too embarrassed . . ."

Wednesday watched as Emily sank her head into her hands

"What did you do, Mrs Dolby?"

"That's the problem; I did nothing, nothing at all."

"And what should you have done?"

"I don't know exactly, but I shouldn't have stood on the sidelines. I was his mother . . ."

Emily's train of thought was leading Wednesday a merry dance, which she was struggling to follow. Clearly Emily wasn't coherent enough to be interviewed.

Wednesday felt her mobile vibrate in her pocket. She reluctantly looked at and saw it was her stepfather. She knew he only called in extreme circumstances. Wednesday excused herself and stepped outside.

"What's wrong, Oliver?"

"It's your mother. Scarlett phoned and talked about some sort of local cult influence."

"Oh."

"She's been worried ever since, and now she thinks I'm trying to poison her. I wonder if she's stopped taking her meds. I don't know what to do."

Wednesday clamped her hand to her forehead and felt the rapid pulse in her temples. "I'll be right over," she replied as she stepped back inside.

"I'm terribly sorry; I have an emergency to attend to."

Emily looked at Wednesday with concern. "Is it about the missing boy?" she asked.

"No, it's another matter altogether."

Wednesday removed Lennox from the lounge and made a quick exit to the car.

"Where are we going?" he asked.

"To see my mother; well I am, you can wait in the car."

Wednesday hastily lit a cigarette before driving off, whilst Lennox gripped onto the overhead handle. Wednesday caught sight of his discomfort in her peripheral vision. *Wimp.*

She pulled up onto a bumpy dirt track that led to the isolated cottage on the outskirts of the village. The long grass down the middle of the track brushed the underside of the car as though tickling the belly of the beast. Smoke billowed out from the chimney and the nets at the windows were in dire need of a wash. Wednesday felt a pang of embarrassment, but it was too late to turn back now.

She parked next to Oliver's mud-spattered Landrover and tossed her cigarette stub out the window. She wound the window back up to shut out the chilled air, then proceeded to get out. Lennox obediently remained seated whilst staring at her.

"Oh give up with the puppy-dog eyes, come on in with me. But I warn you, what goes on in here remains between us. Understand?"

He nodded and refrained from asking any questions.

Wednesday blustered in without knocking, and called out to Oliver. Lennox followed her into a cluttered, narrow hallway that had muddy boots strewn all over the floor. An umbrella stand in the shape of a giant chimney pot stood at the foot of the staircase, filled with a variety of walking sticks and tatty-looking umbrellas.

"Excuse the mess," she said as she stepped over a laundry basket piled with damp clothes.

"Rather than mess, I see accidental beauty," he replied.

Wednesday raised her eyebrows and rolled her eyes.

They found Oliver in the kitchen standing over the sink, and Wednesday's mother, Joan, sitting at the table. She looked up as they entered.

"Who's he? Has he come to take me away?" she said, looking at Lennox with wide eyes.

"No Mum, this is Jacob Lennox, a colleague from work."

"Is he your boyfriend? I don't want you to be single anymore. You're getting too old to be alone."

"No Mum." Wednesday moved closer to her. "Lennox is a detective like me. We work together." She bent down to kiss her on the cheek.

"How are you?" she said, turning her attention to Oliver. She noticed his angular face looked pallid and drawn, and the light behind his green eyes had faded.

"Just about coping, but I'm worried," he whispered. He gestured with a movement of his head for her to get nearer to him.

"I'm worried I won't be able to stave off calling her doctor."

"You have to do what's best for her."

"She didn't sleep a wink last night, and as you can hear," he pointed, "she's speaking incoherently; no rational thinking."

Wednesday nodded and patted his arm lightly. She filled the kettle and put it on to boil. Leaning back against the work top, she surveyed the scene and felt a lump in her throat. The child within her wanted to cry for the mother she had lost to mental illness, but that child in her had to be suppressed.

Lennox was continually brushing his hand over the top of his head which grabbed Wednesday's attention.

"You can smoke in here if you want," she told him with a half smile, noticing how uncomfortable he looked. "I'm having one once I've made the tea." She threw him her packet in a token gesture of their new and fragile friendship.

"Your boyfriend smokes?" asked Joan as she eyed Lennox wearily.

"Mum, he's not my boyfriend he's . . ."

She realised her words were futile. Her mother was not really lucid enough to absorb the complexity of life. She heaved a sigh as she distributed the drinks, before sitting down next to Joan and placing her hand on top of hers, giving it a gentle pat.

"Mum, I want to call Dr Noble to come and see you. We're worried about you."

"I'm safe in here, but I can't go out there. Scarlett warned me. Where is she, is she safe?"

"She's safe, we're all safe. Scarlett's story is just that, a story."

Joan looked agitated as she shuffled around in her chair, biting the skin around her fingernails. She then picked up her teacup and smelt it.

"What have you put in my tea?" snapped Joan as she tossed the cup onto the table, sending hot liquid spewing across the pine surface.

Oliver rushed over with a cloth, and Joan began screeching as though she was under attack. Wednesday called the doctor.

She could hardly hear the receptionist over the racket in the kitchen. She could see Oliver was beginning to lose control of his emotions. She witnessed Lennox take it upon himself to intervene in the most appropriate manner he could think of. Joan screamed louder as Lennox approached her, so he backed away, looking towards Wednesday for assistance.

"Mum, the doctor's on his way, it's going to be okay." Wednesday sat down next to her and wrapped her arm around her shoulders.

Ten minutes later, the doctor was at the door and twenty minutes after that, Joan was being escorted to the psychiatric hospital in Cambridge. Oliver followed in his Landrover, and Wednesday and Lennox returned to work, with Wednesday promising to visit that evening.

They drove back to the station in a reflective and sombre mood. Dense smog of noxious fumes swirled around their heads and clung to their hair. Lennox cleared his throat before speaking.

"I'm sorry about your mum. How long has she . . . ?"

"Since I was eleven. Generally she is stable, but periodically she is triggered by stress or anxiety, and we go through this." She took a deep drag on her cigarette. "By the way, I don't want my private life dissected at work, so please refrain from conversing with the others about what you've seen."

"Hey, I'm not like that. We watch each other's backs. Is Hunter aware?"

"No he's not and I don't want him to be, either."

"What if you need time off?"

"I'll manage. I just don't want my frame of mind or bad temper to be deliberated behind my back. And I don't want bets being laid as to when I'll enter the funny farm."

"You have a distorted view of your colleagues."

Wednesday smiled before checking her makeup in the mirror. As she got out of the car, cold air smacked her face giving her a hint of colour her cheeks naturally lacked.

The Incident Room was noisy with ringing telephones, and officers moving between desks with bundles of files and photographs. Hunter appeared from his office demanding a briefing in five minutes. Wednesday grabbed a coffee and headed for her office without glancing in Lennox's direction.

Closing the door so the racket became background noise, Wednesday slumped into her chair and put her head in her hands. The torment of the past few hours charged around her mind, making her head spin. She found it almost impossible to recall the morning's interviews; her mind only seemed focused on her mother. She knew she should have gone to the hospital with them. She was sick of always feeling guilty.

Maria Jones tapped on Wednesday's door, beckoning her out for the briefing. Hunter was already standing by the white board.

"Right, I want us to focus on the list of possible suspects. Let's consider Reverend Olong; he appears to show a lot of interest in the local kids. There's already a history of him allegedly being involved with a choir boy in the last parish, any updates on that, Arlow?"

"The boy was interviewed with his mother present, but he refused to talk about it. The church moved Olong here to give him a fresh start, as the rumours amongst the parishioners were too rife for him to stay there."

"Right, nothing particularly useful there," he said before taking a sip of water.

"Stewart Cleveland runs the school all the kids attended. And there seems to be an undercurrent of hostility with Dick Pennymore from The Crow. Tenuous links, but there all the same."

As Hunter paced the front of the room, the clicking of his heels added an unwanted distraction from his speech.

"Then we have Des Wright, whom DI Wednesday believes could be a perpetrator of domestic violence, and a possible bully towards his stepson. One thought could be that he had something to do with Tom's death, Darren witnessed it and was consequently disposed of."

Hunter was interrupted by someone's mobile phone which was hastily switched off, but not before Hunter threw an angry look in the culprit's direction.

"Lastly, we come to Colin Pollock, who is also linked via the school to the victims. Rumour has it he's not liked much by the parents, as he's not from their social stratosphere. But he's liked by the students. Not much to go on, but I want thoughts. Throw them out at me now, come on."

Some officers eyed one another, whilst others tapped pencils on the desks and looked at their shoes.

"Perhaps we should get all four in for questioning and ruffle their feathers. Make them sweat and see what they cough up."

"Okay Damlish, let's work that way as nothing else is working wonders. What about the vicarage; anything else turn up there?"

"No Guv, just the exercise book. The trail went cold for the dogs from the garden boundary," replied Arlow, flicking through his notebook.

"That could mean he was either taken away from there in some sort of transport, or he never left the vicarage." Hunter rubbed his chin, his eyes flicking from side to side whilst deep in thought.

"Wednesday and Lennox, I want you to return to the vicarage tomorrow and have another look around. Make them uncomfortable, my money's on the reverend for some misdemeanour or two. Take a warrant to look for a travel blanket; they're bound to have at least one."

"Them and half the population around here," whispered Wednesday under her breath. Hunter caught her eye and she blushed.

"True, so get a warrant to search all the possible suspects' properties whilst you're at it."

"This is just in from Alex Green," said Arlow, brandishing a piece of paper. "The plaster cast of the footprint from the crime scene of Claudia Edwards has been identified as a wellington boot size seven. The make is Hunter."

The information sent a buzz around the room, as any advance in a case did.

"Okay, add wellington boots to the search along with the travel blanket. And remember a size seven could be a woman's."

Hunter wanted everyone to recommence in the morning with refreshed and alert minds, so he ordered them to go home, leaving the night shift to hold the fort.

"Are you going to manage to get some rest this evening?" asked Lennox, poking his head around Wednesday's office door.

"Hopefully," she replied. She had her back to the door whilst packing her work bag. "Lennox . . . Thanks for today."

"No worries. See you tomorrow."

She watched him through the window as he crossed the car park, his face briefly illuminated as he lit a cigarette. After watching him pull out onto the main road, she caught sight of her reflection in the glass. Her hair was barely contained in its chignon, and her mascara and eyeliner had converged under her lower lashes and in the corners of her eyes. With a resigned sigh, she switched off her office light and bit into a chocolate bar as she headed for her car. She checked her mobile for any messages before starting her engine.

Heading towards the hospital with the melancholic tones of Joni Mitchell drifting in and out of her mind, she wondered what kind of state her mother would be in. Mercifully sedated was her hope. It was probably Oliver who would need the proverbial shoulder.

# Chapter Fourteen

Wednesday's head throbbed through lack of sleep, and her skin lacked the lustre of youth, taking on the patina of someone older than her thirty-seven years. She clanged the kettle onto the Aga and rattled the cutlery drawer, before turning up the radio.

"Good god, sis, you could wake the bloody dead," Scarlett said, tossing her matted auburn locks over her shoulder. She opened the fridge and took out the carton of orange juice, spilling a few drops as she sloshed it into a tumbler.

"Where were you last night?" asked Wednesday.

"I was at the office, putting the finishing touches to my article. Why, where were you?"

"At the hospital being the dutiful daughter to our mother."

"Good for you, how is she?"

"How do you think? She's sedated due to her high state of paranoia and anxiety. She was asking after you in her more lucid moments."

"What did you tell her?"

"I said you'd been caught up at work, but you'd visit her as soon as you could."

"Cool."

Downing the last few drops of coffee, Wednesday was about to throw Scarlett a curt comment, when the doorbell rang, and Scarlett escaped to answer it.

"Can't keep away from me, eh Jacob Lennox?" she said on opening the door.

"I've come for Eva actually." He waited to be invited in out of the pelting rain.

"She's in the kitchen."

He followed her through the hallway, noticing that she was wearing silky blue pyjama bottoms, a faded denim-coloured sweatshirt, and silver satin ballet pumps.

Wednesday checked her watch when she saw him, thinking she must be running late for him to be there.

"I thought you might be tired after yesterday, so I thought I'd drive." Raindrops glistened on his navy coat.

"What a courteous colleague you have," Scarlett said in a child-like sing-song voice, fluttering her lashes at him.

Wednesday clamped her lips together as they left. Climbing into Lennox's car, her mobile rang.

"We're on our way. Domestic at the Wrights' house," she informed Lennox as he started up the engine.

"Nothing like a quiet start to the day," he replied with a wry smile.

Screeching to a halt outside the Wrights' residence, Wednesday noticed the net curtains moving in the neighbour's windows; the ones who had undoubtedly decided to finally call it in.

Striding up the front path, they heard raised voices coming from inside the house; doors slamming and crockery shattering.

Lennox found the front door locked, so he hammered on it with his fist and shouted through the letterbox. After a few minutes, the commotion subsided, and Judith's voice travelled through the door, informing them that everything was okay.

Wednesday looked at Lennox before insisting to Judith that they were let in. Muffled sounds were heard from the other side before the lock was slowly turned and Judith's crimson face peered from behind it.

"Can we come in please?" asked Wednesday, determined to shame Des for his cowardly behaviour. "We have a warrant to search your property."

Reluctantly, Judith opened the door but focused on the floor. Lennox followed Wednesday into the hallway.

"Where's Des?" Wednesday asked, looking over Judith's shoulder.

Judith pointed towards the kitchen then let the pair brush past her. Entering the kitchen they found Des standing by the sink, rolling a cigarette. He had dried blood streaks around his mouth and nose, and a couple of missing buttons on his shirt which was hanging out of his trousers. He looked towards them with darkness in his eyes.

Wednesday surveyed the kitchen and noticed the debris of broken crockery scattered across the floor. Coffee and wine stains dribbled down the walls.

"I'm going to ask your wife if she wants to press charges," said Wednesday.

Des laughed and then lit his roll-up. He inhaled deeply before blowing smoke into her face.

"You can ask her all you want, but I know she'll say no."

"Why, have you threatened her if she dares betray you?"

Des continued to stare out the window, smoking his cigarette. He saw his wife enter the kitchen in the reflection in the window.

"What's the warrant for," she asked.

It was as she spoke that Wednesday noticed the smell of alcohol on her breath. Perhaps it was the domestic violence that drove her to drink, she thought to herself.

"We need to search your property for wellington boots and a travel blanket."

Judith gave her a blank look, then walked over to the table and picked up a mug. "You can look where you want. We ain't got nothing to hide."

Wednesday and Lennox wasted no time and began searching from room to room. The rooms were already in disarray, making the search more arduous. They came across numerous overflowing ashtrays and empty bottles and cans, but no travel blanket or boots. Lennox climbed into the loft, but only found a few boxes containing old records and tatty Christmas decorations.

"We've got nothing of interest here and no evidence of Darren hiding back here either. Do you want to try Judith Wright again to see if she wants to make a statement against her husband?" asked Lennox as he dusted cobwebs from his hair.

"I suspect she'll decline the offer. Come on, let's go to the vicarage, we might have more success there."

The Wrights hardly acknowledged the detective's departure; and when they had gone, the detectives imagined the drinking and brawling would soon recommence.

They arrived at the vicarage in time to see Reverend Olong heading for his car.

"Good morning, Reverend. I'm sorry but we need to speak with you inside," said Lennox as he stood between the reverend and his car.

"I was just on my way to a pastoral meeting, could it possibly wait? Vera's inside. Perhaps she can help you?"

"I'm sorry, Reverend; we need to speak to both of you."

Olong exhaled before returning slowly to the front door.

Vera jumped slightly as the three of them entered the kitchen. "Heavens, I thought you'd gone to your meeting. Hello Detectives."

In his perfunctory manner, Lennox explained what they were looking for, and requested they search the house, garage, and cars. He also explained that afterwards they would be taking the reverend to the station for questioning.

"This is outrageous. I'm a patient man, but you are indeed trying my resolve. I have nothing to hide and nothing to fear."

"Good, then you have no problem with our requests," said Wednesday, scanning the kitchen. Her eyes fell upon a rather troubled-looking Vera.

"Shall I take you to the garage, DI Wednesday?" Vera asked.

Wednesday could see she needed to talk, so she left Lennox with the reverend and departed with Vera.

"This is all rather like *déjà vu*, Detective. All this is causing me great concern. I'm worried for George."

"He's not been charged with anything."

"That's true, but mud sticks and I'm not sure George could take much more. This parish is perfect for us both. It offers the tranquillity we both desire."

"Your husband claims he has nothing to fear, but you seem troubled. Is there something you want to tell me?"

"George and I have a happy marriage, but we don't partake in the physical aspect of marriage, if you take my drift?"

"I don't see the relevance, Mrs Olong."

"What I'm trying to say is just because we sleep separately and he's a reverend, doesn't mean he's gay or fancies choir boys." She visibly shuddered at speaking the words, and her face turned a delicate shade of cherry.

"I'm not in the habit of being judgemental. Your home is not the only home being searched, and your husband is not the only person being questioned, so please don't try and second guess our motives."

Wednesday noticed Vera wasn't appeased by her words. It was the first time Wednesday thought how the name *Vera* did not suit her. To begin with, the name sounded older than Vera looked and acted; she had only recently turned forty-one, although her husband was fifty and looked much older. Deep down, Wednesday was not surprised they no longer slept together.

Wednesday spied some wellington boots in the far corner of the garage. She took out the photocopy of the sole of the boot and walked over to the corner. Bending down, she compared the patterns, and although one pair was made by Hunter, they were a size too small. For a brief moment, Wednesday wondered whether Digby Hunter had a pair, simply because they had his name printed on the front.

"May I check your car?"

Vera obliged but Wednesday found nothing of interest.

"Do you visit parishioners as part of your duties? Only I was wondering if you offered advice and support to women in need."

"I sometimes get involved in that way. Why, who are you thinking of?"

"Judith Wright. Not only has one son gone missing and the other son is in prison, but I suspect she may be a victim of domestic violence. I presume I can talk to you in confidence about this matter?"

"Of course. I don't know the Wrights very well; they rarely attend church and they don't belong to the choir. I have little reason to interact with them, but I could pop in if you think it might help."

"I'm not sure what will help, to be honest, Mrs Olong."

Wednesday decided that she had nothing left to see there, so they returned to the house where they found Lennox and the reverend in the utility room, looking through the laundry basket.

Having had no luck with boots or blankets, the detectives drove the reverend back to the station, leaving his perplexed and anxious wife standing in the doorway.

Arriving at the station, they were in time to see a rather indignant Stewart Cleveland being escorted in, followed by a red faced Des Wright who was muttering under his breath. All three saw one another and quickly averted their eyes.

Each was placed in an interview room, and left to brood over their situation whilst staring at the two empty chairs opposite them. Hunter had given the team orders to leave them alone with their thoughts, which sometimes facilitated an outpouring of truths when the time came.

Wednesday and Lennox began with Stewart Cleveland. On entering the room, he searched them out with an indignant look on his face.

"This is an utter nuisance. I do have an important job to do. I've already told you I have nothing to do with these crimes."

"We were wondering what Dick Pennymore wanted with you. He looked rather angry," began Wednesday.

Cleveland's eyes closed slightly, beads of sweat accumulating on his brow. In his lap, his hands formed fists and his breathing became shallow.

"It's a totally unrelated matter to your cases. It's a private matter and I'd like it to remain that way."

Wednesday sat forward and raised an eyebrow. "When murder is an issue, there are no private matters, Mr Cleveland." She sat back in her chair before continuing. "What you should remember is that we already know the answer to our questions, so if you're lying, we'll know that you are."

Cleveland put his hand to his forehead, and brushed back his fringe.

"Instead of persecuting me relentlessly, why aren't you looking at Colin Pollock? He's the form tutor of all these students."

It was Lennox's turn to lean forward and talk.

"You're evading the question, Mr Cleveland. What did Mr Pennymore want with you?"

Cleveland let out an audible sigh. His shoulders once proud, now drooped as he hunched over the desk.

"I need to know that what I'm about to say won't be made public."

"I'm afraid we can't guarantee what would come out in court. However, it's your duty to aid this investigation into the tragic loss of your students, both dead and missing."

Cleveland put his head in his hands, and began to rock back and forth. The detectives watched and waited for him to explain himself.

"I owe Pennymore money, a lot of money. I've been ignoring him since he told me he couldn't wait any longer for the cash."

"What do you owe him money for?" asked Wednesday.

"I thought you said you knew all the answers, Detective." A smirk traversed his face.

"We'd like to hear the explanation in your own words, Mr Cleveland," she replied coolly.

Her flat response wiped the smug expression from his face as he prepared to divulge his shame.

"I'm a gambler, and I owe Pennymore money, a stupid amount of money, some of which belongs to the school."

The detectives listened whilst he unloaded his shame about his addiction. They allowed Cleveland to drown in his own murky waters, whilst they sat back and watched him suffer.

"Does the gambling take place at The Crow?" asked Lennox.

Cleveland nodded and spread his hands open with his palms up.

"I don't want to get him into trouble."

"We deal with murder. Another team will investigate those activities."

Once Cleveland began talking, he seemed unable to stop. He informed them about being approached by Dick Pennymore to join the gambling fraternity, which met every Wednesday and Friday evening in the back room of The Crow. The stakes were high as they were all professional or business people; hence he had a huge debt that Pennymore was calling in. He refused to divulge the other members as they bared no relation to the ongoing investigation. He did say, however, that Pennymore would be able to back up his alibi.

Having unburdened himself, Cleveland visibly relaxed, knowing that his lack of previous alibis could now be traced to The Crow which took him out of the murder equation.

Before terminating the interview, the detectives advised him that another thorough search of the school and the grounds would be taking place, and that they would be seeing Pennymore to corroborate his story.

Wednesday and Lennox moved into the next room, where Reverend Olong sat patiently nursing a plastic cup of weak tea. His demeanour did not shift as they entered the room.

Wednesday was aware of Hunter's suspicion that the reverend had something to do with the murders, and she did not want to disappoint him. Piece by piece, they moved through the reverend's movements, who he saw, and who could corroborate his story. His relationship with his wife and his previous position in the former parish.

"My wife said the trouble in the last parish would come back to haunt us, and here I am, having to defend myself again."

He sat and listened to their questions before answering them with clarity and unfaltering sentences. Tough nut to crack, thought Wednesday to herself, as she also wondered if Hunter was watching the interview through the two way mirror. Instinctively, she ran her hand over her hair to feel how many strands had worked their way loose.

The reverend finally said they could contact his superior to corroborate his story, and with that, he sat back in the chair and placed both his hands in a prayer like position.

"The puzzling issue that you can't explain, Reverend, is why was Darren's school book in your attic?" said Wednesday, who subconsciously mirrored the position of his hands.

"I have no answer to give. The only thing I can say is that it wouldn't be difficult for a young person to find a way into the vicarage undetected. Maybe he was running away from his home life and he thought he'd be safe there, and he only ran away once you started searching the property with your men and dogs. You can ask him when you find him."

Everything he said could have been true, thought Wednesday, and currently they had no proof to think otherwise. No proof and no body.

As they escorted the reverend out, they heard the recognisable voice of Des Wright echoing down the corridor. The reverend turned to them before leaving.

"Perhaps the truth is closer than you think."

The detectives returned to the Incident Room and began writing up their reports. The relative calm in the station was interrupted by the occasional expletive that rumbled down the corridor from Des Wright.

Forty minutes later, Arlow and Damlish returned to the Incident Room looking irritated and hot; neither had seemingly managed to break Des regarding the murders, his missing stepson, or the issue of domestic violence.

Jones wrote on the white board that neither the wellington boots nor the travel blanket was found in the searched properties. Each time the telephone rang, everyone hoped it would bring the breakthrough they were looking for.

Wednesday noticed an undercurrent rippling around the office, with several officers looking towards her, only to turn away as soon as she saw them. She was about to ask Lennox if he had disclosed her personal affairs, when Damlish walked over to her and showed her a copy of *The Cambridge Times*. Across the front page was an article by Scarlett Willow suggesting they may have cult activities taking place in the community.

"Hunter isn't best pleased with this," said Damlish. "I heard him yell that you need to keep your sister under control."

"Half-sister," she replied curtly. "Where is Hunter, by the way?"

"Gone to a meeting with the commissioner, won't be back until later."

Wednesday and Lennox decided to go outside for a smoke, expressly so she could escape the humiliation caused by Scarlett. She wound a cashmere scarf around her neck before lighting her cigarette.

"How's your mum?" he asked.

"Surviving, as we all do when this happens."

Lennox nodded, brushing the top of his head with his free hand. He wanted to ask her more questions, but she didn't seem in an accommodating mood. They smoked the remainder of their cigarettes in silence before returning inside to finish their reports.

Wednesday pulled up on her driveway and eased herself out of her car. Approaching the front door, she saw a small mound-like shape on the step in the porch. Moving towards it with caution, thinking it might be a hedgehog searching for snails, she bent down and saw it was a dead rat. A tingling sensation scurried down her back. Not wanting to touch it with her bare hands, she moved inside to find a carrier bag.

Scarlett was sitting in the kitchen, hunched over her laptop and seemingly too engrossed to notice Wednesday's presence.

"How long have you been home?" asked Wednesday as she put her work bag on the floor.

"A few hours. Why?"

"Because there's a dead rat on our front doorstep."

"Yuk. It must have just died there."

"Highly unlikely. This had better not be connected to your bloody article."

"Wow, if it is then I'm onto something big," she exclaimed, finally taking her eyes off the screen.

Wednesday shook her head then returned to the porch, after which she washed her hands until they were almost red and sore.

"Have you been to see Mum yet?"

Scarlett shrugged her shoulders and returned to the keyboard, tapping away lightly. Wednesday made herself an Earl Grey before sitting opposite Scarlett.

"Work is tough at the moment, so we need to share the care with her. Your dad can't do it all."

"You know I can't abide those places. They're just recycling bins; all the nut bars are sent there to be recycled into mainstream people who can respond normally in a mad world. You and Dad are strong enough to cope."

Wednesday took out a cigarette and offered one to Scarlett.

"Do you know that some mad people smoke to self medicate themselves through stress?" said Scarlett before lighting hers.

"I'm not sure of the scientific evidence for that. Are you worried that you, too, may become ill like her?" Wednesday blew out a trail of smoke towards the ceiling, watching Scarlett through half-closed eyes. "If it helps, I secretly worry that the same fate awaits me; we're more susceptible because she's ill," she continued before taking a sip of drink and waiting patiently for Scarlett to process her thoughts.

"I don't know why you're worrying; we may have the same mad mum, but you're dad is sane—if somewhat boring—but my dad is a fruit cake. What hope is there for me?"

"Do I take then that you are worried about your future sanity?"

"No sis, I'm truly not." And with that, Scarlett closed her laptop and headed up for a bath.

Wednesday felt she ought to phone the hospital or Oliver to check on her mum, but she was exhausted, and did not feel she had the head space for any more trauma.

Forty minutes later as she lay in bed, she put her book down on the bedside table, switched off the light and settled down to sleep.

During the dark hours, the sound of gravel crunching under-foot entered Wednesday's dream until her mind alerted her to the fact that it was coming from outside her bedroom window. Lifting her head off the pillow, she listened more closely. The sound stopped and then started again.

She climbed out of bed without switching on the light and moved to the window. She pulled back the curtain very slowly and peered between the velvet swathes. She could not make anything out in the teeming mass of shadows. So, believing her imagination was in overdrive, she stumbled back to bed and drifted into a much needed sleep.

The following morning, Wednesday found she was still trapped in spiralling destructive thoughts about mental illness.

Creeping out of her room and reaching the bottom of the stairs, she saw a newspaper on the door mat. Picking it up, she saw scrawled on the front page, the words "DIE BITCH" with red pen lines slashed across the photograph of Scarlett.

Behind her, she heard Scarlett coming down the stairs.

"Morning sis, is that the paper?"

"You appear to have made an enemy," Wednesday replied as she thrust the newspaper at her.

Scarlett's face lit up. "Or a fan," she replied as she danced around, holding the paper aloft.

"Scarlett, you're not taking this seriously. First the dead rat and now this. I want you to drop the features on a supposed cult in the area."

"You can't tell me what I can and can't do in my job. This is big, sis, it could set me up as a serious journalist."

"It could set you up as a victim, think about that."

Scarlett laughed in her face then skipped to the kitchen and put the kettle on. Wednesday followed her and flopped into the carver chair. She watched the steam from the kettle undulate across the ceiling whilst she contemplated what to do.

"You always twirl your hair when you're stressed," said Scarlett, placing a mug of coffee in front of Wednesday. "Please don't worry about me, I can look after myself."

Anger mushroomed in Wednesday as she thought how irresponsible Scarlett was being. Irresponsible not only to her own safety, but to the safety of their home. She was angry with Scarlett over several issues, but she had to pick her battle, and the current battle was really about their mother. What really aggravated her was that Scarlett was not even being supportive to her own father.

Wednesday's appetite had vanished, so gulping down her coffee, she grabbed an apple and set off for work. Scarlett was too lost in her own world to notice.

In the Incident Room, Jones was busy collating information given by the night shift, whilst the rest of the officers were gathered around the coffee machine. The only person who noticed Wednesday's arrival was Lennox, and after pouring her a coffee, he strode over to her office and tapped on the door.

"Morning, Boss. How are you?"

"Tired and feeling like crap, seeing as you asked. Or did you want the potted version of just a *yes?*"

He smiled. "How's your mum?"

"Still mad, but thanks for asking," she whispered.

Lennox brushed across his sharpened hair follicles and was about to walk away, when Wednesday spoke.

"I'm not sure why I'm telling you this, but I found a dead rat on the doorstep last night, and then this morning I found this."

Wednesday threw him the newspaper which he perused before handing it back.

"It's this damn cult angle she's taking," she said, placing it back in her bag. "I don't want to tell Hunter about this just yet."

"Not sure what you want me to do about it. Would you like me to come over after work?"

"That won't be necessary; I'm just running through my thoughts with you. Scarlett thinks it's a hoot quite frankly."

"Spunky girl, your sister."

"Half-sister."

Wednesday sat in her office searching through the paperwork, trying to look for links between the cases, chewing on a pencil as she thought about the individuals and wondered what she was missing.

A message alert rang on her mobile from Scarlett who had forwarded a text which she received. It read "BE CAREFUL WHAT YOU

WRITE. WE ARE WATCHING YOU." Scarlett concluded the text with a smiley face and an exclamation mark.

Wednesday sat back in her chair and closed her eyes. Maybe she would take Lennox up on his offer.

# Chapter Fifteen

Vera Olong rang the doorbell and waited for Emily Dolby to answer. She was slightly taken aback when James Dolby came to the door, recoiling as he saw her. He called to his wife and as Emily's frail figure glided towards them, he stormed back inside.

"I didn't expect to see you," said Emily in her petite voice.

"I felt I should come. Hope you don't mind."

Emily looked over her shoulder before whispering to Vera that she could enter, but they would have to sit in the kitchen.

She put the kettle on and busied herself putting biscuits onto a bone china plate.

"I can't begin to imagine how it must feel to lose a child," offered Vera as she accepted the china cup and saucer from Emily.

"It's like a piece of you dies, leaving a black clump attached to your heart forever. I will never be free from that clump of debris," replied Emily.

Vera gazed at her and smiled weakly.

"You and the reverend don't have any children. Why is that?"

"We . . . well especially my husband, are dedicated to God, the church, and the parishioners. There's little time or space in our lives for children."

"Did you know you would be childless?" whispered Emily. "Because I never imagined I'd end up that way."

"I didn't know for sure, but I suspected as much. God is all knowing and magnificent in his supremacy. He leaves little to chance."

"James has renounced his belief in God, so I pray for our souls, including Tom's. I need God more than ever. Do you believe, as I do, that Tom just wasn't right for this world?"

Vera put the cup on the saucer, making a little chinking sound. "My husband would be the right person to respond to that question, not me. But as you ask, perhaps he could only be healed in heaven."

An awkward silence hung in the air. Vera clasped her hands tightly together in the lap as she looked around the kitchen.

As if ordered to evaporate the tension, the doorbell rang. Emily got up to answer it before her husband could beat her to it.

"Detectives, were we expecting you?"

"No, Mrs Dolby, we've brought Tom's laptop back," replied Lennox as he handed over the machine.

"Please come in."

As they entered, they met Vera in the hallway. She acknowledged them with a nod of her head.

"Mrs Olong, carrying out parishioner duties I see," said Wednesday to her as she skirted along the wall to get passed them.

She smiled weakly, before disappearing down the garden path. The detectives followed Emily into the lounge and sat on the overstuffed sofa.

"Is your husband around?" asked Wednesday.

"He must be in his study. He's not that keen on Mrs Olong."

Wednesday noticed Emily's penetrating stare and her avoidance of Lennox. His people skills enabled him to pick up the same sentiment, so he excused himself to make a phone call in the hallway.

"Do you have children, DI Wednesday?"

"No I don't, and I can't pretend to know how you must be feeling right now."

"I think you'd be shocked if I told you," she said, averting her gaze.

"I'm not here to judge you, but I am here to listen."

"Part of me is relieved at no longer having to contend with the teenage angst and behaviour in the house." She paused to quickly glance at Wednesday. "I didn't really want to be a mother in the first place, I did it for James." She bowed her head and toyed with some thread hanging from a button on her blouse.

"Once you had Tom, did your feelings change?" Wednesday asked hesitantly.

There was a weighty pause before Emily continued.

"Of course I loved him, but I didn't find motherhood a natural process. James, on the other hand, revelled in fatherhood." She covered her mouth as she coughed. "Perhaps I am a wicked mother," she said before coughing once more.

"Do you think there was a particular reason for Tom's anger?"

"We couldn't figure it out, so we thought the church influence would quell his devil-like temperament, but it didn't seem to help."

"I understand his behaviour was never a problem a school."

"No, he liked his form teacher, Mr Pollock. I think that's why geography was his favourite lesson."

Wednesday smiled lightly and sat up straight as Lennox and James returned.

"Glad to see that bloody woman's gone," said James, ignoring his wife's scowl.

"You don't like the reverend's wife, then?" asked Lennox.

"I find her a little creepy, can't explain why, I just do."

"But you don't mind attending church?"

"No, it was the reverend I go to listen to."

Lennox informed them that they needed to search the house for some boots and a travel blanket. Neither person refused the request nor asked why.

They did find a travel blanket in the back of their car, but the colours were wrong. No wellington boots could be found.

Wednesday and Lennox excused themselves and left the couple in the lounge with the glacial atmosphere they had cultivated.

"Heaven preserve me from marriage again," Lennox said as he climbed into the car.

"It doesn't have to be like that. I bet they were a happy couple until the death of their son," responded Wednesday.

Lennox ignored her remark and let smoking take over from conversation until they pulled up outside the home of the Wrights.

They were surprised to see the front door opening as they walked up the path, only to find themselves crossing paths with Vera Olong once more as she exited the house. She walked towards them with her hand covering her left cheek, only just obscuring a red mark.

"Is everything okay?" Wednesday queried.

"I heeded your words, but this is the reaction I get for consoling folk in the name of God," she replied as she continued walking down the path.

"Do you want to make a complaint?"

Vera shook her head before climbing into her car.

They knocked on the open door and called down the hallway. Within seconds, the burgundy face of Judith Wright appeared. She snarled at them with her stained teeth.

"I thought you were that snooty, interfering church cow come back for some more."

"We've brought Darren's laptop back. May we come in?" Lennox asked, handing over the computer and putting his foot on the doorstep.

"You might as well. The nosy neighbours don't need more excuses to look down on us."

The cluttered hallway still felt oppressive as they made their way to the kitchen. Wednesday moved a pile of local newspapers and celebrity magazines, to free up a chair for herself.

"We'd like to get more details on your first husband and your eldest son, Mrs Wright," Wednesday said.

"They've got nothing to do with my Darren going missing."

"Is it possible Darren could have run to him, or even have been taken by him?"

"Not likely, last I heard he was living on some commune thing in Scotland," she replied, pouring the dregs of a bottle into a tea-stained mug.

"Your eldest son is in prison for five years, I understand. How did Darren cope with his incarceration?"

Judith Wright raised her eyebrows and looked at Wednesday with her blank, bloodshot eyes.

"Was he upset when his brother was put away?" she tried again.

"Course he was, but he likes having the bedroom to himself."

Wednesday had learnt at the station, that Robert Giles had a string of offences, beginning his career as an eleven-year-old young offender until finally progressing to the heady heights of aggravated burglary of a dwelling and assault.

"Do you get to see him often?"

"Plymouth is too far away, train fare is expensive. I send him a card at Christmas and his birthday."

No glimpse of shame or embarrassment fleeted across her face as she swallowed the last drops of wine, leaving reddish-purple stains at the corners of her mouth, making her look like The Joker.

"Is your husband out?" Wednesday enquired.

"He's gone to the shops. Why, are you worried he's been beating me up again," she replied before letting out a gravelly snigger.

Wednesday dug her nails into the palm of her hand and looked directly at Judith. She was about to speak when Judith spoke again.

"Anyway, why are you wasting your time here? You should be out looking for my son."

"We're doing everything we can, Mrs Wright."

"What about my Darren's book being found in the vicarage? Has that reverend done something to my Darren?"

"We have no other evidence to support that notion, currently."

"I feel he's already dead. Call it a mother's hunch." She reached across the table with a shaky hand to grab a packet of cigarettes.

Wednesday wanted to leave the macabre and toxic surroundings, but was prevented from doing so by the arrival of Des Wright who strode into the kitchen and dumped two carrier bags onto the work surface. The contents of the bags chinked. Des pointedly ignored the two detectives, brushing past them to go into the garden for a smoke.

Wednesday looked at the shopping bags and then at Judith Wright, before raising her eyebrows in an unnecessary gesture. Judith's eyes were drawn to the bags, and she took the opportunity to grab one when Wednesday was distracted by her phone.

At a glance, she saw the phone call was from Scarlett, who had apparently received a package at work containing a dozen beheaded red roses. Wednesday excused herself and called her back straight away.

"Tell me more," she asked, stepping out the front door.

"It came addressed to me and the note attached reads 'with sympathy'. The office is positively electric, and I've found some interesting info about cults on the web."

"Never mind that now. I need you to get everything to the lab at the station straight away. Don't let anyone else touch it."

"Always the dramatic one, sis. I'll do it after I've had a photo taken of everything for a future article."

Wednesday was about to reproach her for her lackadaisical manner, when Lennox arrived behind her at the simultaneous moment that Scarlett hung up on her. She'd missed her moment.

"What's up?"

"I'll tell you on the way to the station."

Once back at the station, Lennox urged Wednesday to inform Hunter of the incidents involving Scarlett. Against her better judgement, she moved towards Hunter and requested a word in private.

"My half-sister—"

"The journalist," he interrupted.

"Yes, Scarlett. She's been receiving threatening messages at home and her office. I've asked her to bring the items in for the forensic guys. I believe it has something to do with her cult article in the paper."

Hunter was looking at the computer screen as he listened, clearly not entirely interested in Wednesday's information.

"She's probably tapped into the lunatic level in our society who have latched onto her crazy notion. She's given meaning to their misplaced paranoia."

He tapped on the keyboard until Wednesday's fixed gazed finally aroused his attention.

"Is there something else?" he asked, looking directly at her.

"She seems convinced that she's on the right track because of the attention it's got her. I'm wondering about her safety, that's all."

"I'm sure she'll cope. But if you're really worried, do you want protection for her? Not that I've got the manpower at the moment," he replied, barely drawing a veil over his loathing.

"I'll keep an eye on her and have a word with her editor."

She felt dismissed by Hunter's stubborn silence. Unbeknown to her, Lennox watched her flounce off in the direction of her office and firmly shut the door behind her. Rubbing the back of his neck he walked over to her.

Entering, he found her snapping off a chunk of chocolate and throwing it into her mouth. The bulge in her cheek made her face look like a hamster. She frowned and waited for him to speak.

"Look, Hunter may not have taken you seriously, but I do. Why don't I spend the evening in your home, in case anything else occurs?"

Wednesday, having swallowed the chocolate, sat back and stared at him. "If it's home cooked food you're after, you're in luck, but I can't guarantee the company."

"That's settled then," he said before walking back to his office.

Wednesday curled her toes in her shoes.

Wednesday was very conscious that Lennox was driving behind her. She pulled up onto her drive and switching off the engine, her hand slipping on the door handle as he pulled up alongside her.

On opening the front door the warmth embraced their chilled bodies, but she was embarrassed about the stale tobacco smell that lingered in the air. She had smoked more than she intended to last night without airing the kitchen.

Wednesday opened a bottle of red wine and poured two glasses. She smiled as she handed him a glass.

"Got any modern stuff," he asked as he perused her small shelf of CDs.

"I don't suppose you consider folk as modern?"

Lennox shook his head slowly. "Never mind. What's for dinner?"

"Chicken thighs, homemade potato wedges, and spring greens, or I could throw it altogether to make a curry. Any preference?"

A shrug of his shoulders indicated that it was her choice, so she chose the former.

"Did Scarlett bring that box of flowers to the station?" he asked.

"No, I'll take it in myself tomorrow. She's not taking this seriously."

"Are you taking it too seriously, perhaps?"

"I don't consider threats to a member of my family as a light matter." She tossed the potato wedges in the sizzling garlic oil, aware that she had snapped at him.

The smell of the chicken crisping in the Aga infused the air and enveloped the pair in a comforting embrace.

As she served up the food she suggested that they call a truce and discuss something other than work as she was keen to know more about him.

Between mouthfuls of food, Lennox talked about his seemingly idyllic childhood, when he spent a great deal of time fishing and building inadequate camps with his two best mates. As he spoke, Wednesday realised he had a dry sense of humour, and she suddenly saw the charm she suspected all the women at the station saw in him.

Lennox was working his way towards discussing her mother's health, when the front door opened, funnelling a torrent of cold air into the kitchen.

"Well don't you two look cosy," Scarlett said as she threw her coat over a chair.

"There's some food in the oven," replied Wednesday, disregarding the less than subtle comment.

"So, Jacob Lennox, to what do we owe this pleasure? I hope it has nothing to do with me?"

"I thought I'd offer my support in light of the recent incidents."

"I'm touched that you care enough about me to do that."

Scarlett flicked her flame curls over her shoulder and peered at him from underneath her heavily made-up eyelashes. She poured herself some wine and ran the tip of her finger around the rim of the glass as she fixed on him with her mottled green eyes.

"Have you read my article?"

"I've glanced at it," he replied, pushing his knife and fork together.

"I must be on the right track, otherwise I wouldn't be getting these threats, don't you think?"

"There are a lot of cranks out there."

Scarlett pouted, took a sip of wine, then with her best dulcet tone asked Lennox if he thought she was in danger, and if so, what could he do about it? Wednesday scraped her chair back and fetched a new packet of cigarettes that nestled between a fruit bowl containing a blackening banana and a kiwi. She turned around just in time to see Lennox's cheeks fill with colour as Scarlett slowly placed one of his cigarettes in her mouth. The glow from the cigarette lighter enhanced her Cupid's bow.

"There is a wealth of evidence on the web about cults," she said, allowing the smoke to drift out of her mouth. "I could show you later, if you like."

Lennox sat back in his chair rubbing the top of his head, all the while keeping his eyes on Scarlett. The smell of garlic oil and rosemary lingered in the air.

"You know society fears the very notion of a cult, as it's deemed to practice mind control. They coercively persuade people to do as they are told." Scarlett could see that she had hooked Lennox, encouraging her to keep going.

"Apparently, the charismatic leader targets people who are seeking love and recognition."

She talked about her research of American sites. "The cult leaders seek out people who are already outside of the nucleus of the community. After a while, the members can actually fear the end of the world and being separated from their charismatic leader, therefore they commit mass suicide." She paused to draw on the cigarette.

Wednesday could see that she was enjoying being the centre of attention.

"The freaks of society experience unconditional love, acceptance, and attention from the enigmatic leader. The cult practises something called 'love bombing', which entails providing constant affirmations to a person, until they feel secure in the group and they feel special."

"And you think such freaks, as you call them, live around here?"

"They say the countryside is full of eccentric misfits, ideal for an up-and-coming cult."

"I don't understand how you came to the conclusion of a cult in relation to these crimes."

"The internet can throw up diverse scenarios. It's the journalist in me that sifts through the trash and comes up with the gold."

Lennox allowed Scarlett to refill his glass whilst he listened intently to her reasoning.

Wednesday opened the back door and stepped outside to gaze up at the canopy of stars. She heard the others talking without hearing the words.

She was transported back to the time when Scarlett had reached maturity with all the grace and beauty of a swan gliding on water. Wednesday had never experienced that and felt virtually invisible to the male population. She smiled to herself and moved quietly back to the table where she noticed Scarlett had placed the box she had received at work.

She poured herself another glass of wine and then slipped away to bed.

"I got the impression from Eva that you didn't like journalists," Scarlett said, picking up the bottle to refill both of their glasses. Noticing it was empty she got up and retrieved another one from the fridge.

"I don't, but you're growing on me; or perhaps it's the wine." He half smiled at her and then covered the top of his glass with his hand.

"It's okay, you're staying the night," she said, removing his hand and filling the glass.

George Olong pecked his wife on the cheek before trudging off for his lay preacher meeting, having been given police approval. She watched him go before unhooking her tweed coat from the rack and wrapping it around her, in preparation for the walk to the village hall for choir practice. The house had an eerie stillness and she thought she heard someone whisper her name.

The village hall did not offer her the change of mood she desired. Recent events and gossip circled around the group. The elder element gravitated towards Colin Pollock to see if they could glean any gossip with regards to the school's role in the recent crimes. In his gruff, antisocial manner, he informed them that the school bore no relation to the heinous events.

Clusters of people eyed Vera as she moved around putting music sheets on the chairs. Questions draped over the tips of their tongues, but no one dared utter the words.

The choir sang half-heartedly, with Vera struggling to summon up any enthusiasm or meaningful harmony from the group; or indeed from within herself.

Relief swelled in her heart as ten o'clock arrived and the practice was over. One by one, they drifted out into the velvet night, with some members stopping to chat and gossip just outside the door. Vera gathered the music sheets and waited for the last stragglers to exit before locking the door.

George took a slow drive home, his mind whirring with uncomfortable thoughts and rumours. As he drove along the main High Street, he saw Vera standing outside the village hall, talking to someone. He could not make out who it was, but he could see it was a man by the long trench coat and trilby hat. He pulled up alongside them and wound down the passenger window. Vera ducked down and stuck her head through the gap.

"How fortuitous," she said, smiling at her husband. She stood up and mumbled something to her companion before climbing into the car.

"Did you have a good evening, dear?" she asked, trying to see his facial expression in the yellow glow from the street lights.

"The bible produced answers that I wasn't expecting. It threw up discord in the verses so I have come away with turmoil and sadness in my heart."

Vera was used to her husband's verbose ramblings, but she often drifted off so that she only half heard what he was saying. She caught sight of the reflection of her face in the window, and was pleased to notice age had still not scarred her face.

Arriving home, she climbed out of the car and followed him into the vicarage. She switched the kettle on then took off her woolly hat and tweed coat.

"Who were you talking to?" he asked.

"Colin Pollock. We can't agree on the song choices for the Christmas concert."

She placed two cups of tea and a plate of biscuits on a tray before moving to the lounge. "Did you find any answers to explain how people can be so cruel to others?"

"We all have the potential to unleash evil, but most of us have the moral clamp-down to stop ourselves from relinquishing to the dark side."

"Well I can't believe that someone in our community would harm children. I believe it's an outsider." She stared at her husband, waiting for some kind of response, but he just stared into his tea cup.

"What do you think about the article purporting to a cult in our midst. It made me feel quite edgy," she said, keeping her eyes on him constantly.

"I'm not sure what to believe anymore, dear. I sometimes wonder whether we truly actually know anything about anyone." He dunked a ginger biscuit into his tea then popped the whole biscuit into his mouth. "You might as well go to bed. I want to spend some time alone in contemplative prayer," he mumbled, putting his drink down on the coffee table.

Vera let out a silent sigh before heading to bed with only the shadow of loneliness as her companion.

George picked up the receiver and dialled.

# Chapter Sixteen

The morning was cloaked in darkness, and Wednesday was hung-over with guilt. She should have rung the hospital or Oliver before going to bed. Instead, she let the selfish gene rule so that she could relax in the company of an interesting and attractive man. Now, she realised the latter was futile whilst Scarlett lived with her, and the former should have been essential.

The rich aroma of strong coffee breathed through the percolator. As she poured the black liquid, she heard footsteps heading for the kitchen. Eager to keep out of Scarlett's way, she grabbed her cigarette packet and opened the back door.

"Shall I just help myself?" Lennox said from behind her.

Wednesday swung around to see him standing there in one of Scarlett's silk dressing gowns, looking dishevelled.

"I didn't know you were still here," she said as she lit her cigarette, trying not to stare at his chest hair protruding from under the pale lemon garment.

"I didn't plan to be. Your sister's rather persuasive."

Wednesday cocked her head and prodded the doorstep with her foot. She gazed at the cracks in the stone slabs, analysing the complex situation they found themselves in.

She was acutely aware of being dressed in faded striped pyjamas, with her un-brushed hair skimming her shoulders. Remnants of smudged mascara lay cloying under her bottom eyelashes, and her lips lacked moisture making her mouth look pinched.

She crushed the partly smoked cigarette underfoot before closing the door. "I'm going to get ready, we've a briefing first thing," she said, brushing past him. She could smell his aftershave intermingled with Scarlett's perfume; the odour made her feel nauseous.

After a shower and getting dressed, she set off for work without calling goodbye.

She was in her office checking her e-mails when Lennox entered the Incident Room wearing yesterday's clothes. As he looked in her direction, she turned her gaze to the computer screen.

Hunter clapped his hands to get the briefing underway. He stood by the white board, searching the room with his steely stare. Once the required hush had descended, he began.

"Another anonymous call has just come in, saying there's a body in the rambling hut in the woods. First officers on the scene say it matches Darren Giles's description."

A low murmur splintered across the room, which Hunter curtailed by spreading out his hands and sighing loudly.

"Wednesday and Lennox, get yourselves there now. If it turns out to be the body of Darren Giles, send the family liaison officer to the Wright's to tell them the bad news."

Wednesday and Lennox stood to leave.

"I then want you two to go to the vicarage and bring both the Olongs in for questioning. Reverend or not, something isn't sitting right with that pair, and the evidence is stacking up against them."

A fine layer of drizzle dotted across the windscreen. The wipers periodically smeared the droplets to one side before more settled again.

Wednesday drove, staring silently at the road ahead, whilst Lennox flicked through his notebook to refresh his foggy head. Although the Wrights were not a couple society would have much empathy with, it was still going to be hard to hear that their son was no longer a missing person.

The walk in the woods was becoming a familiar affair for the pair. Approaching the clearing around the hut, they saw it was already established as the crime scene, with officers performing finger-tip searches around the parameter.

Alex Green gave a wave of acknowledgment to the pair as they ducked under the crime scene tape.

"By the way, the splinters from Tom Dolby's clothing match the wood from this hut."

Wednesday mouthed her appreciation to him. He blushed.

Inside the hut, they found Edmond Carter crouched over the body. On hearing their footsteps on the bare wood, he eased himself up and turned to them.

"Looks like the lad died the same way as the first one. Asphyxiation. His body has also been placed in the same peaceful manner."

"Time of death?"

"Without all the empirical evidence, I'd say he was killed in the early hours of the morning."

The pair looked at the slight figure of the boy. There was no doubt it was Darren Giles. He lay in a prone position, with his arms placed at his sides. There was no evidence around them to suggest the murder happened in the hut, the table and chairs continued to occupy the centre of the space.

With procedures in full swing, it was time for them to turn their thoughts to visiting Des and Judith Wright.

As Wednesday pulled up outside their house she saw Janice Parker had just arrived.

After knocking on the door a few times, Des Wright arrived and stood motionless, looking at the three officers.

"We'd like to speak with you and your wife, please," asked Wednesday.

"Come to arrest us?"

Wednesday dodged the answer until they were all crowded in the chaotic kitchen.

"I think you should both sit down," Wednesday began, observing the swaying motion of the couple.

Wednesday could see that Judith Wright was struggling to focus, so she made two strong coffees as Janice began the job of imparting the painful and disturbing news.

Wednesday placed the chipped mugs in front of the stunned couple then leant against the work surface, ready to administer more hot drinks, tissues, and support.

The normally permanent redness in Judith's face faded at the news of her son's death. Her eyes were already red rimmed and watery, so it was hard for Wednesday to gauge her emotions. Des remain silent whilst rolling a cigarette.

"So that's that then," she said before slugging back some wine straight from the bottle that sat on the table.

She slammed the bottle down with such a force, it made Wednesday jump. "That rev's wife's got some nerve, saying how sorry she is when it's him that done the killings."

Des jumped up at her words, and lumbered towards the back door.

"I advise you not to go to the vicarage," said Lennox as he stood up straight.

"I'm going out for a smoke," Des replied as he disappeared into the overgrown garden.

Wednesday asked Judith if she would like Janice to stay awhile.

"I don't want no one hanging around. I want you all out of my house. Now."

Grief produces a range of emotions in individuals, and it appeared Judith was at the anger stage. They left the couple to muddle through their alcohol-drenched emotions.

Arriving at the vicarage, they saw the forensics van and numerous officers milling around in the drizzle.

A rather harassed reverend answered the door and let them in.

"It's rather crowded in here," he muttered as he wrung his hands together and led them into the kitchen.

"Is your wife here?" asked Lennox.

"She's gone shopping. This was upsetting her."

"I'm sorry but we're going to need to question you both at the station."

"What for? I have no idea how the dead boy's body ended up in the hut. Somebody is using me to hide their crimes, but God will guide me. I can trust him."

Through the window, Wednesday could see Alex Green approaching the house from the side garden. His head was bowed to shield him from the drizzle that was driving towards him.

"Can I see you a minute, DI Wednesday?" he asked, stepping inside.

"I found this next to the body," he said as he handed over an evidence bag containing a wooden toothpick. "We found one next to the other boy's body, I seem to recall. No DNA on the first one though."

Wednesday twirled a strand of hair as she gathered the pieces of the jigsaw in her head. Her gut instinct was telling her she was close to finding the answer.

Alex stepped a little closer to her. "Something you might want to be aware of," he began, "is that the lock wasn't broken or tampered with, so it was either already unlocked or someone used the key. Edmond also wants you to know that the body was moved, and had probably been stored somewhere cool, like a cellar or a garage."

"Excellent work, Alex, thanks for that," she said before moving back to the kitchen, where she found Lennox and the reverend sitting at the kitchen table.

"Reverend, does this house have a cellar?"

George Olong lifted his head up from his prayer-like position. His dusky blue-grey eyes seemed void of any emotion, staring blankly at Wednesday like a lost child in a supermarket.

As though controlled by a puppeteer, he rose from the chair, arms flopping by his sides, occasionally twitching, with fingers outstretched. He moved into the hallway and opened a heavy, arched door and switched on the light.

"I won't come down if you don't mind. The stairs are a bit steep for me."

The stairs were indeed steep and narrow, and the air held the damp smell of a wet flannel screwed up on the side of the bath. Wednesday held onto the slim wooden banister, which felt no bigger than a broom handle, as she descended the stairs. Lennox followed closely behind.

The poorly lit cellar contained a range of boxes, an old marble washstand, and a row of shelves on which stood jam jars full of home-made preserves ready for the church fete. A chest freezer stood against the back wall, with two old bicycles propped up against it.

Wednesday brushed the cobwebs which had attached themselves to her hair and rummaged in her bag to extrapolate a torch. The bright beam somehow made seeing more difficult.

With his gloved hands, Lennox lifted the freezer lid fully until it rested on the wall behind. An ineffective freezer light shone a yellow glow onto the mountain of produce that was stored in it. Wednesday shone her torch in for extra light, but they only found boxes of frozen foods and a multitude of bags containing home grown vegetables.

"We'll have to get the forensic guys in to check this area," Lennox said as he closed the lid and snapped off his gloves.

Olong was waiting for them as they mounted the stairs. Wednesday noticed he looked pallid and had clasped a shaky hand over his forehead.

"Are you all right?" she said as she stepped closer to him.

He swayed slightly, complaining of feeling dizzy, when suddenly he doubled over and crumpled to the floor. Wednesday set about loosening his dog collar and making him comfortable, whilst Lennox called for an ambulance. She knelt beside him as he drifted in and out of conscious-ness, until the blue lights of the ambulance flickered through the cross-shaped glass panel in the front door.

Wednesday and Lennox followed the ambulance, and ensured that Vera was contacted about her husband's condition. Wednesday's skin felt clammy at the thought of being in a hospital; she felt she should be with her mother and not some suspect in a murder case. Lennox passed her a cigarette which she smoked silently, inhaling the fumes deep into her lungs as her guilt mounted.

Having parked the car, they walked towards the hospital only to see a taxi pull up and Vera Olong jump out. As she turned to pay the driver, she saw the detectives approaching.

"I blame you two for this. Harassing my husband into an early grave. I will be speaking to your superior about this."

She did not wait for a response from either of them. Instead, she rushed inside to find her husband.

"How is the Reverend Olong," Wednesday asked a staff nurse as she flashed her badge.

"He's having tests done. You won't be able to question him now."

They had suspected as much, so they went off to find Vera who was sitting in the family waiting room.

"Any news?" asked Wednesday, noticing the faint smell of vomit lingering in the air.

"No, and I don't really want to talk to you two."

"I'm afraid you don't have much choice. The rambling hut is owned by the church and you both had access."

"He may have been found there, God rest his soul, but it doesn't mean we had anything to do with it, Detective. You have narrowed your investigation to focus only on us, when the real killer is carrying on with life outside of your radar."

"The forensic team are going to examine your cellar. So, now is a good time to speak you have anything pertinent to tell us, Mrs Olong."

Vera raised her head and looked at Wednesday with red rimmed eyes.

"I have nothing to say. You can test and fingerprint the whole damn vicarage for all I care, we have nothing to hide."

At that moment, a doctor entered the room and advised Vera that she could sit with her husband, although he needed peace and rest. Vera turned to them with an icy stare and checked she could leave.

"Is he talking?" asked Lennox.

The doctor shook her head and suggested they try the next day. As they considered returning to the station, Wednesday's phone rang. It was Maria Jones advising them that Stewart Cleveland had gone missing. Arlow and Damlish were on their way to the school to interview the staff, and Hunter had requested they go to his house; a warrant was being issued for the search.

Wednesday drove them to Cleveland's house, aware that her stomach was growling much to Lennox's amusement.

"Make yourself useful and get the chocolate bar out of the glove compartment," she said, barely able to hide her irritation.

Arriving at the flat, Lennox rang the bell several times before using his key tools to let them in. They moved cautiously from room to room, checking for Cleveland or evidence of a disturbance.

Everything appeared to be where it should be except for empty drawers in his bedroom, and forlorn hangers in the wardrobe. His toothbrush and toiletries were also missing.

"Looks like he's done a runner," muttered Lennox. "Dog's gone."

"Perhaps Dick Pennymore will know more."

As they descended the stairs Wednesday got a message on her mobile.

"It's from Scarlett. She's had her tyres slashed outside the office and she's asking me to give her a lift home later. Perhaps you would like to do that. I imagine you'll be a house guest again tonight."

Lennox shook his head. "Two nights in a row looks too much like a relationship. I don't subscribe to that concept."

Wednesday breathed a deep sigh and clamped her lips together as they left the house. "Let's go to The Crow and see what's what."

"I'm surprised you haven't given me a lecture about not hurting your sister," he said, climbing into the car.

"You're both adults, although she is a lot younger than you. I'm not some spinster in the twilight of her years needing to live vicariously on other people's relationships."

"Point taken."

The Crow car park was virtually empty as it was only lunchtime. Walking inside, they saw a couple of ramblers huddling around the roaring fire, and a game keeper in muddy boots and a wax jacket standing at the bar chatting to the barmaid.

"Is Dick Pennymore in?" asked Wednesday as she flashed her badge.

"Afraid not, he's at the brewery. Can I help?"

"Have you seen Stewart Cleveland recently?"

"No, not for a few days now. Dick's looking for him too. Shall I say you called?"

Wednesday nodded before she and Lennox reluctantly left the cosy atmosphere for the raw air outside.

"You never liked having my Darren around," spat Judith Wright at Des who had just walked in through the back door. "I bet you're secretly glad he's dead."

Des could see there was nothing he could do to dampen the molten fury in Judith's inebriated mind.

"I'm going to lose the child benefit now, so we'll have less money than before. You're a useless lump," she yelled as she launched a heavy glass ashtray in his direction. It missed him but managed to make another dent in the already mutilated kitchen door.

"If you were less ruled by alcohol, you may have been the mum he needed."

Des instantly regretted verbalising the truth as he saw her stagger towards him with her gnarled hands clenched in fists. As she was too small to reach his chin, she punched him in the groin. He doubled over in excruciating agony. As his head lolled forward, she raised her knee and made contact with his nose. Big, fat drops of blood splashed onto the floor, mingling with the muddy footprints he had brought in.

Des gritted his teeth and screwed up his eyes, fighting the inner turmoil to lash back at her. He wanted to strike her and fling her across the room; but that was what his father had done to his mother—and she died. His father was sent to jail as the jury struggled to believe he was the victim of domestic violence, not the perpetrator.

He felt another blow on the back of his head before she pushed him, knocking over a chair as he rolled towards the floor. Her laugh rang in his ears and then he heard the familiar sound of liquid being sloshed into a mug. He knew she would be subdued for a period of time. He dragged himself along the floor and moved snake-like out into the hallway. As he reached the front door, he stood up, brushed himself down, and made a silent exit. He needed to rid himself of his internal rage.

As he walked along the road, he wiped the blood from his face and rolled a cigarette. He allowed the breeze to carry the grey plumes from his mouth; his neck muscles tightened as he relived the past few moments and the tension began pounding in his head.

Reaching his destination, he threw the stub end to the ground and crushed it under foot. He marched into The Crow and ordered a pint.

Arlow and Damlish received a frosty welcome from the receptionist at Markham Hall, but undeterred, they interviewed all the staff members that were available at that time. The last teacher was Colin Pollock.

"Let's talk about the headmaster. Did you have occasion to meet him after work?"

"Mr Cleveland and I don't mingle in the same social circles."

"What do you do in your spare time?"

"I'm a geography teacher, so I like to hike around the countryside and get involved with nature. I'm also a member of the local choir."

"Are you a religious man?"

"Religion is a drug for the weak and fearful. But I do sing in the choir so I'm there on Sundays for the music, not God."

Arlow raised his eyebrows then looked down at his notebook. "Is there anything else you would like to add?"

"Not that I can think of. Can I go?"

Arlow nodded and waited for him to leave before turning to Damlish. "We've got nothing to offer Hunter here," he said gruffly, flicking through his notes.

"Let's try the receptionist. They're usually a good source of gossip," replied Damlish.

They scraped back their chairs and headed for the front office, where they found Nina Prince engrossed in marking the attendance sheets.

"Could we have a word, Mrs Prince," said Arlow after glancing quickly at her name plaque on her desk.

"It's Ms Prince."

"Right. Is there anything you can tell us about Mr Cleveland's time-table over the past few days?"

She sat up straighter in her chair and shuffled forward on her buttocks. "He'd been getting unscheduled visits from some unsavoury looking men over the past few days. Mr Cleveland hadn't booked them in his diary either, so I can't tell you who they were."

"What do you mean by 'unsavoury'?"

"Well," she began in a conspiratorial tone, "they looked like the type of men who could have an unhealthy interest in the students, if you know what I mean?"

"I'm not sure that I do, could you clarify that?"

"Call yourselves detectives? They looked like paedophiles. It's the shifty eyes and shaven heads."

Damlish stifled a snigger with a cough, although Nina Prince knew exactly what he was doing. She chastised him with an arched eyebrow.

"And what do you think they were doing with Mr Cleveland, unless you're implying that he, too, is hiding something?" Arlow asked.

"Goodness no!" she exclaimed, her eyes darting from one man to the other.

"If you hear from Mr Cleveland, or some of those visitors call for him, please contact us straight away."

They made their way to the front entrance, relieved to be leaving the building that smelt of teenage body odour and plimsolls.

Arlow was conscious of his rumbling stomach. Looking at his watch he realised lunchtime was a couple of hours ago.

Walking towards their car, a young girl loitering by a tree caught their eye. She turned away, but not before the detectives saw her looking troubled.

"What's your name?" asked Damlish, walking towards her.

"Freya."

"Was there something you wanted to tell us?"

"It's just . . ." She paused, scuffing her shoes in the carpet of damp, brown leaves. "I was wondering whether what happened to Claudia will happen to someone else?"

"Is that what's worrying you?"

"Well I'm a girl, and everyone says I'm prettier than Claudia, so I'm bound to be a target for the freak."

"We're actively searching him out, and we will get him. Keep yourself safe at all times, be vigilant of your surroundings and make sure your parents know where you are at all times."

"They're saying she was sacrificed to appease him."

"Who's saying that?"

"The rumour is all around the school."

"Perhaps you should return to your lesson, and not listen to gossip."

The girl flicked her sleek hair over her shoulders before prancing off in the direction of the school entrance.

"The kids seem to have lost their innocence these days, don't you think?" asked Damlish as he watched the girl tug on the entrance door before sliding inside.

"The girls are too aware of their sexuality. It's disturbing."

Damlish looked at his partner and shook his head. "Disturbing is perhaps pushing it."

"If you had a new baby daughter, you'd find it disturbing."

Wednesday pulled up outside Scarlett's office and saw her immobilized car a few spaces along. Anger burgeoned within her. Scarlett had brought this on herself.

After waiting five minutes in the car, she called Scarlett on her mobile, but it went straight to voicemail. Nagging worry intruded her thoughts as she watched the staff leave. When she saw a reporter she recognised, she wound down the window and called to him.

"Shaun, is Scarlett still up there?"

He moved towards her and bent down so they were face to face.

"Hiya Wednesday. No, she's not up there. She said something about meeting a friend for a drink. Don't know where, though."

Wednesday rolled her eyes and thanked Shaun before winding up the window. As much as she wanted to have a soak in the bath whilst drinking a glass of wine, she switched on the engine and drove towards the hospital. Muttering under her breath she gripped the steering wheel so tightly her knuckles turned white.

Visiting time was almost over by the time she arrived. Walking down the windowless corridor that echoed with foreign sounds, Wednesday tried not to breathe in the clinical stench of insanity by holding her finger under her nose.

The charge nurse let her onto the locked ward, but warned her that she only had twenty minutes. Thanking him, she went off in search of her mother, whom she found sitting up in bed with her knees pulled up under her chin. Oliver was sitting on the chair next to her.

He raised his heavy eyelids to greet her. He looked like he was being slowly eaten by the chair, with stubble speckling his chin.

"I'm sorry I couldn't get here sooner—work's rather hectic. How is she?"

"She isn't deaf or stupid, she is sitting right here," Joan said in a child-like voice.

"Sorry Mum, didn't mean to ignore you."

"Was that said with feelings of sincerity or guilt?"

"Please don't start," replied Wednesday as she dragged a chair over to sit next to Oliver.

He leaned in to her. "She's been like this all day," he whispered as he patted her knee.

"I'm still here, you two. I know you're colluding with the doctors to keep me in here 'coz you want a rest." She jabbed an accusatory finger in Oliver's direction.

He took her hand and kissed it, but she withdrew it sharply and folded her arms across her chest. Oliver exhaled quietly.

"Why did you stop taking your meds, Mum?"

"I was feeling better. The tablets slow me down and dull my artistic flare. I paint better when I'm drug free."

"You know it's the meds that are making you better. When the levels are back up, you'll soon be home."

"Only when I'm subdued like a ragdoll."

Wednesday turned to Oliver. "Are you looking after yourself?"

He nodded and patted her knee again, as though she was a worried seven-year-old who was concerned about her parents arguing.

"Where's Scarlett?" asked Joan.

"Busy at work."

"She's not got mixed up in that cult thing has she?"

"No Mum. There isn't a cult around here anyway."

"There must be if Scarlett's written about it. She doesn't lie, my Scarlett doesn't."

Wednesday felt a twinge zip across her chest at her mother's words. *Scarlett's no ruddy angel.*

"Is everything okay, you're looking tired," asked Oliver.

"Oh you know, work is rather harrowing. The death of young people is always difficult to come to terms with and sometimes, my brain just won't switch off."

The next ten minutes were spent watching Joan drift in and out of sleep. Periodically, her mouth would twitch as though she was speaking to the ghosts in her head.

"I'm here if you need me," Wednesday said quietly to Oliver. His face crumpled into a million creases and folds as he smiled.

"Please try and encourage Scarlett to come. I'm sure it would help your mother."

"She's not always easy to pin down, but I'll try."

A nurse announced that visiting time was over, so they both bent down and kissed Joan before tiptoeing out of the door.

Wednesday's eyes began welling up with forgotten tears. Her deep, compounded fear was that she would follow in her mother's footsteps and weave herself a mad future, where her only source of company would be the staff on a psychiatric ward. She remotely unlocked her car, got in and helped herself to a cigarette before heading home.

The house was in darkness when she arrived home, and part of her was glad Scarlett was still out, as she was in no mood for confrontation. But another part of her worried.

She picked up the post and placed it on the console in the hall. It was then that she noticed the note from Scarlett, saying she had found out some juicy facts on Reverend Olong. The article would be published tomorrow.

Wednesday frowned. Scarlett was prying too closely to her own casework. She made an Earl Grey tea before moving upstairs to run a bath.

As she lay amongst the fragrant bubbles, her mind drifted to the recent interviews to try and figure out what she was missing. The school, the church, and the complicity of the village all held some mystery with regards to the murders.

Emerging from the bath with skin a deep pink colour, she picked up her mobile and called Scarlett. Voicemail kicked it. *Where the bloody hell is she?*

# Chapter Seventeen

Wednesday trundled downstairs, rubbing her sleep sore eyes. The house was as quiet and as untouched as when she went to bed, six hours earlier.

Whilst the coffee brewed, she tramped upstairs to speak to Scarlett; she was going to tell her that she had to visit their mother that evening, no excuses.

Wednesday tapped on the bedroom door, and when she got no reply, she tapped harder and called out to her. The resounding silence began to unnerve her, so very slowly she opened the bedroom door and peeked around it.

The bed was untouched. Wednesday's heart started to pound in her temples and she began scouring the room for any evidence to indicate where she had got to.

On the dressing table sat Scarlett's burgeoning make-up bag and range of perfumes; but Wednesday knew that she carried a more compact version of both items in her handbag. Nothing was missing. She ran back downstairs to get her mobile, dialled Scarlett's number and got the voicemail once again.

Just then, she heard the sound of keys in the front door, and turned to see Scarlett breeze in.

"Bloody hell, where have you been?"

"God sis, what a welcome."

"We agreed to let each other know if we're staying out all night." Wednesday gabbled her words. Her face flushed.

Scarlett just stared at her and shrugged her shoulders.

"Well?" said Wednesday.

"I went for a drink with Niall Barclay, the editor. We got talking about my articles, and one thing led to another. You know me."

"Yes I do, but you normally bring your conquests home. I was worried about you, especially with what's going on."

"You fuss too much. Is that coffee I can smell?"

Wednesday sighed and moved to the kitchen to pour two mugs of coffee.

"Isn't it a bit too close to home, sleeping with your boss?"

"Says the woman who slept with her work colleague."

"That was years ago, and it was a bloody mistake. Now stop deflecting the conversation."

Wednesday drew a cigarette from the packet and offered Scarlett one.

"No thanks, I'm off for a shower," she replied before taking a mouthful of coffee then disappearing upstairs before Wednesday could rope her into further discussion.

She lit her cigarette and sat pensively, allowing relief to wash over her anger. The letterbox flapped as the paper fell to the floor but she did not move, preferring instead to finish her cigarette. After stubbing it out, she buttered some toast to take up with her whilst she got ready for work.

As she passed the front door, she picked up the paper to sling on the console table, when the front page caught her eye. In bold letters, the headline read "Reverend not as angelic as he seems," by Scarlett Willow.

Wednesday began reading as she slowly mounted the stairs, butter dripping down her chin. She was stunned, but not overly surprised, to read Scarlett's finger-pointing ascorbic words, backed by her terrier-like journalistic research.

She sat on the edge of her bed and continued reading. According to Scarlett, it would appear that the reverend had brought similar trouble to Warsbury from his previous parish—Bethnal Green—and she alluded to the fact that a youth club was a ploy he also used to get closer to the youth element.

The story went on to talk about a teenage foster child in the last parish. He was fostered due to being abused by his own father. According to sources, the boy complained to the foster parents that the reverend was getting too personal, and wanted intimate details from the boy about the abuse he suffered. The boy reported that the reverend was persistent, which made him feel uncomfortable. The foster parents reported their concerns to the dean and it was shortly after that the reverend and his wife were relocated.

Wednesday put the paper on her bed and rubbed the back of her neck. She was going to have to speak to Scarlett about her sources and about her articles that had a bias against one of the suspects. She also knew that Hunter was going to be on her case when she got to work.

Scarlett was still in the bathroom and Wednesday was running late; the conversation was going to have to wait.

Greg Edwards brought his wife a cup of coffee in bed, and placed it on the bedside table.

"I wish we could have stayed in London a little longer," she said as she leant upon her elbows.

"I know, but I need to get back to work."

"I hate being here with the pitying stares from the neighbours, I feel reassuringly incognito in London."

Greg moved to the window and opened the curtains so the grey sky was visible over the bare and sleepy garden.

The morning song of the blackbird combined with the cooing of the collar dove made for a heady mix of country sounds that were suddenly repulsive to Lucinda. She longed for the rumble of the black cabs and squeaky-braked buses, intermingled with the shrill of car alarms.

"I'm disconcerted with the distance you've put between us since Claudia's departure," she said before taking bird sips of coffee.

"Seeing as this is turning into a candid discussion about our feelings, I'm taken aback with how quickly you seem to have come to terms with her death." Greg began to pace up and down in front of the window, his hands thrust into his cashmere blend trouser pockets.

"Are you insinuating that I loved our daughter less than you did? Because I'll tell you this, you were always more focused on her rather than me when she was alive, and even more so now that she's gone."

"I never took you to be the jealous type," he roared as he deliberately turned his back on her and stared out the window.

"I'm not, but I'm surprised you've noticed anything about me these past few years."

"Don't," he muttered as he turned around to face her again.

"You always saw her as a pure, angelic girl. You never saw the flirtatious young woman she was turning into."

"That's twisted."

"Well, perhaps you prefer it now she's dead, as that way she can remain your little angel forever."

James took three large strides towards her and struck her across her face with the palm of his hand. Her cheek stung and so did his hand. But worse than that, was the sentiment for both of them that the relationship they once had was now over.

On entering the Incident Room, Wednesday saw Hunter standing by his office door. His face vivid crimson and the look in his eyes compelled her to run; only her legs disobeyed her orders.

"In my office now," he bellowed.

On his desk lay a copy of *The Cambridge Times*, with the front page headlines facing upwards. Wednesday swallowed hard as she waited for the volcano to erupt.

"I asked you to be careful around your sister."

Wednesday was about to respond when he raised his hand in a motion for her to stay silent.

"Not only is she continuing to write her own version of things; she's compromising our case. The reverend will now argue that any jury— should we get that far—would be biased against him, thanks to this," he said as he slapped his hand onto the newspaper.

"I haven't spoken to her about it, Boss."

"So she came up with the idea of checking the reverend's background all by herself, did she?"

"Yes she did. I mean two bodies have been found in the vicinity of the vicarage and we're crawling all over the place. It wouldn't be hard to figure out he is a possible suspect. Journalists dig—that's what they do."

"And what about these so-called facts from his last parish?"

"Again, all down to her. I hate to say it, but she's found out more than we did."

"And hate it you should. The commissioner is going to have a field day with all of this. I won't be able to defend you."

"I don't need you to defend me; I've done nothing wrong."

Wednesday regretted her shrill tone of voice as she caught the anger flaring in his eyes. She apologised quietly and left his office after he dismissed her with a wave of his hand.

Stepping out, she became aware of a multitude of eyes watching her as she walked towards her office. Her fury towards Scarlett boiled inside her, and she vowed to thrash it out with her that very evening. But first, she needed to make more headway on the case in a different direction as she was not convinced the reverend was as guilty as people thought.

"Scarlett, we weren't expecting you. Eva told us you were busy, but we're glad you're here, aren't we Joan?" Oliver said sitting up straight in the unforgiving hospital chair.

Joan was in a drugged haze but she managed a weak smile for her daughter who lingered by the bed. With her outstretched arm she attempted to connect with Scarlett, until she saw the haunted look in her eyes.

"Are you afraid of me?" she whispered with her dry throat.

"I'm afraid of this hospital, not you," she replied as she wrung her hands together and gazed at the floor.

"Is that why it took you so long to visit?" Joan asked, fighting to keep her expressionless eyes open.

"I hate this place. The sterility and hushed madness. I don't want this to happen to me."

"Well right now it's about your mother, not you," Oliver said as he shifted around in his chair, finally standing up to stretch his long legs. His drawn face looked ghost-like against the magnolia walls.

"I don't see Mum as being ill. I see her, and you come to that, as eccentric. Where does eccentricity end and madness begin?"

Oliver moved towards Scarlett and put his hands on her shoulders.

"Who we are is constantly evolving. We're not set in stone as a child, Scarlett." He squeezed her shoulders, feeling the rigid knots of muscle under his fingers.

"I'm sorry that I'm a daily reminder of your possible unstable future. Maybe I shouldn't have had kids." Joan closed her eyes, before pulling the sheet over her face.

"I think perhaps you should go now. It's not doing either of you any good," Oliver said in a hushed tone.

She knew he was right, so she kissed him on the cheek and blew her mother a kiss. A weight lifted from her shoulders as she walked down the corridor, but the weight returned as she passed patients milling around in a visible catatonic state.

Driving back to the office, Scarlett's mood lifted. And by the time she was walking up the stairs thinking about her articles, she felt positively elated.

# Chapter Eighteen

"I've made a pot of tea and sliced some cake for both of us," said James Dolby as he carried the tray into the lounge and placed it on the coffee table.

Emily continued staring out the window, and as the darkness fell, she began to see her own reflection instead of the naked trees. She was a shattered woman with no meaning to her life, whilst her husband tip-toed around her as though she would splinter into a thousand shards if the air around her moved.

The doorbell summoned him to the front door, and he was strangely relieved to see the reverend's wife standing there.

"I thought I'd call in and see how you were both doing. Is now a convenient time?"

"I'm not sure she'll talk to you, but could you stay with her whilst I nip out, if you don't mind?" He stood back to let Vera Olong in and followed her to the lounge.

"I'm off to get a few things, Vera will stay with you." He waited for a response for a few seconds before quietly slipping away.

He took a few deep breaths of fresh air as he walked down the path. It was exhilarating after the stale air in the house.

"How are you today," Vera asked, as she sat next to Emily.

Emily wriggled in her chair, pushing her body into the arm of the sofa. "How do you expect me to feel? Does God understand how I'm feeling or should I be talking to your husband for that answer?"

Vera smiled and suggested she make some tea, noticing the half empty cup.

"That's all anyone seems to offer me."

Vera stood up and walked to the window where she could still see

Emily behind her. She watched as Emily twisted her wedding ring around her finger, over and over again.

"What have you said to the police?" Vera asked.

"Nothing, but I imagine they're interested in you because of where he was found." She spoke the last four words in a whisper.

"We have spoken several times, but the mystery still remains. The past week has been a burden upon all our souls."

Emily looked at the newspaper on the table next to the armchair. "Is that all true?"

Vera turned and followed her stare. "Lies that have damaged George. And now the rumours have followed us here."

Vera returned to sit next to Emily and picked up her hand, which she stroked lightly. "If you ever feel the need to talk, you know where I am. You need to speak with someone who understands your pain. Remember that."

Emily pulled her hand away and placed it back on her own knee, smoothing the creases in her skirt. "You haven't got any children, so I'm not sure you would totally understand; if you don't mind me saying."

Vera pursed her lip and gazed into the distance before replying.

"I am a woman; hence I have the softness in my heart that allows me to absorb other women's pain. I can travel the road with you even though ultimately we have different destinations."

Emily closed her eyes and allowed the tears to seep from under her eyelashes. Travelling down her cheeks, they pooled in the corners of her down-turned mouth. She opened her eyes partially and gave Vera a sideways glance whilst she cleared her throat in readiness. The cogs in her mind turned as the words formed, but her parched mouth prevented the phrases from being uttered.

"Perhaps I should leave you in peace. Call me if you need to talk," Vera said as she squeezed Emily's arm before rising from the sofa. "I'll see myself out."

Emily's shoulders relaxed as she heard the front close softly. She picked up her now cold cup of tea and took a tiny sip, letting the liquid slowly travel down her throat. The calm lasted for only a few minutes as she heard the front door open and the sound of her husband's footsteps on the wooden floor. He paused outside the lounge door, before moving towards the kitchen.

He put the carrier bag on the worktop and took out the bottle of malt whisky—something normally reserved for Christmas. He poured the bronzed liquid into a glass before knocking it back in one mouthful. It hit the back of his throat, bringing tears to his eyes, but it was not enough to dull his senses, so he poured another.

Both needed each other, but both harboured thoughts of darkness which they could not divulge to one another. They feared reprisal should they voice their concerns or open up suspicions, so they remained in separate rooms—both sipping on a very different cold, golden-brown liquid.

# Chapter Nineteen

Stewart Cleveland's bank account showed no signs of activity and an extensive search by officers did not deliver any evidence of his whereabouts. His passport was still in his home, although all ports and airports had been given his description.

The atmosphere in the Incident Room had plummeted as it was Friday evening and weekend leave had been cancelled again. Wednesday was aware of murmurings around the team because of Scarlett's article on the reverend. Hunter was clearly avoiding her, which perturbed her more than she anticipated.

She watched the team through her window, and caught sight of Hunter striding across the room towards Maria Jones. She felt as though she was on the edge of the action, in a dream-like state, and had been forgotten by those around her. She was not ready to interact with another human being when Jones knocked on her door.

"There's been a possible sighting of Stewart Cleveland in Bethnal Green in London. They're sending us the details now, and trying to locate him to bring him in."

Wednesday followed her into the Incident Room where a certain frisson was ripping through the room. Perhaps at last, a suspect was about to be caught.

Hunter came out of his office, talking on his mobile. With the mobile still clamped to his ear, he beckoned Wednesday and Lennox towards him. They stood before to him like obedient children, waiting for him to finish his call.

"Right you two, you're off to Bethnal Green—your old stomping ground, Lennox—to check out these leads. It looks like Cleveland is holed up in a local bed and breakfast down there. Bring him back, we need to know what or who he's running from."

Wednesday grabbed a few strands of hair and began twirling them around her finger. "He may just be running from his debts with Dick Pennymore, Guv."

Hunter looked her directly in the eye and rubbed his chin. "That may be part of it, but we can't ignore the school as a link with these deaths. He may be involved in some other way."

"I'll drive seeing as I know the way," said Lennox.

Hunter watched the pair leave before swallowing a couple of paracetamol for the pounding headache that was gripping his head.

The drive down the M11 towards London was spent in unyielding silence. Wednesday's cheeks were burning as she read the report from the metropolitan police, whilst studying the grainy picture of what looked like Cleveland. Lennox drove at a steady pace whilst chewing on some gum.

Wednesday was relieved when her mobile rang, giving her some form of human contact. After listening to the voice at the other end, she turned to Lennox to impart the news.

"They've got Cleveland at the station, but he's not talking. They're hoping he'll open up to us."

"Not sure about that. He's not our greatest fan."

They entered the station and flashed their badges at the sergeant behind the desk, who duly waved them through. They found Cleveland sitting in an interview room with a female officer—who clearly recognised Lennox—standing guard. Cleveland raised his head and let out an audible sigh.

"God, not you two. What the bloody hell have I done to deserve such a visitation?"

"Going on the run during a murder enquiry. Does our visit sound reasonable now?"

"I'm not responsible for the murders. I can't see what right you lot have to keep me here."

He looked rather dishevelled and wide-eyed, and smelt faintly of stale sweat and urine.

"Lots of people are worried about you, Mr Cleveland. Didn't you think your disappearance would cause concern?"

"I think that certain people may be worried because I've begun to work things out. Things to do with the murders."

Wednesday and Lennox looked at one another before sitting opposite him. The sound of their chairs scraping along the floor made Cleveland wince.

"We're listening," said Lennox, not expecting to be enlightened.

They listened as he spoke about seeing Des Wright frequently with Dick Pennymore at the pub. He believed that Des Wright was working for Pennymore as a debt collector, which was the main reason he had disappeared. He feared for his life. He had seen Des doing a lot of work around the pub, mainly odd jobs and gardening. Cleveland sat back in his chair and complained of having a dry mouth, so the officer brought him a cup of water before he continued his tale.

He believed that Pennymore had something on Des which enabled him to use Des as cheap labour.

"But how do you know he isn't paying Des a fair wage?" asked Lennox who was feeling they were wasting their time.

"Because I've heard him telling people when he sits on the pub wall drinking. I've seen him be two-faced about Dick. Nice as pie to his face, then slating him with unsavoury words behind his back." Cleveland took a large gulp of water and let the liquid moisten his cracked lips.

He continued to hypothesize, telling them he believed Des had killed Tom Dolby when he was round his house; it was well known he had a temper. It was not well known that Judith did too, thought Wednesday to herself.

He went on to say Darren must have been present and so he had to be silenced. He stopped and rested his chin on his prayer-like hands. "So?" he said, as though expecting a round of applause.

"It's a nice theory but one that we'd already considered. It's based on fantasy, not fact. You have no substantial evidence for your claims, Mr

Cleveland." Lennox brushed his hand over his hair, all the while maintaining eye contact with him.

"I knew you wouldn't believe me. Look," he started as he bent over the table to get closer to the detectives. "I know that Des has been a beater for the shoot Pennymore organises each year; he'd have been aware of the hut in the woods."

"As would every dog walker in the village," said Wednesday.

Cleveland paused and looked at the floor, chewing on the inside of his cheek.

"You're no help," barked Lennox, tired of being strung along by him.

"You two may see me as a worthless mutt. But as a headmaster, I am influential and know people in high places."

Lennox clamped his teeth together, flexing the muscles in his jaw.

"Detectives, I want protection when I return. I fear Des Wright will harm me." He leant forward again and stared at them both with a wild look I his eyes.

"We don't have the resources for that, Mr Cleveland," said Wednesday. "What I suggest you do is keep your doors locked at all times, only open the front door to people you trust, and call us if he turns up at your house or place of work and threatens your safety. Right, we need to get you back."

Cleveland sat behind Lennox in the car for the journey back to Cambridgeshire. Periodically, Lennox looked in his rear-view mirror to see Cleveland gazing out of the window with a pensive look upon his face.

He also noticed that Wednesday kept glancing at her watch.

"Do you get on with the teachers at your school," he asked, drumming his fingers on the steering wheel to imaginary music.

"I'm not there to be their friend, but seeing as you ask, yes I do. I command respect from them, even the younger ones."

They dropped Cleveland outside his home and checked he got in safely before returning to the office.

"Any plans for the evening?" asked Lennox.

"I thought I'd visit my mum then call in on Oliver."

Lennox made a humming sound in response as he pulled into the station car park.

Wednesday succumbed to eating another chocolate bar from her stash whilst she finishing her paperwork. Periodically, she looked up to see Lennox at his desk generally gazing into space. He had been quiet since their visit to Bethnal Green.

She finished her report before turning off her office light. She was unaware of Lennox staring at her as she walked past his office.

Sitting at his desk in his dimly lit office, he picked up his mobile and made a call. A softly spoken voice answered at the other end.

"I know it's late, but I wondered if I could call in on my way home?"

"You know you can stay, don't you?"

Lennox smiled before closing down his computer.

# Chapter Twenty

Lennox pulled up outside the house and threw his cigarette butt through the crack in the window.

Scarlett answered the door promptly, dressed in an oversized jumper and faded jeans, with her fiery hair cascading down her back. She smiled as he walked in and brushed passed her.

"I'm glad you're here. I'm feeling rather defenceless with all that's going on."

"Defenceless is not a term I'd use to describe you."

He followed her into the kitchen where she poured the Bordeaux into two long-stemmed glasses.

"My research is throwing up all kinds of scenarios that could be happening round here." She gestured for him to sit opposite her before she offered him a cigarette.

She talked about an underlying section of Christians who still believed in exorcism, and if they felt someone had the devil residing within, they had a duty to rid that person of the infliction.

She blew grey smoke towards the ceiling. "Do you think the reverend could be a fanatical freak? He comes across as a quiet and reflective man. Just the type we should be looking out for, according to the web."

The candle light danced in her eyes as she spoke in her animated fashion, hypnotising Lennox.

"Where does the research say this goes on?"

"Well, so far, it's mainly found in the USA . . ."

Lennox interrupted her by making a loud snorting noise as he rocked back in his chair. "These crimes took place in a quaint English village. I don't think we're overrun with zealous clergymen casting the devil out of un-pure teenagers."

The wine bottle made a heavy clunking noise as she slammed it down on the table after refilling her glass. "You police are so quick to dismiss anything you haven't found out yourselves."

She inhaled then blew smoke in his direction. He refrained from quipping, preferring to maintain a dignified silence. Something he could do when not in a meaningful relationship.

"Okay, Miss Marple, what do you suggest we do? Round up the rev and all the church goers and tell them to leave the devil well alone." His face was glowing with the combination of wine and mirth at his own brand of humour.

"I didn't think you wanted to come over to make me look foolish. I thought there was more to you than that."

Lennox apologised with a smile and told her that they were not closing their minds to any scenario.

"With that in mind then, would it be okay if I shadowed you for a few days. Make my reports more cutting edge, so to speak."

Lennox suddenly felt a fool for thinking his inimitable charm was the reason she wanted his company. "Why don't you ask Eva?"

"Because there is such a thing as sibling rivalry. She's always been jealous of my allure and effervescence. She sees herself as the career woman, and she won't help me up the ladder for fear that I will be better at that too."

Lennox sucked in the air so it whistled over his bottom teeth.

"Doesn't sound like the Eva I know. Anyway, if you shadowed me, you'd be shadowing her too, and I'm sure that would piss her off."

He was glad he had only had a small glass of wine, as all he wanted to do now was go home and unwind to the sports channel whilst eating the fish and chips he would buy on the way.

As he rose to leave, he thought he saw panic flash across her eyes.

"Please don't leave me. I'm worried they will get me because of my articles."

"Eva told me you weren't taking the threats seriously. Why the sudden change?"

"There are a couple of steaks in the fridge. Why don't I cook them up for us?" She topped up his glass, and before he knew it, the air was filled with the aromatic smell of steak and black pepper.

Wednesday tipped the crisp packet into her mouth to get the remaining crumbs. She blushed as she caught Oliver watching her.

"Sorry, I'm starving," she said as she screwed the packet up and put it on the coffee table, where it began to noisily expand and pop.

"I could rustle you up something. Soup and a bread roll perhaps."

"Please don't worry. It's already late, I should be getting home."

Oliver hoped that if food could not keep her, then gossip may. He was desperate for some adult company that did not involve measuring moods.

"A mutual acquaintance bought another vase from me today. Nina Prince."

Wednesday frowned. She knew the name but that was all.

"The receptionist at Markham Hall. You're down there a lot by all accounts." Whilst he spoke, he took a variety of cheeses and pickles from the fridge, and placed them on the table with a crusty loaf. Wednesday was hooked.

"She's quite the gossip about what goes on at that school, and she told me a lot. Not realising that we're related. Certain students seem to rule there, by her reckoning."

Wednesday was eyeing the food on the table, rather than paying attention to what he was saying. "What were you saying about the students?" she asked, cutting the bread into thick slices.

"There's an elitist element led by the boys of local businessmen," he began before cutting off a piece of brie. "She mentioned some names, so as soon as she'd gone, I wrote them down. I thought they might be useful to you."

He got up and opened a drawer in the welsh dresser, and pulled out an envelope on which he had scrawled the names.

"Ralph Sanders is the son of the golf course owner. James Almond's father owns the five star hotel and restaurant just outside Cambridge, and Tony Pennymore's father owns The Crow pub."

"I didn't know Dick Pennymore had a son. He seems an unlikely mix with the other two boys," she said, suddenly sitting upright in her chair.

"I bet it's got more to do with the kind of business his father has. Alcohol on tap, if you see what I mean."

"I wonder what goes on with this so-called elite group." Wednesday said, spraying a few bread crumbs on the table, which she brushed off with her hand.

"I'm not sure; Miss Prince didn't specify that deeply. But she thinks even the headmaster is afraid of them."

Wednesday pondered his statement as she opened the jar of pickled onions. "Perhaps we should all be wary of them. Who knows what they can and have done, if the group does truly exist."

She finished her last piece of cheese and pickle then pushed back her chair to get up.

"Can't I persuade you to stay a little longer?" he said as he moved to put the kettle on.

"I'm sorry, I'm working all weekend and I need some sleep." She looked at her watch and saw that it was nearly eleven o'clock. Part of her wanted to stay as she could see he was starved of company. But she wanted to be alert at work. She did not want to give Hunter any reason to say she was not up to the job.

The headlights picked up the droplets of drizzle as they merged on the windscreen, before being erased by the wipers. The noise of the wipers acted like a metronome causing Wednesday to fight the urge to sleep.

Approaching her house, she recognised Lennox's car parked outside. With a heavy sigh, she pulled up on her drive and switched off the engine.

The house was in almost total darkness, except for a soft glow emerging from the kitchen. She followed the light and found the source; the candles in the centre of the table. She was angry to find them unattended. She then saw the remains of a steak meal on two plates. Tempted as she was to storm upstairs to confront the thoughtless pair, the last thing she needed to see was Lennox in a state of undress.

She felt in need of some comfort, so she put a pan of milk on the Aga to make a hot chocolate, and put some Mahler on the music system. She felt her shoulders relax but her thoughts still remained sharp and focused—she knew they had the answers to the cases right in front of them, they just could not see them.

The chinking of the teaspoon against the sides of the mug masked the sound of footsteps coming down the stairs. Wednesday had just lit a cigarette when Scarlett appeared at the door.

"Oh, didn't hear you come in," she said as she walked over to the fridge.

"I'm sure you didn't," Wednesday replied as she caught sight of Lennox out of the corner of her eye.

He looked unkempt and slightly embarrassed to see her.

"Did you have a good evening," he asked, avoiding direct eye contact.

"Not really, but I can see you did," she replied before stubbing out the barely smoked cigarette. "I'm off to bed," she announced as she blew out the candles and picked up the mug.

Scarlett and Lennox watched her disappear, leaving a trail of extinguished candle smoke behind her. Scarlett turned to Lennox and rolled her eyes.

Vera Olong tiptoed down the stairs to get a glass of water; it was past midnight and she did not want to wake her husband sleeping in the adjacent bedroom.

Walking towards the kitchen, she saw a light coming from underneath his study door. It was unlike him to be awake at such a late hour, so she tapped lightly and pressed her ear to the door. She thought she heard him mutter a reply, so she opened the door slowly to see him hunched over his desk.

"Are you all right, George?"

"Not really," he sighed. "Life is troubling me and God doesn't seem to have the answers I seek." He buried his face in his hands and took a few deep breaths before continuing. "Man must plough his own furrow, and plant his seeds of destiny as seen fit in the eyes of the Lord."

"I hate it when you talk like that," she replied, moving towards the chair in front of his desk.

"In what other way should I talk?"

"Like a man. Not always like a reverend." Her face was flushed as she spoke, and her hands trembled slightly as she reached out to take a sip of water from his glass. Swallowing the liquid, a look of surprise covered her face.

"Are you drinking gin again?"

He nodded taking back the glass and staring into the clear liquid. The occasional bubble from the tonic water rose to the surface. His gaze returned to the photographs of the choirs he had led over the years.

"I know no other way of speaking or thinking. I am a reverend through and through."

"I think that is where the problems lies, George. You used to be so much more."

Vera stood up and headed for the door. Reaching it, she turned around. "I hope we're not going to be moved from here, too," she said before vanishing into the darken hallway.

George remained, shifting through the memories splayed out on his desk. Life was easier when he was the choir master. He had all the answers then. He downed his drink in one large gulp, before switching off the desk lamp. The shadows in the corners of the room seemed dark and menacing, and the various shades of black and grey played tricks with his tired eyes. Paranoia closed in on his mind, telling him that he was being watched, and that not only God knew his dark thoughts and deeds.

Upstairs, Vera stood by the window watching sheets of rain cascade against the pane. She could see the anticipation in her face in her reflection as she rubbed her stomach in slow circular motions.

The following morning, a low hum resonated around the Incident Room as the officers gathered around the desks, hugging their mugs of cheap instant coffee.

"What's this weak piss they're giving us?" said Lennox as he sidled up to Wednesday.

She sat up but avoided any eye contact and informed him that it was to do with the budget cuts. Filter coffee was now considered a luxury. Lennox shrugged his shoulders and perched on the table next to her.

Out of the corner of her eye, Wednesday could see two female officers gazing longingly at him before giving her an envious look. She wanted to shake her head at them and tell them he was sleeping with her Scarlett, so their longing was pointless. No one could compete with her.

"We've just received a call from the hospital. Stewart Cleveland was brought in after being found in a bunker on the golf course. He's suffered quite a beating," Jones said, handing over a fax of the hospital report.

"Hunter wants you to go and interview him now, if he's fit enough. Then interview the owner of the golf course, Mr Sanders."

Lennox jangled his keys and indicated with his head for Wednesday to follow him. Sitting in the passenger seat, she read the report aloud.

"He's suffered a broken arm, two fractured ribs, and a dislocated jaw. He was found by Ralph Sanders, the owner's son."

"Is that the same Ralph we saw at Markham school after Claudia's death?"

Wednesday realised she had not recounted the information supplied by Oliver last evening. She briefly relayed the news about the possible elite group of boys, who all had rich fathers.

"Could mean something and nothing. I imagine that secretary loves a good gossip."

They found Cleveland lying in a bed in a side room, having his intravenous drip tended to by a male nurse. When he saw them standing in the doorway, he let out a low moan which made the nurse turn to look in their direction.

"DI Wednesday and DS Lennox," Wednesday said, addressing the nurse. "We'd like to ask Mr Cleveland a few questions."

"Make it short, detectives, he's in quite a bit of discomfort, and will tire easily."

They pulled up two chairs next to the bed and waited for the nurse to leave.

"You've taken quite a beating, Mr Cleveland," said Wednesday unbuttoning her coat. "Do you know who did this to you?"

Cleveland slowly parted his cracked lips and winced. He moved his eyes from side to side.

"I'll take that as a *no*," she said.

"How many were there?"

Cleveland whispered that he did not know and that he was tired.

"We want to catch who did this to you. Is it connected to the money you owe Dick Pennymore?" persisted Lennox.

"I don't know," he whispered, his lips barely moving. "But I told you I was in danger." He closed his eyes and made no further effort to answer their questions, or even acknowledge their presence. They watched his chest rise and fall in slow rhythmic movements.

As they rose to leave, Cleveland made a feeble whistling sound and then lifted two fingers. "I think there were two," he rasped, his eyes firmly closed.

"Thank you. We'll come back when you're stronger," replied Wednesday in a hushed tone.

"What do you make of all that, then?" asked Lennox, eyeing a nurse bending over the reception desk.

"The nurse or Cleveland?"

"Oh, ha-ha. The nurse is rather tempting, though."

Wednesday play slapped him on the forearm before picking up the pace.

Arriving back at the station, they saw the reverend walking towards them.

"Just the people I wanted to see," he said as they drew level to him. He fished around in his waterproof coat pocket and brought out a crumpled piece of paper.

"This came through the door this morning, and I thought you should see it." He handed the note to Wednesday and waited for her to read it.

"WE KNOW IT'S YOU. GET OUT NOW OR DIE."

"Succinct and to the point," said Lennox, peering over her shoulder.

"Did it come in an envelope, and have you still got it?"

The reverend rummaged around in his pocket again and retrieved a dog-eared envelope that had his name on the front, using cut out letters, just like the note.

"I'll get this to the forensics lab. Would you mind coming in to make a statement, Reverend?"

He made a guttural sound and followed the pair inside. He refused a cup of tea as he sat in the interview room, anxious to move things along so he could get back to work.

"I don't want Vera to find out about this, she'd only fret. I'm sure I've nothing to be afraid of."

"You may not be able to keep it quiet for long if the threats increase," replied Lennox.

"You think I might get more?"

"It's a possibility. Now has anything unusual happened lately, people treating you differently, things like that?"

George sifted through his thoughts and activities over the past few days, but nothing stood out to him. He repeated his request to go home as he still had a sermon to write.

The detectives watched him trundle down the corridor before returning to the Incident Room, where they found Arlow waiting.

"The guv wants you to interview Des Wright about the attack on Cleveland, then onto the golf club to view any CCTV that may be available."

Lennox scowled until Arlow said he and Damlish were occupied with the Tom Dolby case.

Wednesday drove to the Wright's home where they found a barely sober Judith all alone. She leant against the door frame and refused to let them in.

"If it's Des you're wanting he ain't here. He's working on the pub garden."

"The Crow?" Wednesday asked.

Judith nodded in a jerky fashion before stepping back inside and shutting the door in their faces.

They drew up and parked next to a filthy pale blue van with visible rust displayed on the wheel arches. They heard the sound of a chainsaw whirring coming from behind the pub, and walking around the side, they saw Des cutting back the perimeter hedge. He was unaware of their presence.

With caution, they put themselves in his eye line to indicate they needed to talk with him.

"What now?" he yelled after switching off the machine. He kept his visor down and the chainsaw brandished in front of him.

"We'd like to know where you were last night," Lennox asked.

"At home, pissed, with the old woman. Why?"

"Stewart Cleveland was assaulted last night . . ."

"So every time something goes bad around here, I'm to expect a call from you guys, am I?" He straightened his back and rolled back his shoulders, staring directly at Lennox.

"No, we're making enquiries and your name came up."

"Let me guess, by Cleveland."

"Now why would he bring up your name?" Lennox said, raising his eyebrows.

"He never liked me. He made that clear if I went to that damn school about Darren."

"In what way," continued Lennox, keeping an eye on the chainsaw.

"I dunno. It was obvious he thought I was a dumb piece of shit, not educated like him."

"Could you raise your visor?" asked Wednesday.

He did as he was asked, revealing the faint mark of a new bruise on his right cheek.

"Where did you acquire that bruise?"

Des said nothing and let the chainsaw drop to his side.

"It looks suspiciously new. If this is a result of some home dispute, you could report it to us," said Wednesday in a low voice. "But if it's some fight, we'll need the details to verify your story."

Des guffawed at her comments, saying the bruise was a result of him staggering into a door frame when he was drunk the night before. He snapped down his visor and revved up the chainsaw, returning his attention to the hedge.

As they turned to walk away, they found Dick Pennymore standing behind them.

"Anything wrong, Detectives?"

"Just making enquiries. Where were you last night after closing?" replied Wednesday.

"I had a private party going on in the back room until about two in the morning."

"Could anyone corroborate that?"

"Sure. I can give you a list of names."

"If you would." Wednesday held her pen over her notepad.

Pennymore sighed and proceeded to reel of the names.

She saw him watching them leave in her rear-view mirror, before turning around and heading back towards Des.

The drive to the golf club took them along hedge lined roads that opened up onto windswept, barren farmland. Despite the chill in the air there were plenty of cars in the golf club car park. However, they were more salubrious that those of the clientele in The Crow. They noted a couple of sports models, three Range Rovers and one Silver Lady Rolls Royce.

"Impressive," said Lennox as he perused the mechanical marvels.

"I suppose, if you're impressed by ostentatious, materialistic paraphernalia," replied Wednesday as she gazed around. "There's a CCTV camera up there. Hopefully it'll have captured something."

Crunching up the lavender lined gravel path, the pair found the double door entrance to the club at the front, overlooking the green. The door was flanked by two tall bay trees. Window boxes and hanging baskets containing winter pansies were interspersed around the perimeter. The tables and chairs on the veranda were covered over for the winter.

A gust of warm air blasted their faces as they stepped inside and walked towards the reception desk.

Lennox introduced them as they flashed their badges. "We'd like to speak to Mr Keith Sanders, please."

The overly made-up woman dialled through, and within seconds, a man in an expensive looking suit with black patent shoes arrived in reception and introduced himself.

"I suppose you've come about Mr Cleveland. Shall we move to my office?"

Wednesday and Lennox followed him into his plush office, with a bottle-green leather couch, walnut desk, and a showcase full of golfing trophies.

"Most of those belong to my son," he said, noticing them looking.

"Would that be Ralph?" enquired Lennox as he moved closer to the cabinet.

"Yes, he's on his way to becoming a professional golfer. He's got a big future ahead of him."

"It was Ralph who found Mr Cleveland, I understand."

"Yes, he practices every morning before school. I told you, he's aiming high so he has to put the hours in."

"How has Ralph been since the death of Claudia Edwards?"

"He's been fine. He knew her, but not all that well."

"You wouldn't have classed them as dating then?"

Sanders gave a throaty laugh, and said absolutely not, stating again that his son had no time for frivolous activities such as dating girls. Girls were a distraction.

"Is Mr Cleveland a member of this club?" Lennox asked.

Another look of mirth from Sanders confirmed that Cleveland was not a member, although he was trying to find a sponsor so he could be. He went on to say that Cleveland may be well educated, but he did not have the aristocratic or esteemed background other members had.

"People pay a lot for exclusivity," he said, before there was a knock at his door.

His secretary entered and whispered in his ear before giving him something to sign. After her departure, they discussed the CCTV footage which only covered the clubhouse and the car park, which is locked at eleven thirty, after the closure of the clubhouse. No problems had ever been reported at the club, and he had no idea what Cleveland was doing there. Nevertheless, Wednesday asked for the footage to take back to the station.

"If there's anything else I could do, just ask."

They asked if they could have a look around before they left, and that they would need to interview Ralph about the discovery. Sanders waved his hand in agreement.

They walked around the green and found the bunker where Cleveland was found earlier that day. The area had been swept by officers, but nothing pertinent had been found.

"There's no way of seeing people arriving through the woodland. It's secluded down here. Anybody could have dumped him here without being seen," said Lennox as he looked around. "Come on, let's get back to the station, we're just wasting time here."

Wednesday took a last look around before striding out to catch up with him. Once in the car, she reclined her seat and leant her head on the padded rest. Images of her mother in emotional crisis interspersed her logical thinking about the murders. She closed her eyes for a few seconds to attempt to blot out the disturbing visions.

Arriving at the Incident Room, Arlow approached them.

"We're releasing Tom Dolby's body to the parents today. They want to have the funeral in a couple of days."

"I suppose Hunter will make us attend that," said Lennox, rolling his eyes as he headed for his office.

Wednesday's mobile rang. It was Scarlett.

"Thought you'd be interested to know that a wreath was delivered to the office for me a few minutes ago, with a message that reads 'May your soul be damned'. What do you make of that? Isn't it just divine?"

"Good god, Scarlett, this is getting serious. I'll send an officer to collect it and get a statement from you."

"Don't blow a fuse, sis. I'm okay, and I'm sure Jacob will be my body-guard again tonight."

Wednesday glared in the direction of Lennox's office as she disconnected the call. She sent an officer to Scarlet's office then marched straight over to Lennox.

"We need to talk about Scarlett," she said as she closed the door behind her.

"What about?"

"Two things really. The first being she's just received another threat in the form of a wreath, and secondly, I hope that you don't intend to hurt her feelings."

Lennox indicated for her to take a seat, which she declined.

"Firstly, I hope she's taking the threat seriously, and secondly, I hope she's not taking me too seriously. You know how I feel about commitment."

"Oh indeed, *I know*. But I'm not so sure Scarlett does."

"Perhaps you should enlighten her."

"That's not my job, and I'm not the guardian of your love-life. I've avoided mentioning her until now for the sake of our working relationship."

"There's nothing to worry about. I'm sure she's strong enough to deal with a transient liaison."

Wednesday exhaled loudly as her mobile rang again. Snatching it from her pocket, she saw it was a call from the psychiatric hospital. She hurried from his office without saying another word to him.

Shutting the door to her office, she listened as a nurse informed her that her mother was being discharged next week, and that they would like her to attend a pre-discharge meeting, along with Oliver. Wednesday checked her diary and knew there was never going to be the right time in her work schedule, so she reluctantly agreed for a meeting on Monday afternoon.

Her reluctance made her feel guilty, which in turn made her unearth all her fears about the future. She could not comprehend how, as a family, they were going to cope with her mother's increasingly fluctuating mental health and suicidal ideation. Oliver was showing signs of compassion fatigue and Scarlett displayed a marked lack of interest, hence Wednesday felt she needed to be the one to cope with the caring demands as well as the demands of her own career. Her shoulders drooped and her head began to throb.

Looking up she saw Hunter standing outside her door holding a copy of the local newspaper.

"I see your sister is hard at work, stirring up mass hysteria again. I thought I'd asked you to get her to tone it down," he said as he slammed the paper on her desk.

"Sorry Guv. She doesn't listen to my requests or demands, and now it's getting her into more trouble."

"More?"

Wednesday's cheeks flushed as he stood over her desk, waiting for clarification.

"She's just received a wreath at work."

"And what do you want me to do about that?"

She felt like a schoolgirl in the headmaster's office. He remained standing, with his arms folded across his chest.

"An officer is bringing in the wreath for examination. She's just winding up the religious section of the community talking about cults."

"Well we don't know that for sure. In fact, we don't know much about anything at the moment, which is bloody unsatisfactory to say the least."

Jones appeared at the door and asked Wednesday what she wanted her to do with the wreath that had just arrived. Hunter looked at her before exiting, leaving a frosty atmosphere in his wake.

"I'll take it downstairs," she said, taking the wreath and heading to the laboratory.

She found Alex Green hunched over a microscope; he was so absorbed he did not hear her knock. He finally looked up thanks to her theatrical coughing.

"Who does that belong to?" he asked, looking at the wreath.

"It was sent to my half-sister, so I want it processing for fingerprints. See if there's anyone in the system we can trace it to. It was paid for in cash, anonymously at the florist."

With gloved hands, Alex took the wreath and placed it on a table. "It's not priority. I've still got loads to do for your cases. Besides, there were no latent prints on the other items from her."

Wednesday understood albeit unenthusiastically.

Instead of returning upstairs she headed for the courtyard. The air was damp, but it did not deter her from lighting a cigarette. Her mother's delusional voice kept appearing in her mind, saying over and over that they were trying to poison her; "they" being the hospital staff. She wished her troubles could evaporate in the air, much like the cigarette smoke.

"Thought I'd find you here," said Lennox, pulling out a packet of cigarettes. "I need to ask you a favour."

She eyed him suspiciously through the murky smoke.

"You remember me telling you about my difficulties with my two sons?"

Wednesday nodded and took a deep drag from her cigarette.

"Well with all this cancelled leave, I've missed a few visits. So, I'm taking them bowling in London this evening."

"Sounds like a great idea. What do you need from me?"

Lennox scuffed his shoes along the ground, blowing clouds of smoke into the air.

"I need to have a quiet word with Archie about his aggressive behaviour, and I need Alfie to be distracted whilst I do that."

"You want me to tag along to be the distraction? Why don't you ask Scarlett?"

"Because I don't need another adolescent to care for. I need another adult for support."

Wednesday liked his description of Scarlett, but disliked the idea of an evening with two unknown teenagers, and especially disliked the notion of wearing other people's smelly shoes.

Driving down to London, they refrained from smoking in the car for the sake of the boys.

"How are you going to introduce me?" Wednesday asked as she tucked a strand of hair behind her ear.

"Hadn't occurred to me what to say. How about work colleague?"

Wednesday nodded. She envisaged a mountain of complications over the course of the evening, but it was too late to change her mind as they pulled up next to a tree outside his ex-wife's house.

She watched Lennox walk up to the front door of the modern semi-detached house and ring the bell. She noticed him stand up straight with his shoulders back as the door opened.

His ex-wife was tantalising out of view, and even when Wednesday unbuckled her seatbelt and leant forward as far as she could, she still could not see her. All that was visible was a shadow of the mother of his children, cast out by the light coming from the hallway. The interaction was brief and before long, Lennox was walking to the car with his two sons in tow. The eldest was almost as tall as his father, whilst the youngest still had a way to go.

Both backdoors opened simultaneously and the car rocked as the boys threw themselves in before slamming the doors. The smell of cheap aftershave pervaded the air, and Wednesday barely received an acknowledging grunt from either of them as Lennox introduced her.

Lennox tried to engage the boys in conversation about school and football. Wednesday found it painful to witness, and her irritation with Archie was mounting as he persistently pushed his foot into the back of her chair. She could see Lennox gripping the steering wheel. She wanted to reach out and touch him on the arm; only that would be miscon-strued by everyone.

Lennox had hardly stopped the car, when both boys jumped out and made their way into the bowling alley.

"I'm sorry," said Lennox, pulling on the handbrake.

"No worries. I remember being a teenager . . . But you owe me." She smiled to reassure him, even though she meant the owing part.

Before she knew it, she was standing alone with the younger boy whilst Lennox took Archie off to buy the drinks.

"So, are you my dad's girlfriend?"

"No, we just work together."

"I don't know why you're here then," he replied, looking at her with his inquisitive hazel eyes, which were a brighter, livelier version of his father's.

"I don't quite know myself. Shall we set up the game?" she asked, hoping to distract him until the others returned.

Out of the corner of her eye she could see Lennox returning with a tray of drinks in tall plastic containers with fluorescent straws. Archie was looking very red in the face and gesticulating wildly with his arms.

"You have no right to tell me how to behave. You left us. Is that how to behave?"

"Don't be so rude."

"There you go again, telling me what to do. We hardly see you and when we do, you think you're in charge."

Wednesday and Alfie watched Archie spew his bitterness over his father.

"Look son, I'm just worried about you, and so is your mum."

"Don't bring her into it. I hate you," he threw his large carton of Coke on the floor and stormed towards the exit.

"Watch him," said Lennox, indicating with his head in Alfie's direction as he dashed after Archie.

Wednesday turned towards Alfie who stood open mouthed as his father disappeared through the crowd.

"Shall we play?" she asked half-heartedly.

He shrugged and turned away from her before slumping into a seat. He repeatedly rammed the toe of his trainer into the table leg, with his head hung so low Wednesday could no longer see his face under his floppy fringe.

Five minutes later, Lennox returned with Archie and announced that they were leaving. His news was met with a mixture of sighs and drooping shoulders. But Wednesday was relieved that the nightmare evening was almost over.

Throughout the return journey, Archie continued to push his foot into the back of Wednesday's seat. She fumbled with the packet of cigarettes in her pocket, longing to draw one out and light it. Lennox had given up on small talk, so the subdued atmosphere lasted until they arrived back at the boys' home.

Once again, Wednesday could not see the front door clearly, but she heard raised voices and then heard the door slam as Lennox returned to the car. She held out her packet of cigarettes as he clicked his seatbelt into position.

"Sorry about this evening," he said before lighting up. "My plan didn't pan out. Sorry you had to witness my crash and burn."

"No worries."

Small talk was off the agenda again and as he pulled up outside her house, he let her out before driving off revving his engine briefly.

On entering the hallway, Wednesday heard voices coming from the lounge. Standing in the doorway, she was surprised, and not too happy, to see Vera Olong standing in front of the fireplace, talking to Scarlett.

"DI Wednesday, what a surprise. Is this your home?" She was composed as she spoke, her face the same paleness as always, contrasted against her raven hair. Wednesday suspected she dyed it.

Wednesday nodded and sat on the couch, awaiting an explanation.

"I was asking Miss Willow if she could cease writing inflammatory articles about my husband and whether we have a cult festering away in our community."

"I see. How did you know where she lives?" said Wednesday, leaning forward in her seat.

"A friend told me. Look, George is getting quite depressed over recent events, and I feel these articles are fuelling the gossip. You know how small-minded people can be."

"I've already told Mrs Olong that I will tone down focusing on the reverend, but the cult issue is big news. I can't stop that," piped up Scarlett.

"Listen DI Wednesday, I'm worried that someone is trying to implicate my husband in the recent deaths by planting evidence at the vicarage. It needs to stop before it tips him over the edge."

"I'm not in charge of Scarlett. You've taken it up with her, so if you're not satisfied, I suggest you see the editor of the paper. I would prefer it if you didn't call here again, but go to her office instead."

"I'm sorry, I was hoping to be less formal, appeal to her human nature rather than go the formal route via her boss."

Wednesday rose and Vera took the hint. As they reached the front door, she turned and looked at Wednesday. "Do you believe my husband is guilty in some way?"

Wednesday frowned. "I can't discuss ongoing cases with you, Mrs Olong. We are still investigating many leads and suspects."

"One of which is my husband."

Wednesday pursed her lips and opened the front door. "Goodbye Mrs Olong," she said before quietly closing the door.

Wednesday headed straight for the kitchen and reached for the open bottle of wine in the fridge. She poured herself a large glass then sat in the carver chair at the head of the table. She rubbed the back of her neck and closed her eyes, letting the memories of the day wash around her mind. She opened her eyes on hearing Scarlett enter the room.

"That was awkward and positively annoying," said Wednesday. "I don't like my work life to enter my home via osmosis. It could cause complications."

"Geez sis, you worry too much. She wasn't threatening me, just asking me to go easy on the rev."

"All the same, I don't feel comfortable with people feeling they can drop in and discuss the cases in any way, shape, or form."

"All right already; message received." Scarlett poured herself a glass of wine and was about to leave the kitchen when Wednesday stopped her.

"There's the discharge planning meeting on Monday to discuss Mum coming home. You should be there."

The glass hovered at Scarlett's lips before she took a sip. "You know how I loathe those places."

"It not the place you loathe, it's the staff."

"Meaning?"

"You're worried that some doctor or nurse will see your own madness. The madness you deny so frequently."

Scarlett moved closer to Wednesday and slammed her glass on the table, causing droplets of wine to slosh over the table.

"I may be excitable at times, but at least I don't live my life on the flat level like you."

"We have insanity in the family. You never seem to worry about that."

"Why worry? That alone can lead to insanity."

Wednesday's head pounded and Scarlett's raised voice was intolerable. She rubbed her temples contemplating her next move, but before she had a chance to challenge Scarlett's viewpoint, she'd already left the room and was clomping up the stairs. The slamming of her bedroom door signalled the end of their conversation.

Wednesday was a light sleeper, so when she heard footsteps on the gravel path, in the early hours, she moved quickly to the window and peeked through the curtains. Her eyes adjusted to the darkness, but they also played tricks with the shadows so she could not be sure about what she was seeing. The security light suddenly lit up, casting a glow over the two cars. Wednesday waited to see any movement and then she saw a cat stroll out from the shadows. She waited some more before returning to bed and pulling the quilt over her head.

The smell of coffee and the chatter on the radio roused her from her slumber. Scarlett was already sitting in the kitchen, reading the Sunday paper.

Wednesday skirted around the table to grab herself a coffee. "I'm sorry about last night."

"Already forgotten, sis."

"I've got to get ready for work, but perhaps we can have a chat later about the meeting tomorrow."

Scarlett mumbled incoherently as she buried her head in the paper.

"Are you sure you can cope with this morning's service?" asked Vera, looking at George over the breakfast table.

He sat with his elbows on the table, nursing a mug of steaming tea. "God will give me the strength I need," he replied.

Vera vigorously tapped the top of her soft boiled egg before decapitating it, freeing the yolk so it oozed down the shell's exterior. "You could always ask a lay preacher to take over just this once."

"Then it would look like I have something to hide. People are talking enough as it is." He drank the last of his tea then excused himself from the table, leaving Vera alone with her thoughts.

"I don't want to move again," she called out before hearing his study door close.

As the church bells chimed, George paced up and down in the vestry, wringing his hands and mumbling a prayer to God. He stopped midflow as Vera knocked on the door to check that he was okay.

"Of course I am," he replied before recommencing his pacing routine.

Standing in the pulpit, George was acutely aware of the thinning congregation. Reliable church members such as Emily, and the returning James Dolby, continued to keep their faith in God and in him.

As the opening hymn began, the strength and depth of the voices was noticeably lacking, as one by one, the parents had removed their offspring from the choir, leaving mainly adults such as Colin Pollock to keep it going. Even though Vera was in charge of the choir, it appeared that no one believed her strong enough to protect their loved ones from her husband.

Vera valiantly conducted whilst singing at the top of her soprano voice. She caught her husband's eye, and he responded with a gentle nod of his head.

After the hymn was over, everyone sat down and waited for him to speak. He opened his sermon by discussing the Ten Commandments; his hands shaking underneath his cassock and his mouth becoming so dry that his lips stuck to his teeth.

"What evil have you brought upon us?" called out a voice from the pews.

The congregation stirred and people turned around to see who had spoken. People began murmuring and twitching nervously, until again, this time in a faltering voice, the question came again.

"What evil have you brought upon us, Reverend?"

George recognised the voice as did the congregation as they shuffled in the pews to gaze at Emily Dolby. The reverend leant on the lectern with his hands clasped together in a prayer-like position.

"Dear Emily, I'm not sure what you mean."

Emily stood up whilst her husband looked up at her in bewilderment; the colour draining from his face.

"Life around here may have been a tad dull but it was safe. Then you came along, and all these . . ." she paused to swallow hard. "All these deaths have happened to our children. It can only be you."

She remained standing, gripping onto the pew in front to keep her balance as she swayed back and forth. Colour flooded her face until her cheeks were glowing as though she had been slapped.

Vera had discreetly sidled up to George and whispered something in his ear.

"My dear Emily, I can see you are very troubled. So may I suggest that we discuss your concerns after the service?"

James tugged on his wife's sleeve, encouraging her to do as he suggested. She finally gave in and sat down.

Unfortunately, her outburst had unsettled the congregation and the reverend struggled to draw them back into the words of God. He indicated to his wife to start the next hymn, which everyone reluctantly joined in with.

George ended the service by mentioning the three adolescents by name, which provoked muffled cries from some people. He walked down the aisle and stood by the arched door with Vera, ready to thank everyone for attending the service.

The congregation was slow to disperse, not wishing to miss out on the confrontation between the reverend and Emily Dolby. For some people, the battle between the pair offered up the opportunity for gossip and intrigue.

With the final person dispatched, George and Vera moved inside. He positioned himself in the pew in front of the Dolbys, sitting sideways so they could converse easily. Vera placed herself discreetly a few pews behind.

"I'm sorry for my wife's outburst, Reverend. She's been under a lot of stress of late."

Emily looked at her husband and placed her hand on his arm.

"We have both had a stressful time," she began, "and I don't need my husband to apologise on my behalf." She faced George once more. "I want you to explain things to me."

"I will do my best," he replied, as he clenched his hands together.

"Before you came here, we were a good Christian community. Then you arrived and suddenly we appear to have a cult that is killing our children. We heard you were forcibly moved here. Have you been involved in a cult movement before? Is that why they sent you here?"

George remained impassive. Emily took a deep breath and waited for him to answer.

"The cult story is fictional and the finger is being pointed in my direction as I'm an easy target. Religion can bring one's downfall in society, from both the scared and the nonbelievers. Even James, had momentary lapse of faith."

James blushed and gazed at his feet.

"Jesus came across his fair share of doubters," finished George.

"You're skirting the issue, Reverend. My son is dead, and I don't know who to blame. I need to know the truth."

"The search for the truth is not for the faint-hearted," said George as he looked towards Vera.

"Shall we go to the vicarage for some tea? We want to soothe your soul before you return home," offered Vera.

"No thank you, I just want to go home," replied Emily.

The Dolbys stood up and shuffled down the pew. Neither gave eye contact to George or Vera, although James did attempt to raise a farewell hand.

George rubbed his forehead and screwed up his eyes.

"It will soon blow over," said Vera. "Let's go back for a cup of tea."

Suddenly feeling weary and old, George followed his wife to the vicarage. It was going to take more than tea to bolster his soul.


"Shall we grab a bite to eat in the canteen?" asked Lennox as he stood in Wednesday's doorway.

Wednesday shook a packet of cigarettes at him. He laughed. "Cigarettes aren't a meal replacement. Come on, food first."

It was a fine, but cold day, and squirrels scampered across the car park as the pair walked to the canteen.

Lennox bought a plate of fish and chips, whilst Wednesday bought an egg salad sandwich. The smell of the vinegar on the chips made her mouth water and the sandwich less satisfying.

"How are your sons?"

"Archie won't talk to me on the phone and Alfie just answers monosyllabically. My ex balled me out for thinking of my girlfriend before my sons."

"Didn't you explain . . . ?"

"I tried to. To be honest, it was already brewing. It would've happened whether you were there or not."

Wednesday stirred her cup of coffee incessantly, until Lennox finally told her it was getting on his nerves. She placed the spoon on the table and rocked it back and forth with her middle finger, until Lennox whisked the item out of her reach.

"Spit it out," he demanded.

"Look, I need to be somewhere tomorrow at three. Could you cover for me? I'll only be gone an hour."

"Okay, but assure me you're not putting yourself in danger."

"It's not work related, it's of a personal nature."

"Therapy session?"

Wednesday prodded her egg sandwich, pushing her finger further into the doughy bread; and Lennox knew at once he had made a faux pas.

"Are you implying I'm unhinged?"

"I can have that effect on women."

He sat back in his chair, displaying a wide grin on his face, which faded as he saw the seriousness in her eyes.

"Sorry, Guv, I didn't mean to wind you up."

"They are discharging Mum next week, and I need to go to a meeting to plan for her care once home. If I'm honest, I'm not sure how we'll cope as a family this time around. Oliver is getting tired, I'm overloaded at work, and Scarlett is, well, Scarlett."

The trouble was, once she started opening up to him, she could not stop. She even mentioned that she was worried about Scarlett's emotional wellbeing, until she remembered he was sleeping with her.

"Sorry, I shouldn't have said that last bit. I'm just a colossal worrier."

"Does that mean you, too, could potentially be two people and I won't know who you are at times?"

Wednesday expelled a deep sigh. "Firstly, schizophrenia doesn't mean being two people. They function differently from the rest of society. They can often lose touch with reality, be ambivalent to life."

Lennox placed his cutlery on the plate and pushed it to one side.

"Is this why you've kept it a secret from Hunter?"

"Yes, I suppose so. Look at what you thought. I don't want him to see it as a potential weakness. He'd scrutinise every move and mistake I made so he could blame it on my state of mind."

Before they had time to resolve each other's concerns, Damlish blustered into the canteen and approached their table.

"Colin Pollock has brought something of interest to the station. Thought you ought to see it."

Wednesday left her half eaten sandwich and followed the men out.

They found Colin Pollock sitting in an interview room, tightly clutching a plastic bag. He shuffled about in his chair as they walked in and sat down.

"I found this on my doorstep this morning. I got up late, so I don't know how long it's been there."

Wednesday donned some gloves and opened the bag. She pulled out a blue-green travel blanket.

"Have you touched this?" she asked Pollock.

"Well yes, I was curious."

"We'll need to take your prints for exclusion purposes."

Wednesday carefully turned the blanket over and then placed it back in the bag.

"What made you think to bring this here?" she asked.

"I remember you searching for one and I thought it could be relevant. Or it could just be a prank."

"Who would do that, Mr Pollock?"

"I truly have no idea. I'm a teacher at a secondary school, so it could be anyone. It's your job to find out *who*, Detective."

Wednesday thanked him for coming in, before an officer took him away for fingerprinting. She then took the bag and blanket down to the lab, where she found Alex Green on his mobile. She hovered around until he had finished.

"I think this could possibly be the blanket that was used to kill Tom Dolby. Could you process the blanket and the bag?"

"This could be a lucky break if I can lift any prints from the bag, or find hairs or skin cells on the blanket. I'll make it my priority."

Wednesday hoped he was right. If ever there was a time when she needed good news, now was that time.

# Chapter Twenty-One

Weak winter sun hit Wednesday's bedroom window, piercing through a chink in the curtains, tapping her unwelcomingly on her face.

Normally, she was not affected by the Monday blues, but the hospital appointment in the afternoon was playing on her mind. Guilt was crushing her abdomen as she had not visited her mother as often as she should have. It did not matter that she and Oliver understood how time-consuming her work was, she still felt as though her mother deserved better, considering the life she had led.

With the Aga offering comforting warmth, she was soon ensconced in the carver chair—with her feet tucked under her body—and the local paper and a mug of coffee to keep her company. As she unfolded the paper, she saw the front page article shouting the words "London cults spreading our way". Wednesday shook the paper straight with both hands and then placed it on the table and smoothed it over with her palms.

The article, written by Scarlett, informed the reader of her trip to London to meet a secret source who explained the growing underworld of cults in the capital city. It went on to explain that cults were organisations with radical views and behaviours that jarred with the accepted views in the mainstream community. Not mind blowing so far, thought Wednesday as she lit a cigarette before continuing to read.

The leaders of such organisations are often charismatic people, who proclaim they have been chosen by a higher power. They encourage the members to isolate themselves from family and friends.

Wednesday blew a long stream of smoke from her mouth as she released the tension in her shoulders. She discarded the paper to one side and drank the last of her coffee. No movement from upstairs, so she got ready for work without the opportunity to challenge Scarlett for continuing to stir the chattering masses about a cult killing their children. Never mind the promise she gave to Vera Olong.

Wednesday grabbed a notepad and scribbled the time of the pre-release meeting that afternoon for Scarlett, knowing full well that she would not attend, but she hoped the note would prick her almost non-existent conscious.

Joni Mitchell's voice oozed out from the car stereo as she drove to work, with her third morning cigarette dangling from her mouth. As usual, Lennox's car was already parked in his space, and she could see Damlish walking towards the station entrance, clasping a take-away cup of fashionable coffee.

The morning dragged for Wednesday, chasing up forensic results and completing reports. Even the interaction with Alex Green did nothing to distract her. She kept herself locked away in her office until it was time to leave.

Lennox gave a gentle nod of his head as Wednesday left her office. Maria Jones had brought in cakes to celebrate her birthday, making it easy for Wednesday to slip out unnoticed by the rest of the team.

The drive to the hospital was easy enough. However, finding a place to park proved difficult, so by the time she reached the ward she was out of breath with a faint whiff of smoke clinging to her clothes.

Oliver stood up with outstretched arms, and gave her a wide smile as she arrived in the waiting room.

Within five minutes, a nurse appeared and asked them to enter the meeting room. Wednesday gave one last look towards the main door.

Joan was sitting quietly on a chair to the right of the psychiatrist. She looked pasty and barely acknowledged the presence of her daughter and husband, and the psychiatrist seemed to over-compensate with theatrical gestures and a jovial voice. As he spoke, his handlebar moustache jiggled with a rippling effect. Wednesday found it distracting, so she turned her attention to Oliver.

His face was drawn, accentuating the lines from his eyes and down his cheeks. His curly hair lay in clusters on his head, jutting outwards randomly much like the springs in an old mattress.

Joan, on the other hand, had obviously had her appearance dealt with by the staff so she conformed to the social norms. Nevertheless, her eyes betrayed an inner dullness that was not the mother Wednesday knew, except for episodes after a hospital admission.

Wednesday listened whilst the consultant spouted the same psychobabble she had heard before. Impatient for him to get to the point, Wednesday decided to speak.

"What happens if Mum stops taking her meds again?"

"It's quite the norm for people like your mother to stop taking meds when they feel well. They are convinced they are better."

"I know that," said Wednesday. "So what can we do about it?"

The consultant brushed his ring finger over his moustache before replying. "Constant encouragement and vigilance for her to remain on her meds, and remind her that her urge to stop is normal but not advised."

The advice was repetitive and never seemed to change. She found the whole matter discouraging and wearing.

The nurse appeared with Joan's suitcase and placed it at Oliver's feet. They all stared at the inanimate object as though it was going to offer the solution they all sought.

The psychiatrist stood up to leave and wished everyone well, leaving them in muted confusion.

"You couldn't give us a lift home, could you? I couldn't face the parking, so I came by bus," said Oliver as he leant in to Wednesday, with pleading eyes.

As sanguine as ever, Wednesday nodded, even though she was keen to get back to work. She was not sure how long she could leave Lennox without him confessing to her whereabouts.

Joan linked her arms through theirs and the three of them shuffled out of the ward, towards the car park. Oliver carried the suitcase, and Wednesday carried a plastic bag full of medication and the appointment card for follow-up visits. Joan had hardly uttered a word, except to say during the meeting that she wanted to go home.

"Is Scarlett safe?" she whispered in Wednesday's ear.

"Of course she is. Why shouldn't she be?"

"Writing those stories."

"We've been over this, Mum."

"I know dear, I know," she replied, giving her daughter's arm a little squeeze.

On entering the house, Wednesday wished she had had the forethought and time to tidy up before the homecoming. Old newspapers were strewn over the arms of the two sofas; mugs lay dotted around, half full of cold tea with scum floating on the surface. The chilled air smelt stale and vaguely like a brewery.

Joan appeared oblivious to the state around her, choosing instead to trundle to the armchair by the unlit fire. She sat bolt upright and stared into the middle distance until Wednesday brought her a cup of tea, whilst Oliver set about lighting the fire.

"I really do have to get back to work. I'll call you later. Take care," she said to Oliver as she pecked him on the cheek. She then bent down and said much the same to her mother. As she reached the lounge door, she looked back to see the gentle, yet wretched scene. She hoped she was not seeing a vision of her own future life.

Wednesday returned to the station to find the Incident Room rumbling with gossip about Scarlett's article. She feared she was going to be overloaded with questions from her colleagues, but Hunter got to her first.

"Close the door," he asked as they entered his office.

"I suppose you've seen this," he said, throwing the newspaper on his desk.

"I have, Gov." Wednesday remained standing with her hands clamped together behind her back.

"What are your thoughts?"

"It's her take on the crimes, based on nothing but rumour. I don't take it seriously." She rocked from one foot to the other, waiting for him to speak again.

"This London angle is potentially interesting." He sat down and looked directly at her. "I want you to accompany me to the vicarage, I want to get the reverend's take on this," he said before picking up the telephone receiver. "I'll meet you in five. You're driving."

Wednesday left his office with her cheeks burning a gentle hue of cherry. She looked over towards Lennox's office and noticed that he wasn't there

"He got called away to a family emergency," said Jones, noticing Wednesday's puzzled look.

She checked her mobile to see whether he had left her a message, but he had not. Wednesday quickly gulped down a coffee, almost scolding her throat, before she saw Hunter striding out of his office and beckoning her towards the door.

As they climbed in her VW Beetle, Wednesday was embarrassed by the overwhelming smell of cigarette smoke. Even Hunter's aftershave did not mask the stench. Switching on the engine, they both opened their windows even though the weather was bitter.

Hunter sat in the passenger seat looking pensive and drumming his fingers on his knees, whilst Wednesday drove at a steady pace without smoking or playing any music, even though she was desperate for both.

She drove up to the vicarage and parked next to the reverend's burgundy Volvo.

Vera opened the door before they knocked; evidently Hunter had called them about their imminent arrival. Her frown displayed her displeasure at seeing them. Without speaking, she stepped back and waved her arm to usher them in. She then pointed them towards George's study.

A steady and clear voice beckoned them in, where they found him sitting behind his modest desk. A green glass desk lamp stood next to the telephone on one side of the desk, and a pile of papers sat on the other. His hands were in a prayer-like position between the two piles.

They both sat down before Hunter began the conversation by asking George his perspective on the cult angle pursued by the local paper.

"You're not the first person to ask me that today."

"Oh?"

"I've been approached by several parishioners asking me the very same thing."

"And what did you tell them?"

"The same I'm going to tell you. I have no evidence of such an abomination. It's the paper's way of selling more copies. That Scarlett Willow has a lot to answer for." He shot a glance in Wednesday's direction.

Wednesday was used to having anonymity. However, after Vera's visit, she knew that cover was blown.

"Who in particular was asking you?" asked Hunter.

George gazed towards the ceiling and twiddled his thumbs before answering. "Emily and James Dolby were rather upset by the insinuation that their son may possibly have been involved in a cult. It's got all their neighbours whispering, apparently."

He wrung his hands, and his face glistened with sweat. The change in his demeanour did not go unnoticed.

"Reverend Olong, if you know anything about these murders, then I urge you to speak now, before the person strikes again."

Hunter leant back in his chair and waited for George to respond, but he remained in the same position, his eyes fixed on the swirls in the patterned carpet.

"I am unaware of anything untoward happening in this community, or the surrounding villages," he said finally, his eyes moving upwards to briefly look Wednesday in the eyes.

"Could you show us around the church?" Hunter said as he stood up.

Dark circles harboured under the George's eyes, exhausted by their very presence. He begrudgingly eased himself out of his chair and walked around the desk to stand next to Wednesday. He unhooked a grey duffle coat as they past the rack by the front door.

The gravel crunched beneath their feet as they made their way across to the Norman church. George turned the large pewter coloured knob and led them into the church, where it was a few degrees colder than the exterior.

A shiver went up Wednesday's spine as they walked down the central aisle towards the vestry. Feeling insecure she turned her coat collar up around her neck.

"Is there a crypt?" she asked.

"Of course. I'll take you to see it."

They followed George through a door and down some stone steps. The air felt as still and as chilled as the inside of a fridge. The damp smell of stone infused the air. The lights shed very little illumination into the corners of the vast space, and it took a while for Wednesday's and Hunter's eyes to adjust to the gloom.

Pockets of rooms without doors led off from the central vault, and each space contained books, relics, or nothing at all. Wednesday used her hand to gently guide her along the wall, when her foot brushed against something that rustled. She bent down and patted the ground with her hand until she came across an empty crisp packet.

"Do people often come down here?" she asked George as she put the packet in a plastic bag.

"Only to put something in or take something from storage, such as the candles."

"Who has access?"

"Many of the lay preachers find the damp troublesome for their joints, so I'm the one who usually comes down here. However, the door's not locked, so theoretically, anyone could."

"And when were you last down here?"

"I really don't know. A couple of weeks perhaps."

Hunter suggested they return upstairs and he would get the forensic team to check out the crypt. As they reached the top, Wednesday and Hunter squinted, but George was unfazed by the contrast in light.

"How is business?" said Hunter.

"I beg your pardon?"

"Numbers in your congregation."

"Immediately after Tom's death, the numbers multiplied. However, since the local paper started writing about my past and a cult, numbers have dwindled." He stood in front of the altar, wringing his hands and stumbling over his words. His face glistened in the light that filtered through the stained glass windows.

"Thank you for your time, we can see our own way out," Hunter said as he began walking away.

"Is a cult a real possibility?" Olong called out as they were almost through the door.

"We have no evidence to corroborate the story. It's probably the fabrication of someone's overactive imagination," replied Hunter, giving Wednesday a sideways glance.

"Let's go to the Edwards' home," he said.

As Wednesday drove, Hunter was on his mobile, instructing the forensic team to process the crypt. His manner was clipped and precise, he commanded the air around him, and Wednesday wished she had the same ability. She feared her gene pool would eliminate her chances of having such power over her entourage, unless it was the power of fear.

Lucinda Edwards answered the door, looking as fragile as ever. She raised a spindly arm in a greeting and allowed them in.

"Greg is working in his home office today. Would you like me to get him?"

"In a minute, Mrs Edwards, we'd like a chat with you first," Hunter said.

The affluent environment did not manage to extinguish the cloying sober air of bereavement around them.

"Have you found the person responsible?" she asked with perfect diction.

"We're still making enquiries, Mrs Edwards. We would like to know more about your daughter's life. See if we're overlooking something," replied Hunter as Wednesday produced her notebook and pen.

Lucinda Edwards's eyes glazed over, until she was prompted by Wednesday to begin with Claudia's school life.

She recounted how her daughter was in year eleven at Markham Hall School. With her poker-straight light blond hair and translucent blue eyes, she was a popular girl with the boys—not that Greg knew that fact. She was only five-foot-three and petite in build, so her father never saw her as a teenager, instead preferring to see her as "his little cherub." Claudia was apparently considered mature for her age, and when Hunter asked for clarification, Lucinda blushed and looked towards Wednesday for support.

"Do you mean that she was aware of the sexual connotations of life? Was she sexually active?"

Lucinda nodded and lowered her voice as she gave an account of a conversation she had with Claudia about going on the pill. It had taken Lucinda by surprise, and she had never discussed the conversation with Greg, as she knew he would have been furious.

"Did she have a serious boyfriend then?" asked Wednesday, equally quietly.

"She never mentioned a name. Anyway it was all elementary; she was gone before we got that far." Tears welled in the corners of her eyes at the mention of her daughter's demise. The word *gone* was more palatable than the harshness of the word *died*.

"What about her social life," said Hunter, keen to move the conversation forward.

It emerged that Claudia was in the habit of receiving countless messages on her iPhone, and spent many hours on the internet, on various social networking sites.

Hunter turned to Wednesday and checked that Claudia's laptop was being processed, and she confirmed it was.

"Thank you for your time. You've given us a more complete profile of your daughter," said Wednesday as they all rose to their feet.

Lucinda went to the lounge door and opened it, peeked around the corner, then closed it again.

"I have one more thing to say, but you must promise that it doesn't go further."

The pair waited for her to divulge the information.

"You may eventually find this out for yourselves anyway, but . . ." An awkward pause arose whilst she visibly drew deeply through her mouth for breath.

"Claudia had a termination at the beginning of the year. And no, she never disclosed who the father was. I took her to a private clinic in London, on the pretext of having a mother-daughter weekend." The colour drained from her cheeks and her shoulders drooped as the burden was lifted from them.

"I know there were three boys who would visit her here, and they'd also go to the cinema." She searched the ceiling for a few seconds. "Ralph, Tony, and James."

"Do you think one of these boys could have been the father?"

Lucinda shrugged her shoulders and studied the ostentatious emerald ring on her hand, turning it around and around her slender finger.

Wednesday and Hunter had got more information on Claudia than they had imagined, and there, perhaps lay the motive for her murder. They both thought Mrs Edwards should have disclosed the fact earlier, but understood, up to a point, why she had kept it a secret.

Driving towards the Dolby household, Hunter was deep in thought.

As Wednesday pulled up outside the house, they saw James Dolby park up on the driveway. He got out, briefcase in hand, and looked their way as he heard their car doors slamming. His face inanimate in response to their greeting.

"Have you come with news or more questions?" he asked in a flat tone as they walked up to him.

"More background questions, I'm afraid, Mr Dolby. May we come in?" asked Wednesday.

He audibly sighed, bemoaning that he had already had a difficult day at work, but allowing them in all the same.

Emily's face blanched as she saw the detectives arrive with her husband. James quickly told her that they had only come seeking more answers, and that he was going to have a shower.

Emily's cheeks burned bright red as she led them into the kitchen, where it was warm.

"We would like to gather more background information on Tom if that's okay," Wednesday said, before offering the frail-looking woman a gentle smile.

"I think we've said all there is to say, but I'll try if it helps you find the killer."

After Emily made a pot of tea, she recounted how quiet and bright Tom was at school, but that he was more outspoken and temperamental in the home. He had very little respect for her as he hit his teens, and was frequently arguing with his father.

"What did they argue about," asked Hunter, as he struggled with the tiny handle on the teacup with his stubby fingers.

"The usual things, I suppose. What time he could go out and come home, where he could go and with whom."

"We understand that he was good friends with Darren."

"Well yes, I told you on that awful night. It was a bone of contention with us. We didn't think Darren or his family were the kind of people we cared to fraternise with."

"What concerned you about them?"

"You've met them. The mother is often seen drunk during the day, his brother's in prison, and the stepdad is violent."

Wednesday kept her eyes on her notebook as she wrote. Gossip, whether it was the truth or fantasy, was often rife in villages. There was always currency in gossip.

They heard her husband walking around upstairs, and Emily looked up to the ceiling as though she could see right through it.

Hunter coughed to draw her attention back to the room. "Did Tom have a girlfriend?"

Emily looked at her hands, and shook her head very slowly. "I never mentioned it to James, but I secretly wondered whether our son was, you know . . . gay." Her voice trailed off at the end of the sentence, so the word *gay* was little more than a whisper.

"Would that have been a problem?" Hunter asked.

"We are a religious family, so my husband would have undoubtedly banished Tom from our lives. I would have tolerated it, so as not to lose hm." She pulled a handkerchief from her sleeves and dabbed her eyes.

Wednesday was about to ask what had led her to believe Tom was gay, when James arrived in the kitchen in a pair of brown twill slacks and a roll neck jumper. He smelt of soap and talcum powder.

"Have you got all the answers you need?" he asked as he poured himself a glass of fruit juice.

"Almost. Could you tell us what kind of things you and your son argued over," asked Hunter.

James frowned and looked towards his wife before answering. "Are you a father?" he asked Hunter.

"He's at university."

"Well then you should know; it's no bed of roses when your son starts to believe he is becoming the man of the house because youth is on his side. He needed putting in his place more than once, and by that I mean grounding and or restricting the use of the computer, not violence."

"Thank you for your time, Mr and Mrs Dolby. We'll see our own way out," Hunter said.

He slumped into the passenger seat and shut the door harder than Wednesday liked. He yawned loudly and instructed Wednesday to drop him back at the station so he could pick up his car.

Wednesday finally arrived home, exhausted and drained. On opening her car door a cloud of cigarette smoke billowed out and she noticed Scarlett's car was parked in the drive, but the house was in darkness—which could have meant one of several things. Either she had taken a taxi to go on a drunken night out, or she was already in bed with the residual hangover or with someone she had just picked up.

Wednesday traipsed to the kitchen in the semi-dark, and grabbed whatever she could from the fridge to make a sandwich. She found an already opened bottle of red on the counter and poured herself a glass.

On turning around, she almost dropped her glass as she saw Scarlett slumped over the kitchen table.

"Good god Scarlett, are you okay?" she said, rushing towards her.

Bending over her, she recoiled from the stink of alcohol coming from her open mouth. Angry at being made to feel concerned, she shook Scarlett by the shoulders.

"Have mercy, sis, please . . ." she rasped with her dry mouth.

"What the hell is going on?"

"I've had a shit day. Someone's put pressure on the paper to quash my cult story. I mean, how sick is that?" She slurred her words as her head rolled around on her unstable neck.

"It's not surprising. It's upsetting people, and there's no proof."

Wednesday put the kettle on to make Scarlett a coffee.

"Everything's hopeless. Nothing will ever go right for me," she sobbed.

Wednesday's heart sank. She had been there before with Scarlett. Terror swelled in her as she thought about the baying sleepless nights, the duvet days, the wailing, the drinking, and the black cloud of despair suspended over the house. Scarlett's highs were more bearable—if a little exhausting—than the lows, but both could be more manageable if she agreed to see a doctor, grumbled Wednesday to herself.

"Have you eaten anything?" Wednesday asked, believing she knew the answer already. She placed a mug of coffee in front of her.

"No. I thought I'd eat something with Jacob but he's not answering his mobile. I've left loads of messages."

Wednesday rolled her eyes. "He's got a family emergency. Not everything in the world revolves around you."

Scarlett shrieked and tossed her head around, sending strands of wild curls swirling around her shoulders. "I need him. I should come first. It's so unfair. I bet he's running back to his wife." Scarlett banged her fist on the table, making the crockery chink.

Wednesday firmly believed Lennox was not going back to his ex-wife, but chose not to tell Scarlett for fear of raising her hopes about cultivating a genuine relationship with him.

"I think we should go to bed. You'll have the mother of all hangovers in the morning and I'm plain shattered. Come on," she said, linking her arm underneath Scarlett's armpit to lift her up.

As they staggered upstairs, Scarlett kept moaning in Wednesday's ear that she wanted Jacob to hug her in bed, as though believing Wednesday could do something about it.

Once she had tucked Scarlett into bed and placed a bowl on the floor next to her, she made her way to her own room. Her mind shifted through the events of the day and it appeared all the people she had interviewed that day had one thing in common. A secret sadness or a silent misery they kept secret from the one they professed to love.

Malevolent relationships could be the loneliest place in the universe, she thought to herself as her eyes began to close. The last thing she heard ringing in her ears was the sound of Scarlett vomiting into the bowl.

Lennox was already in his office, hunched over his desk, when Wednesday arrived. She grabbed herself a mug of coffee before knocking on his door. He signalled for her to enter then raised his hand to stop her from talking first.

"Before you try to dissect my personal life, Alex has given me—although I believe he was looking for you—the results from the blanket Pollock brought in."

Wednesday pulled up a chair and leant towards him, nursing the mug between her hands, her cheeks glowing softly.

"It's certainly the blanket used in Tom Dolby's death. The fibres match, and they found skin cells matching Tom's DNA. No prints were found on the plastic bag, except for Pollock's."

"Can we trace where the blanket was purchased?"

"Already underway."

"Let's visit the school now to interview the boys with their parents?" she said before finishing her coffee.

Lennox nodded, scraping his chair back to stand up so Wednesday could see his crumpled suit. She then noticed his face bore the shadow of stubble.

"By the way, I got a hell of a lot of messages from your sister yesterday," he said with a degree of emotional detachment.

"Sorry about that. She's having a rough time at work, so she got drunk, and when she's drunk she can become rather obsessive."

Lennox raised his eyebrows and then muttered under his breath how that was an understatement. As she followed him down the corridor, she noticed he did not have the familiar scent of musk that she liked so much. In fact, from behind, he wasn't the same immaculately dressed man at all.

# Chapter Twenty-Two

Winter sun streaked through the clouds and shone in their eyes as they drove towards Markham Hall School. Lennox drummed his fingers on the steering wheel, with a cigarette hanging from his lips so smoke circled around his head. Ash fell from the tip and landed on the lapel of his coat.

Getting out of the car, they heard children's voices chattering and shouting, although they were not visible. On entering the building, they realised they had arrived as a lesson had finished, so the corridors were heaving with students jostling one another with their rucksacks.

The receptionist greeted them with the same chilled cordiality as she had always afforded them. Within minutes, the interim head, PE teacher Patrick Gould, walked towards them with his arm extended out.

"Detectives, the three boys and their fathers are waiting for you. They're very busy men, and the boys have lessons, so I hope you won't keep them for long."

"We'll keep them as long as we need to," snapped Lennox.

Gould led them towards the waiting group lined up in the corridor. He begrudgingly allowed the detectives to use his new, temporary office. Wednesday offered a smile to the gathered group, but was met with a frosty reception.

"Ralph and Mr Saunders please," said Lennox as he opened the door for Wednesday to pass through first.

Father and son appeared very similar in stature and colouring. Both were tall with broad shoulders which tapered to a slender waist.

"I'm not sure what we're doing here. The woman on the phone was very cryptic. I can't imagine my Ralph being in any kind of trouble," said Mr Saunders, brushing the seat with his hand before sitting down.

"He's not in trouble, but some more information has come to light involving Ralph which we wish to clarify."

Ralph shuffled in his seat but kept his head high. He listened intently as Lennox recounted Lucinda Edwards's conversation about him being a boyfriend.

"And does this make him a suspect for her murder?" asked the father as he folded his arms across his chest.

Ralph sat up straight, and looked towards his father for reassurance.

"No, Mr Saunders, but it does connect him to Claudia, and we need to find out what she was doing, and with whom, in the days before she died. When was that last time you saw Claudia, Ralph?" asked Wednesday, turning to him.

He gave a quick look in his father's direction, and was encouraged by the nod he received.

"I told you already, I saw Claudia at school on Thursday and she was hyped up because she had the house to herself again."

The adults looked on as he cleared his throat and continued recounting.

"She asked me to go round that evening," he gave a sideways glance at his father and drew a deep breath. "She wanted me to stay over, you know, the night." His face was now as red as a lacquered pepper, and even his father looked tight-lipped.

"Would you like to speak to us alone?" Wednesday suggested.

"I'm not leaving," said Mr Saunders, jutting out his chin.

Ralph remained silent, so Wednesday took that as her cue to carry on.

"Claudia was pregnant at the beginning of this year. Did she mention that to you?" she asked, keeping her focus on him constantly.

Ralph's face drained of colour. His father, looking clearly shocked, turned to his son and demanded that he reply.

"I didn't know about that," he exclaimed in a cracked voice. "It couldn't have been me . . . not me." He was almost pleading with Wednesday to end his misery, and allow him to leave the room.

"Are you saying that you never slept with Claudia, or that you had protected sex?"

Mr Saunders got up and paced to the window, where he stood gazing out onto the autumnal garden, waiting to hear his son's answer. Ralph looked in his father's direction and then replied in a low voice.

"We only did it once, and it was safe, you know, I used a condom." After speaking, he hung his head and crushed his hands between his thighs.

"Were you aware she had an abortion?"

"Hell no."

"Now you have all you need, I presume we can go," Mr Saunders said as he walked over to his son and made him get up by tapping on his shoulder.

"Thank you, we'll get back to you if we need to," replied Wednesday as she stood up and extended her hand. Mr Saunders ignored her gesture and hurried Ralph out the door, leaving a chill in their wake.

Lennox then invited Tony Pennymore and his father, Dick, into the room. Both looked uneasy and subdued, and neither relaxed when Wednesday informed them that she wanted to know more about Tony's relationship with Claudia.

"Relationship is a strong word to use. Kids are never serious at this age," said Dick Pennymore, relaxing visibly.

"Claudia was pregnant. Did she mention that to you?" she asked Tony.

"Not bloody likely," replied Tony, sitting up straight. "She wouldn't sleep with me. I wasn't good enough for that, I was only good to flirt with and tease. I was an easy way to get some alcohol."

Tony slumped in the chair once more, but kept his eyes locked with Wednesday's.

"Did that make you angry?" she asked, maintaining his gaze.

"I see what you're getting at," interjected Dick. "You think my lad killed her 'coz she wouldn't sleep with him." He rose to his feet and glared at Wednesday.

"Sir, enquiries sometimes lead us to ask difficult and uncomfortable questions. Rest assured that presently we are only gathering information."

Dick Pennymore remained standing and was about to tell his son that they were going, when Lennox spoke.

"Please sit down and allow us to finish," he said as he gestured for him to sit.

"When was the last time you saw Claudia?" continued Wednesday.

"On Thursday in geography. She was buzzing about something; I saw her whispering into James's ear. They sat together."

"Who would you say was Claudia's boyfriend? Was it James?"

Tony rolled his eyes and shrugged his shoulders, not caring to answer the question.

"Did you want to be her boyfriend, or was she dating all three of you and you all found out that Thursday?"

"Again, you're insinuating my son's a murderer. Come on Tony—we're off."

He yanked Tony up by the arm and dragged him out of the office, startling James and his father, Keith, as they sat waiting in the corridor. Lennox beckoned the pair in and closed the door behind them.

Wednesday ran through the same batch of questions, waiting for a similar response to the previous pairs, from both father and son, and she was taken aback by the coolness of the pair.

"Claudia and I were having sex on a casual basis—did it every time her folks went away to London, actually." James held his head high and looked proudly over to his father after he had spoken.

"Were you aware that she was pregnant?" she asked, watching him closely, but he never flinched.

"Nope, it never came up."

"Is it possible that you were the father?"

"Could have been. We usually used condoms, but who knows?"

"You said 'usually' and yet you don't seem that concerned. Were you aware of this, Mr Almond," asked Wednesday as she turned towards the father.

"I remember what it's like to be a teenage boy, all those hormones bouncing around. But I didn't know she was pregnant. James knew what to do if that happened."

Wednesday raised her eyebrows at James and waited.

"He means get rid of it. Dad said he'd pay if I got into a fix."

"So, had Claudia got you into a 'fix', so to speak," asked Wednesday, feeling irritated by the pair's casual attitude to sex and relationships.

"I think my son has already answered that question, Detective."

Wednesday sat back in her chair and folded her arms, whilst she crossed one leg over the other.

"I would imagine that your father owning a hotel is a bonus, all those bedrooms to choose from. Did you ever use the hotel with or without your father's knowledge?" asked Lennox.

Wednesday gave him eye contact fleetingly, admiring his cool thinking whilst she had become entwined in her anger at the chauvinistic viewpoint echoed by father and son.

"We don't have secrets, apart from those we keep from his mother," replied Keith Almond with a glint in his eye as he nudged his son.

"When did you last see Claudia, James?" Wednesday said, interrupting the father-son jovial moment.

"Not sure. I suppose it was on the Thursday."

"The same Thursday you sat next to her in geography and she told you her parents were away."

James cocked his head, and for the first time during the interview, his cheeks blushed a gentle shade of pink.

"Yes, just like you said. We already told you she said we could go over that evening. Tony was going to get a bottle of vodka from the pub like always."

"Were you all dating Claudia at the same time?"

James snorted and then placed his hands behind his head as he tilted back on two chair legs.

"None of us were actually going out with her exclusively. We were all just having fun."

"Was Claudia having fun too?"

"Oh yes," leered James.

"So what happened Thursday evening?" asked Wednesday, ignoring his ego trip.

"Like we've already told you, we all met at her house and kept ringing the doorbell, but she wasn't in. We assumed she'd chickened out, so we hung around together in the maze garden at my dad's hotel and drank the vodka."

"Did you not wonder where she was?"

"No, and once the alcohol kicked in, we'd forgotten all about her."

Wednesday closed the interview and thanked them for their time. As they left she turned to Lennox and declared that they had gleaned very little from their time there.

"I'm not sure what to make of Claudia now," said Wednesday, climbing into the passenger seat.

"Does it make any difference? She didn't deserve to die like that."

"I know that. It's just she's not the girl her father painted, half the girl her mother painted, and a whole other person as painted by the boys."

"We're all different people to the various people around us."

As Lennox started the engine, Wednesday received a call from the forensic team—it was Alex. Wednesday made humming noises whilst writing notes down. After thanking him she relayed the details to Lennox.

"Forensics have found Darren's DNA on the sleeping bag from the vicarage attic, but only unidentifiable smudges on the crisp packet from the crypt."

Lennox stared straight ahead, keeping his focus on the road.

"We'll need to visit the vicarage again, but now I think it'd be useful to visit Claudia's GP, to see whether they could enlighten us on the baby's father."

Without waiting for his response, she called the station and left their new itinerary with Jones. She then pushed her head into the headrest and gazed without focusing at the passing skyline.

"Did you want to talk about your family troubles?" she asked without looking at him.

"Not really, can't get my own head around it, never mind trying to explain the quagmire to you."

The journey into town was conducted in silence, broken periodically by Lennox's manic drumming on the steering wheel.

After a short wait in reception, Doctor Hall agreed to meet them both.

"Patient confidentiality prevents me from answering your question," she replied to Wednesday's request to know who the father was regarding Claudia's pregnancy.

"This is a murder enquiry, Doctor. We can wait for a court order if you prefer."

The doctor scanned her notes on the computer, frowning at the screen for a few minutes. "A court order would make no difference, she didn't tell me the father's name. I even spoke to her without her mother being present, but she insisted she didn't know who the father was. Sorry."

"You weren't concerned about her being abused, by her father, for example," asked Wednesday.

"Certainly not. I've been their family doctor for years. Her mother had spoken to me about her concerns regarding Claudia's burgeoning sexuality and interest in school boys, and their interest in her."

The detectives were disappointed by the dead end, but thanked the doctor for her time. They had nothing concrete to take back to the station, and they knew Hunter would be waiting for them to deliver. Had Wednesday been a religious person, it would have been the time to pray.

"Let's head for the vicarage. They are hiding something from us. And finding Darren's DNA on the sleeping bag may force them to reveal their secret to us," said Lennox.

Wednesday relaxed her shoulders and smiled, thinking perhaps God was looking out for them after all.

Reverend Olong looked visibly underwhelmed when he opened the door to them. Without uttering a word, he stood back and let them in.

"Do you need my wife to be present?" he asked in a flat voice.

"That would be useful, thanks," replied Wednesday before following him into the wood-panelled sitting room.

Wednesday sat down on the sofa, which offered her little support or comfort due to its saggy frame. Lennox stood by the soot stained fireplace with his hands behind his back, staring through the window.

"Tea, detectives," announced Vera as she walked into the room, carrying a tarnished silver tray.

Wednesday and Lennox turned down the offer, choosing instead to relay the information of the forensic find on the sleeping bag.

"We are finding it difficult to understand how a sixteen-year-old boy could hide out in your attic without you knowing. He would have moved around, stolen food from your kitchen, and perhaps even used the bathroom." Wednesday looked from George to Vera in order to gauge their reactions; but neither showed even a flicker of concern.

"This is a rambling old house and my wife and I are very busy people with church life. I put any noises down to the creaking floorboards, or the wind whistling through the gaps in the frame and roof."

"You seem to have an answer for everything. The attic, the garden, the crypt—"

"What about the crypt?" asked Vera, suddenly looking interested.

"We found an empty packet of crisps there, but no readable fingerprints. So obviously, the crypt was or is being used for something or by someone."

"That could be anyone. Kids playing hide and seek would probably be a good bet, especially as it's left unlocked most of the time," replied Vera as she walked over to her husband and placed her hands on his shoulders. "My husband and I do a lot for the community and we have nothing to hide or fear. Having said that, we are an easy target for anyone against God or religion. It wouldn't be the first time, as well you know."

Wednesday tried to get comfortable on the sofa by pushing a cushion behind her lower back. Lennox remained rooted to the spot by the fireplace, his hands still clasped behind his back.

"The current crimes are more than someone just disagreeing with your religion. Framing you for murder and kidnapping is far more serious and worrying. Aren't you concerned?" said Wednesday, wishing she had remained standing as Lennox had done.

"We have no need to worry. God will protect us from whatever force you feel we should fear," replied George as he patted Vera's hand that was still on his shoulder.

When Vera returned from seeing them out, she gave her husband a hard stare.

"I do hope that you've not been up to your old tricks, dear."

George bowed his head, before rising from the chair to make his way to his study, where he hoped the bible would offer him some semblance of comfort.

As they left the vicarage, Wednesday felt drained of all emotion and was grateful that Lennox was driving.

"How about a working lunch in The Crow?" He suggested.

Wednesday nodded before saying the vicarage gave her the creeps.

"That's because religion scares you. It's the unknown entity that it represents. You can't figure it out."

"I believe it was you who declared a love of solving puzzles, not me," she replied, flicking ash through the crack in the window. "Anyway, I don't need you spouting psychobabble to me the way your parents obviously did to you."

Lennox gave an imperceptible nod before parking the car in the space next to the pub entrance.

They were the only customers to order food that Tuesday lunchtime. The three other customers were bikers who huddled around the bar, conversing with the affable blonde who was pulling their pints.

"I'm surprised to see you two here," said Dick Pennymore as he walked up to their table with a pint in his hand.

"Even the police need to eat," replied Lennox with a note of irony in his voice.

The barmaid arrived with two plates of cheese-and-onion toasted sandwiches, plus a bowl of chips for Lennox.

"Still looking at my son as the killer, or has some other poor sucker got you two on his tail?" He asked as he hovered above them, swaying gently from side to side.

"Maybe. Perhaps you've heard some rumours being bandied around the pub that might be worth repeating," replied Lennox before shoving two chips into his mouth.

"The word is the reverend's done something like this before, apparently."

"Go on."

"Well apparently the reverend likes boys. God you detectives need things spelling out."

"And how does Claudia fit into that theory?"

"She found out about his goings on, so he killed her."

"Interesting," muttered Lennox.

"Your sister seems to have her own wacky idea, eh, Detective?" Wednesday felt her cheeks redden.

"Whatever she chooses to write about has nothing to do with me."

"But you've got to admit it's intriguing. Perhaps the reverend has a sideline in devil worship and Claudia was a sacrifice." He chuckled to himself before being called to the bar by the arrival of Des Wright with a tatty rucksack over his shoulder.

"I wonder what he wants?" said Lennox, cocking his head in Wright's direction.

"Whatever it is, they obviously don't want us to hear," Wednesday replied as she watched them disappear into the backroom.

"I ache for the days when we could smoke in the pub," he said wistfully.

"You're just showing your age now. Anyway, we should be getting back. We can smoke in your car, seeing as we've broken that rule a million times already."

"I mainly kept it smoke free for my boys. They hated the smell of smoke."

That was her cue to bring up the subject that had piqued her interest all morning. Nudging a cigarette from her packet, she offered him one before he switched on the engine.

"We can either talk about your family crisis, or we can talk about Scarlett. Your call."

Lennox realised staying tight-lipped about his affairs was futile, so he chose the one that was truly causing him pain.

"Archie's been arrested for being part of a gang that were fighting with another gang in the neighbourhood. My ex is going bloody mental over it, saying it's my fault for being an inconsistent father. Kids apparently replace families with gangs these days."

Suddenly, Wednesday felt uncomfortable with the results of her prying. Their job did not cater for a family life or for relationships in general, hence the barren gash in her life.

"So what's happening?"

"He's under the youth offending team, receiving anger management and consequences sessions. That'll be a waste of time, if you ask me."

"Have some hope; he's still young enough to change," she urged as he parked in his designated space.

"I can't offer him hope. I am the foundation of his failing, he knows it and so does his mother."

Back at The Crow, Pennymore and Wright were busy exchanging information on who was attending the gambling club that evening, and who Pennymore wanted protecting or persuading from the list of participants. Wright wanted to ask what the police were doing there, but he trusted Pennymore could see off detectives such as Wednesday and Lennox.

The atmosphere in the Incident Room was subdued, with only the occasional phone ringing and piles of paperwork and files precariously positioned on the officers' desks. Hunter was in his office, pacing in front of the window whilst bellowing down his mobile phone.

"That doesn't bode well," whispered Wednesday.

"Nothing surprises me with these cases. We might as well follow Scarlett's train of thought at this rate."

It was the first time he had uttered Scarlett's name without bitterness resonating in his voice.

Wednesday opened her office door to her phone ringing, and found Oliver on the other end.

"Could you come round later, I could really do with a break," he said in a hushed voice.

"I can't promise, Oliver. Work is hectic at the moment, but I will try."

She felt he already had compassion fatigue, but questioned whether she felt she could do any better. She doubted it, but was not ready to admit it to anyone, least of all herself.

"Have you seen Scarlett today?" he asked, still speaking quietly.

"Oliver, I really can't chat now . . ."

He did not wait for her to finish, his needs were greater than hers.

"I'm worried about my daughter. She seems low in mood . . . you know."

She knew. And she did not want to think about it. The thought of sharing her house again with the malevolent monster clawing into the walls was unbearable.

"We'll talk later," she said before hanging up.

A tap at her door attracted her attention, and she reddened slightly as she saw Hunter standing there. He was dressed in a dark blue suit with faint pinstripes running lengthways, accentuating his lean figure. His shoes were pristine, as was his hair, and he smelt of freshly cut grass. Wednesday stroked down the creases in her jacket and wondered how long he had been outside her door.

"How are you and Lennox getting along?" he asked.

"Fine Guv, no problems to report."

Hunter pursed his lips and shoved his hands in his trouser pockets. "Even though he's dating your sister, which I have to say concerns me."

She tried not to look shocked that he knew. "It doesn't bother me. They don't discuss work as far as I know." She twirled strands of hair around her finger, and avoided direct eye contact, fearing he could see right into her soul.

"That may be so, Wednesday, but you are to monitor the situation to prevent it from diluting our investigation or for pillow-talk secrets to leak into the paper. She's got too much access for my liking." He finished with a sharp nod of his head, before leaving her office and closing the door firmly behind him.

Wednesday put her head in her hands and rested her elbows on her desk, taking in deep, slow breathes to halt the dizziness. If she wanted to have a trusting relationship with Lennox, she would have to relay Hunter's conversation, warn him that eyes were on him. She let out a heavy sigh—life was getting too complicated.

She wandered over to Lennox who was by the coffee machine, when Jones rushed up to them to say a very drunk Judith Wright was at the desk, angry about something that was apparently missing.

Judith was worse than they anticipated when she arrived at the interview room. She was accompanied by an officer who looked so young he could have been her grandson. Wednesday ordered a mug of coffee to be brought to Judith whilst she guided her to a chair.

Judith dropped into the chair so hard that her teeth rattled. Her bloodshot eyes swayed between Wednesday and Lennox, and when she opened her mouth, the stench of alcohol was pungent.

"My Darren had a chain . . . Chain around his neck." The words stumbled out of her mouth as her fist hammered onto the table.

Wednesday encouraged her to sip the coffee, if only to cleanse her breath, then asked her to explain what she meant.

"A bloody chain, woman, around his neck. It's missing, some bugger has stolen it . . . Real silver it was, too."

"When did you last see him wearing it?" asked Wednesday.

"He wore it all the time. It was his lucky Saint Christopher. So where is it?"

Wednesday said she did not recall one being found at the crime scene or on Darren's body. She asked whether Judith had searched in the house, which only seemed to anger her more.

"I keep telling you, he was wearing it. Sterling silver with his initials on the back—DG. His dad got it for him."

"I'll get an officer to search through the evidence bags, and we'll get back to you. I'll get someone to accompany you home; you're in no fit state to be out on your own."

Judith made no comment as her head lolled from side to side. An officer escorted her out and Wednesday was glad to get away from the stale air.

She was about to take Lennox to one side, when Hunter strode up to them. He looked directly at Wednesday as he spoke.

"Cleveland is out of the hospital. I want you to interview him. We need to ascertain whether his assault was connected to his debts or the murders."

He strode off without waiting for a response. Wednesday jangled her keys at Lennox. She wanted to get out.

"Hunter's concerned about your liaison with Scarlett. He wants me to dissuade you from seeing her." She didn't look at him.

Lennox brushed his hand over his hair and stared out of the passenger window. Tall poplar trees lined the road, bending back and forth in the gusts of wind. People walking along the pavement with their heads hung low, scarves flailing and collars turned up.

"Did you tell him about me and Scarlett?"

"Certainly not. I want us to well work together, which so far I believe we do. So no, it wasn't me."

Lennox rubbed his chin, feeling the slight abrasion of stubble under his fingers. "You know it isn't really a relationship. Just a mutual interest in physical exercise."

Wednesday squirmed at his description and gripped the steering wheel harder. "It's none of my business, but tread carefully with her. She's not as resilient as she makes out."

Lennox made no reply and continued watching the scenery pass by until they arrived at Cleveland's flat.

Once inside the building, it took a while for Cleveland to hobble to the door. He peered through the spy hole before removing the security chain.

"Checking I'm safe?" he asked with a half smile.

"We've come to see whether you remember more about your attack," replied Wednesday, looking past his shoulder into the kitchen and noticing empty takeaway cartons spilling all over the worktop.

"Well I can't, so you've had a wasted journey."

"You must at least know whether the attack was due to your debts or something to do with your school."

He looked hard at her with his bloodshot eyes in discoloured sockets. She returned his regard and suggested they move their conversation inside.

"You're a lucky man to work with such an attractive woman, even if she is bossy," he said to Lennox, as they all moved to the lounge.

But Lennox did not bite, returning the conversation to the attack.

"You still remain a suspect in the murder cases, so I suggest you take things more seriously. Your flippant attitude is not ingratiating."

"I didn't realise I had to get on your good side. Are you here to arrest me?" He mockingly held his arms out with his wrists together, and cocked his head whilst looking from one to the other. "I didn't think so," he laughed. "You're at a loss, no real evidence. You're just stabbing around in the dark."

His laughter progressed into a coughing fit which split the cut on his lip. As blood seeped out, he grimaced and swallowed some cold tea to rid himself of the nasty taste in his mouth.

"We understand you're not a member of the golf club, but you would like to be. Is that correct?" Wednesday asked.

"I suppose it was Saunders who told you that. Well, I have no desire for such a membership. And I have enough well-to-do and aristocratic connections at the school to get me what I want."

Markham Hall was not an upper class boarding school for the local gentry, as he seemed to be making out. Cleveland seemed to have a delusional streak where he and his school were concerned.

"Unfortunately, the CCTV footage from the golf club has yielded nothing of value," she continued. "So, could you tell us where they attacked you first and how you came to be on the golf course?"

"All I can say is that there were two of them. They were wearing balaclavas and they were tall and broad. They took me from outside my flat and bundled me into a car or a van. I could sense they left me outside by the temperature, but as I was blindfolded I couldn't say where."

He rubbed his bandaged wrist as he spoke, then placed a cushion on his lap on which to rest his arm.

"Did you recognise their voices?"

Cleveland shook his head slowly before complaining of a headache and wishing to go to bed.

"So they said nothing to you at all. Not even that the beating was a message from someone?"

"Nothing at all. Why ever it happened is of no consequence. I'm afraid to go out now, so what they did worked."

He looked pitiful and Wednesday knew they would get nothing out of him. Gripping onto the door frame with his bruised hand, he saw them out. Hearing their footsteps recede, he turned around to put the door chain on again and then moved to the kitchen. He picked up a bottle of whisky and poured himself a large measure before moving to the lounge to sit in a dark corner, facing the door.

Wednesday drove to her parent's home feeling guilty at wishing she was going to her own place, but she had promised Oliver he could have a break at some point.

Oliver's face lit up as he answered the door, welcoming her in with a meaningful hug. "Your mother will be pleased to see you. I think she may be bored of my company."

Wednesday followed him into the lounge, where Joan was rifling through a cupboard.

"Found them," she exclaimed as she brandished a couple of photo albums in the air.

Wednesday noticed her mother was dressed up and wearing her expensive jewellery. She had applied too much garish blue eye shadow and peony rouge on her cheeks. Her lipstick was a bold fuchsia pink and her nails were the same colour. It was a contrast from how she looked in the hospital, but Wednesday knew that her new appearance was not necessarily a good thing.

"I'm off to play dominoes in the pub. I'll be back later." He blew them both a kiss and scarpered, lest Wednesday should change her mind.

Joan's face closed down for a few seconds before shuffling up to Wednesday and asking whether she thought he was having an affair.

"I doubt that very much, he loves you to pieces. He just wanted to spend some time with his male friends. It's been a stressful time of late."

Her words appeared to pacify Joan as she picked up the albums, suggesting they sit at the kitchen table to leaf through the pages. Wednesday made a pot of tea before they rummaged through images and memories of times gone by.

Joan gazed wistfully at pictures of her as a young girl who was as yet unaware of the trials that lie ahead for her. Her fingers traced the flat outline before she moved on to the next picture. "If I knew then what I know now, I wouldn't have become a mother," she whispered as though talking to the people in the photographs.

"You're a great mum," replied Wednesday as she gently stroked her mother's hand.

"Nonsense. I've had periods of absence in your lives. I disappeared when I was needed, I wasn't there for many of your school plays or parents evening. And worse of all, either of you could end up the same as me."

"We don't know that, Mum," she replied before lighting a cigarette and standing by the back door. She watched her mother flicking through childhood memories stored in a shoe box, spreading the pictures and greeting cards across the table and spilling a few unnoticed ones over the edge. She watched her mother brewing her own personal storm in her troubled mind.

"Scarlett looked so pretty with her hair in bunches and wearing that gingham dress. Pretty and innocent. Do you think she will be all right?"

"In what way?"

"People say how alike Scarlett and I are—and I don't mean in looks. Do you think people see the same madness in her as they see in me?"

"I've no idea what other people see or think and you should know better than to worry about that. People will always gossip and speculate about the lives of others."

Wednesday was feeling the tedium she imagined Oliver felt most days. No wonder he wanted to get out. To save her own sanity, she collected two more photo albums and pulled her chair closer to Joan.

"Let's immerse ourselves in the recollection of happier times," she said as she put her arm around her shoulder.

Lennox paced around his sparse kitchen with his hands stuffed in his pockets. Impulsively, he pulled out his mobile phone and called Scarlett. As he listened to the ringing, he had second thoughts and hung up. He flung the phone on the table and wandered over to the fridge, hoping to find something to fill the void. As he opened a bottle of beer, his mobile rang.

"Sorry I missed your call. I'm glad you phoned," Scarlett said, having pressed call-back.

"I was at a loose end and wondered if you fancied meeting up?"

Scarlett invited him over, saying that Eva was out so they had the place to themselves. There was a different tone to her voice, but he could not analyse it.

After spraying on some cologne, he picked up a full packet of cigarettes and a bottle of Merlot, before heading to his car. He set off in an almost dream-like state, heading for an evening of untold joy and pleasure.

When Scarlett opened the front, Lennox almost thought he had gone to the wrong house. She was not the exuberant and dynamic woman that he knew. Her flamboyant gestures and decadent attitude had been replaced with a sombre, disconnected mood that was hardly what Lennox would have chosen in a companion for that evening. He wanted the physical delights that only a woman could offer.

"Are you all right?" he asked, following her to the kitchen.

"Work is getting to me. I'm having my articles quashed. The editor wants me to get insider info seeing as I live with the DI on the case. What do you think about focusing on a serial killer angle instead? Is that how it's perceived by the police?"

"You know I can't answer that," he said, picking up the corkscrew that lay on the work surface.

"Okay then, but it's a realistic train of thought. Two boys died in very similar circumstances, but the girl was different, almost more personal than the others."

He knew she was talking sense, but he did not want to regurgitate the facts of the day, or resurface the images of the corpses in his mind. He poured two glasses of wine and handed her one. As he did so, Scarlett reached for his wrist with her hand and began rubbing her thumb along the underside of his arm.

"I need you to hold me," she whispered.

Wednesday's words rang in his ears. So this is what she was talking about, he found himself thinking. He gently untwined his wrist from her hand and moved around the table to sit down.

"Let's go to the lounge, we'll be more comfortable on the sofa," she said, following him around the table and linking her arm through his.

Sitting on the sofa, she snuggled into him and rested her head on his chest so she could hear his heartbeat.

"Eva said you had family problems. Care to share?"

"She said too much, and no, I don't wish to talk about it."

"Are you planning to reform your family? Are you still in love with your ex?"

Lennox sat up, dislodging her from his chest and turning to face her. "My personal life is private, and I have no desire to discuss it with you." He picked up his glass and downed a large mouthful.

"Well what did you come round for?"

"I thought that was obvious. The animal side of you is very tempting."

Suddenly, Scarlett was on her feet, nudging the coffee table and knocking over her wine glass. All Lennox could hear was a jumble of words tumbling out of her mouth, whilst her arms gesticulated wildly like a windmill in a gale.

Placing his glass on the side table, he stood up and held her by the shoulders until she focused on his eyes and stopped talking.

"I need you to need the whole of me, not just my body," she finally said.

Lennox released her shoulders and took a step back. He was just about to launch into his free-agent speech, when he heard the front door open.

Wednesday looked weary and unhappily surprised when she walked into the room. Instead of speaking, she turned around and headed for the kitchen. Her head was pounding, and the sight of Lennox with Scarlett had sapped her remaining patience.

Snatching her ringing mobile from her pocket, she found herself speaking to Hunter. Sighing, she returned the mobile to her bag and moved towards the lounge.

"Sorry to tear you love birds apart, but we've got to go to the vicarage. Apparently a very drunk Colin Pollock is hurling abuse at the reverend," she said, looking at the mess on the table and floor.

"Do you both have to go?" asked Scarlett with a pouting mouth.

"That's the way it works," replied Wednesday before turning around and walking out.

Lennox tried to hide his relief from Scarlett as he wrenched himself free from her grip. He called out an apology as he darted out the front door.

Wednesday was already in her car with the engine running and a lit cigarette between her lips. Lennox climbed in, and before he had time to put his seatbelt on, she drove off.

On arriving at the vicarage, they found Colin Pollock, with a bottle of beer in his hand, standing in the front garden, hurling abuse at the reverend, who was leaning out of an upstairs window.

"Be a man, get down here and I'll teach you a lesson," yelled Pollock, punching the air with his flailing arms.

He was unaware of the detectives walking up behind him, and he physically jumped as Lennox placed his hand on his shoulder.

"Let's go and discuss your problem in the car, shall we?" he said, gripping Pollock firmly by the shoulder and elbow.

Pollock wriggled and flinched as he tried to untangle his arm from Lennox's grip, but to no avail. Lennox frog-marched him to the car, and removing the bottle of beer from his clammy hand, put him in the back seat before sitting next to him.

Wednesday talked to George Olong through the window, as he refused to come to the front door. He informed her that he did not wish to press charges, and for the matter to be dropped. Exasperated with how the evening was going, Wednesday returned to her car to see what Pollock had to say for himself.

"It should be him in here, not me," moaned Pollock as Wednesday got into the car.

She wrinkled up her nose as the smell of beer permeated the air, mixed with the lingering whiff of cigarettes. It was reminiscent of the odour in a pub before the ban.

"It's all around the school, you know. The students are full talk about the reverend trying to start a rambling group which was a cover for a satanic cult." He slurred his words and then belched without covering his mouth.

"Did any of the students attend the meetings?" asked Lennox.

Pollock thought for a few seconds before replying. "Well, not exactly. You know what kids are like, a rumour starts and before you know it, they've met the devil himself."

"If that's the case, why on earth are you here hollering at the reverend?"

"Because I got roaring drunk at home and needed someone to yell at." Pollock punched the back of the empty passenger seat with his fist. "I hate living around here. Stuck up people with their spoilt stuck up kids." His shoulders hunched over and he shuddered as he belched again.

"Get him out of my car, he's going to be sick," urged Wednesday, pulling the passenger seat forward.

"I hate two-door cars," replied Lennox as he shoved the delirious man out onto the grass verge.

Pollock landed on his knees on all fours, head bent down like a dog and vomited onto the grass with loud retching sounds.

"I didn't sign up for an evening like this," said Lennox as he noticed vomit splashes on his shoes.

"Obviously not, seeing as you were at my place earlier."

"Have you a problem with that?" he replied.

"No, it's just from where I was standing Scarlett seemed to be a lot more into you than the other way around."

Lennox was in no mood for her analysis, so he scooped up Pollock and threw him into the passenger seat.

The merging smells in the car were turning Wednesday's stomach, causing her to drive at speed to get to his house. Once there, the pair peeled Pollock from the seat and helped him lumber up the path. Lennox took the door keys from Pollock's shaky hands and let them in.

Wednesday put the kettle on, whilst Lennox reclined Pollock on the sofa, without removing his shoes. Wednesday opened several cupboards before she found the mugs. Littered all around her was the debris of a single man, who feasted on ready meals, washed down with copious amounts of beer.

By the time she entered the lounge, Pollock was awake, but complaining of still feeling sick.

"Drink this," she said, placing the coffee on the table. "You're lucky the reverend and his wife aren't pressing charges, although we could still have you for breach of the peace."

"Will the school get to know of my behaviour tonight?" he asked, before taking a sip and grimacing.

"Not unless the reverend tells them."

The detectives left Pollock slumped on the sofa and mumbling into his mug.

The smell of vomit hung around the car as they drove back to Wednesday's place. Lennox looked across at her, but she stared rigidly ahead, chewing on her bottom lip.

"Shall I come in?" he asked as he ran his hand over his hair, which was less spiky due to the dampness in the air.

"Depends on how you intend to behave once inside."

Wednesday parked on her driveway and turned to Lennox.

"Be careful with Scarlett. Don't give me cause to hate you."

Lennox paused then remembered the bottle of wine he had brought earlier. He and Wednesday would cope, he thought to himself, as he followed her in, to be met by a needy, but strangely enticing Scarlett.

Wednesday rolled her eyes, grabbed a glass of milk, and headed to bed. *Alone as always.*

"Had to come back to me, eh?" Scarlett whispered.

"Still had some wine to finish."

"Is this how our relationship is going to be? 'Coz I would like something a bit more regular." She walked her fingers up his chest towards his neck.

"Let's take one day at a time," he replied, grabbing the bottle and leading her upstairs.

# Chapter Twenty-Three

"Where have you been?" snarled Judith Wright as her husband blundered in.

She bumbled down the hallway, knocking into a box of magazines, almost tripping her up. Des suppressed a giggle, which was hard to do with a system full of beer.

As Judith's heavy frame stood in front of him, he could smell alcohol and cigarette smoke, which he had come to associate as her perfume over the years.

"I've been at The Crow, where else?" he replied.

"I don't want none of your cheek. You've been at The Crow all bloody day?"

"I had things to do first, woman, then I played darts. Now I need some grub."

He tried to push past her to get to the kitchen, his own awareness and sense of personal space dulled by alcohol. The push aggravated Judith, stimulating her anger to such a peak that only violence could pacify her inner demons.

She grabbed his wrist and twisted it sharply before pushing it back, causing his knees to buckle. This allowed her to grab hold of his hair and wrench his head backwards. In the melee of his protestations and her verbal tyranny, they both began grappling with each other with their hands; fingernails slicing flesh, muscles flexing and straining.

Before he knew it, Judith grabbed her riding crop, and began beating him wherever she could reach. He bit his lips together to stifle his cries. As he reached out with an arm to try and grab the crop from her, he caught the framed picture of a generic tropical sunset, sending it crashing to the floor.

Above the noise of their scuffles they could hear banging on the wall from a neighbour who was tired of listening to their battles.

"You always have to spoil things," she hissed at him as she held the crop under his chin. "It's your fault we have the police around here so much."

"And I thought it was because of you. Your temper and what you've done to Darren," he replied, pulling himself free and pushing his broad back against the wall.

Judith squared up to him, pushing her body into his, until he felt his lungs constricted.

"I dare you to repeat that," she said through gritted teeth.

"With him out the way, you have more energy to dispense on me."

Judith pulled away from him. Her breathing steadying and her hand slackening its grip on the riding crop. "You don't know what you're talking about. And I hope you haven't been spouting that crap in the pub."

Des shook his head as she backed away to top up her alcohol content in the kitchen. He watched her pour some wine into a mug and knock it back as though it was cold milk. He was not sure what to think anymore, but he knew the beatings would never stop.

Wednesday was disconcerted to find Lennox eating breakfast at the kitchen table. A fresh pot of coffee stood on the worktop. Scarlett was flitting about the kitchen like a nineteen-fifties wife tending to her man's every need. Over the rim of her mug, Wednesday watched Lennox watching Scarlett, with an uncomfortable heaviness in her heart.

"There's a briefing this morning, don't you need to get changed first?" she said.

"I might not bother. That'll get them talking at work, eh?"

His wink towards Wednesday conveyed the message of a childish prank, a school boy joke that only she would be privy to once at the station.

"Like we need to give them more to talk about," she muttered.

Wednesday drove to work, knowing that Lennox was not far behind her, undoubtedly on a high after a goodbye kiss from Scarlett. She focused on the road and turned up the radio. She didn't notice him turn off the road.

Walking towards the station she heard someone calling out her name. It was Claudia's father, Greg Edwards.

"I thought you'd want to know that Claudia's funeral is this Friday. The police normally like to attend, or so I understand."

"Thank you Mr Edwards; it will most likely be me and DS Lennox."

He gave a swift nod of his head as he handed her the black-rimmed invitation.

"Any further forward in finding my daughter's killer?"

"Leads are coming in all the time. We'll get there, sir."

"I'm looking for him too, so you'd better get to him first."

He did not give her the opportunity to say that vigilantism was unlawful. She guessed he already knew that as he marched off with a quickening pace.

Everyone was taking their place as Wednesday entered the Incident Room. She moved quietly around the edge of the tables and took a seat, keeping an eye on the door for Lennox.

When he did finally arrive, she could see he had changed his shirt and tie; she knew he couldn't really cope with wearing a shirt two days in a row. His fastidiousness made her smile.

Hunter, in contrast, was looking fatigued. Dark circles under his eyes spreading further down his cheeks. He called the room to order before pausing to take a sip of coffee to moisten his parched throat.

"We need to narrow the field of suspects. What have we got?"

He looked around expectantly, whilst his team shuffled in their seats or hid behind their coffee mugs.

"Stewart Cleveland is off our list, I would say. His gambling debts are plaguing him, not guilt about murder," said Arlow.

"That would also tie in with the alibi for Dick Pennymore. The gambling club has provided that," added Damlish.

"I suggest we scrutinize the parents of the murdered kids deeper. They must be holding clues or withholding information that would open more leads. I want Arlow and Damlish to re-interview the Wrights and return to the school to re-interview students and staff. Wednesday and Lennox, I want you to visit the Dolbys and the Edwards. Remember, parents always lie."

After Hunter returned to his office, the room broke into a hum of murmuring. Some officers gathered their files and others busied themselves with phone calls. Hunter had demanded progress—he had given them direction—and now they needed to give him some answers.

Arlow and Damlish looked less than happy about revisiting Judith and Des Wright. Jones wandered over to Wednesday and asked her quietly if Lennox was going to the Christmas party.

"I've no idea. You could always ask him yourself."

Jones play-punched her on the arm, unable to hide her glowing cheeks at such a daring suggestion.

"He doesn't bite," Wednesday said, rolling her eyes.

"That's not what I've heard," she replied cheekily before sashaying off.

Lennox had arranged the visits; their first one was to be at the Dolby's house. He was happy to let Wednesday drive, as lack of quality sleep was already catching up with him and he thought he could rest his eyes on the way.

His rest was short lived as he was nudged into action by Wednesday telling him they had arrived.

As James Dolby answered the door, Lennox's eyes watered as he stifled a yawn. He looked apologetically at the bereaved father.

Emily Dolby was waiting for them in the lounge, sitting bolt upright in her over-stuffed chair. She gave a pained smile before offering them a drink, which Wednesday declined on both their behalves.

"You bring us news?" asked Emily quietly.

"I'm afraid not, Mr and Mrs Dolby. We'd like to ask you both some more questions. There may be clues we've overlooked."

Emily's shoulders and head drooped at her response, but James remained upstanding with his eyes fixed upon Wednesday. She asked them to recount the day Tom disappeared.

James stood with his hands behind his back, rising almost imperceptibly up and down on his toes, as he spoke.

He went to work that Wednesday like every other day, nothing special, same dull meeting that he had most days. He had not seen his son at breakfast, as Tom was in the habit of rising late and running to school eating toast along the way. He had seen Tom at dinner time on Tuesday evening, but he was in a sullen mood.

"I told him to buck his ideas up, get an idea of what he wanted to do in the future. Emily wrapped him up in cotton wool. I believe he thought he could live off us forever." James moved to the window and turned his back on everyone in the room.

Emily took the opportunity to recount her last time with her only child. Tom was not a morning person, so she would go into his bedroom at seven and open his curtains, but it would take him another thirty minutes before he would get out of bed.

"He was grumpy when he came downstairs. He'd only grunt when I suggested he eat something. A typical teenager I suppose." A regretful smile touched her lips.

At that point, James turned around and startled everyone by letting out a snorting laugh. "The dead are often seen through rose-tinted glasses, allowing the living to forget difficult and obnoxious behaviour. Emily is offering you that rosy portrait of our son as it is too painful to mention his faults. It feels disloyal."

Emily looked wide-eyed at her husband, disbelieving his words. "You drove him away from us. Always belittling him, never praising his achievements. You never showed him enough love."

She remained seated whilst wringing her hands rapidly. "You wouldn't help me when he was being difficult. It was always up to me to deal with him alone. If he was rude to me in front of you, you never stood up for me or defended me." Tears streamed down her face, pooling in the corners of her mouth. James was unmoved by her exhibition and remained where he was.

"I knew you were blaming me for his death. I was offering him tough love to counter balance the smothering he received from you."

Watching the parental meltdown, Wednesday decided it was time to intervene. She suggested that perhaps they should interview them individually.

"No you don't. You did that last time. We'll be interviewed together or not at all, unless we are under arrest," snapped James.

"This is an informal visit, Mr Dolby. We are happy to speak to you both at once."

Emily dabbed her cheeks with a tissue to compose herself before speaking more candidly about her son. She revealed Tom had a dark side when at home. Her face grew bright red and she could only bear to look at the floor.

"He was always a quiet little boy, never any trouble. It all changed when he started at Markham Hall, I don't know what it was. He just changed."

She sat back in her chair and expelled a long blow of breath. She took a sip of water to moisten her arid mouth. She looked up at James and hesitated, as if waiting for his permission to continue speaking. When he gave no indication as to his emotions, she heaved a sigh before continuing.

"Tom became friends with Darren, and I think it was through him he saw another side of life. A side we'd always shielded him from." She leant forward and whispered, "Domestic violence and alcoholism," before leaning back again.

She paused to blow her nose. "He began to treat us, well, me especially, like uneducated fools who had no understanding of the world we live in."

Out of the corner of her eye, Wednesday could see Lennox tapping his foot in rapid succession and running his hand over the top of his head. In many ways, she felt just as irritated by the slow process of Emily's drawn out memories, but if that was what it was going to take to get to the truth behind their middle class facade, then so be it.

"Darren would come here occasionally, although they would just disappear to Tom's bedroom."

"Could you explain the changes in Tom more clearly," said Lennox, finally speaking to keep himself awake.

"Bad tempered, with quick changing moods for no apparent reason, fluctuating appetite and a lack of respect in the home."

"Sounds very much like a normal teenager."

"You didn't see the look in his eyes when he was shouting. They were full of black venom."

"Do you think drugs were involved?" he asked, although aware that no trace was found in the toxicology screen.

"Tom was too bright to go down that path," interjected James. "But I can't vouch for that Darren. I sometimes noticed a smell of smoke around him. I wouldn't be surprised if drugs were sold from that household."

James was proud of his statement, amplified by jutting out his chin. Wednesday disliked the man's egotistical attitude, but tempered her emotions by remembering he was a grieving father.

"Did you address this issue with him?" she asked.

James rose on his tiptoes, with his hands now stuffed deeply in his pockets. A break in the clouds let a few rays of sun form a halo around his head, catching the few white hairs that were beginning to cluster around his temples.

"Emily would say I was too strict, but I treated him like my own father treated me. He was a military man and he expected order and respect, and I expected the same from Tom. I never mentioned drugs."

He looked towards his wife who was now sitting up straight with her hands clasped in front of her, resting on her tweed covered lap. Her face drained of any colour, and her thin lips tightened as she fought back more tears.

"In truth," she began, "I always thought having children would prove difficult as they never live up to your expectations."

Her husband turned his back on the room again and she shuddered whilst still controlling her tears. Tom's death had driven a gigantic wedge between the parents for Wednesday and Lennox to bear witness to. They found they were left with more question than answers, but the turmoil experienced by the parents was not going to help address their queries.

Wednesday stood up and left them the number of a helpline before she indicated to Lennox that they were leaving. Not a sound could be heard as they closed the front door behind them.

They drove along the tree lined road towards the Edwards' home, with the mellow voice of Joni Mitchell singing in the background. Wednesday pulled the visor down to shield her eyes from the low sun, before leaning over to take a cigarette packet out of the glove compartment. Lennox opened it for her and took one for himself before handing her one.

"What did you make of all that?" he asked before flicking the lighter.

"That even outwardly happy relationships harbour deep secrets and misery. The lesson being—stay single."

Lennox laughed, expelling billows of smoke over the windscreen. "I was thinking more along the lines of the father could have killed his son, perhaps through rage before placing him in the graveyard out of misplaced love and respect."

"Plausible, but that wouldn't explain the other deaths."

"We're not even sure they're all linked at this stage," he replied as he wound down his window slightly.

"I think it would be safe to say that both boys' deaths are."

Wednesday pulled up onto the Edwards' ample driveway before brushing dirty-white ash from her trousers. She popped a mint in her mouth and offered one to Lennox.

Lucinda Edwards answered the door wearing a pebble-grey silk blouse with ruffles around the collar, and a pair of wide-legged, dark grey trousers. Her hair was scraped back from her face, showing off her high cheekbones and hollowed-out cheeks. She wore neutral, but expensive looking makeup and smelt of *Chanel No5*.

"My husband is waiting for you in the lounge, I'll go and make a pot of coffee," she said as she lifted her frail arm and pointed towards the lounge.

"How are you both coping?" Lennox asked.

"We're both dreading the funeral tomorrow. I wonder if Lucinda will cope with it all."

Lucinda walked into the room and Greg leapt up and took the tray from her.

"Have you received any calls, cards, or flowers from the boys who knew Claudia?" Wednesday asked.

"Only a card from the school. The school phoned to ask if some of their students and staff could attend the funeral."

"We'll be there to observe who attends and how they react, but we'll be discreet."

"This all feels like a nightmare. I wake up each morning thinking she's in her bedroom and that this is all a mistake," Lucinda said quietly.

"There was nothing untoward on her laptop. Her social networking showed nothing more than innocent banter between friends and school acquaintances. This leads us to believe she knew her assailant rather than meeting up with a stranger from the net."

"Thank God for that," sighed Greg. "A stranger felt like it was her fault."

"Once again, our sincere condolences and we'll be in the background tomorrow. We'll see ourselves out."

On their way back to the station, they hoped that Arlow and Damlish had had better luck at the Wright's and the school, but doubts dogged them.

"We're missing something," said Wednesday, watching the road through the windscreen wipers that sloughed away the downpour.

"I suspect it's well hidden under the web of lies fabricated by one or two of the community members around here," he replied.

"So, are you pursuing a relationship with Scarlett?"

"You women like the relationship word. I'm still fragile and untrusting of women."

"Not fragile enough to resist sleeping with her."

"I didn't say I didn't need sex, that's a different matter altogether.

Why spoil things by turning sex into a relationship?"

Wednesday bit her tongue for the rest of the journey.

Back at the station, no one had had any luck with the families. The atmosphere was stale and leaden with frustration.

"What about Markham Hall?" asked Hunter, taking out a packet of mints from his jacket pocket.

"Nothing new," replied Arlow. "A group are attending the funeral tomorrow, and gossip is rife about Claudia being an offering in a cult ritual."

"We know where that idea sprang from," he said, looking over towards Wednesday. "Wednesday and Lennox, you two to cover the people attending the funeral, and Arlow and Damlish take down all car registrations for a search enquiry."

His abrupt manner always left a tense atmosphere in the room.

Wednesday followed Lennox to his office.

"What are you doing after work?" she asked casually.

"I'm seeing my sons. Taking them out for dinner."

"What a coincidence, I'm having dinner at Mum's. I'm hoping to drag Scarlett along."

Wednesday drove home with the thoughts of attending another child's funeral in the morning—the sight of a small coffin never failed to bring a lump to her throat.

The inky sky offered intermittent glimpses of the stars, and the smell of cigar smoke lingered on her jacket, reminding her how every action left a lingering trace in a lifetime.

The aroma of bacon wafted towards her on opening her front door. Scarlett was singing in the kitchen.

"Have you forgotten that we're eating at Mum's tonight?"

"No, I just fancied a bacon sandwich. Do you want one?"

"No thanks, I'm going to get ready and I suggest you do the same, we're leaving in an hour."

Wednesday trudged upstairs and threw her jacket on her bed. Her feet were cold and achy, and she longed to soak in the bath. She rubbed the back of her neck in an attempt to ease the stiffness.

Oliver let the pair in and embraced each one warmly. The smell of beef casserole and dumplings infused the air making Wednesday's stomach growl.

Strolling into the lounge they found Joan sitting by the fire with a medicated vagueness about her. The orange glow from the wood-burning stove reflected off her skin, and her partially white hair was gathered in a bun on the top of her head.

Scarlett gave her mother an over-exuberant squeeze, and Wednesday bent down and kissed her tenderly on her forehead. Joan took hold of both of their hands and looked up at them.

"My beautiful daughters; you look tired Wednesday, and you, Scarlett, you look otherworldly."

Wednesday sensed that her mother's mind was not settled, and that perhaps madness connected with madness, hence her bizarre observation of Scarlett. Before the whirlwind of conversation could begin, Oliver announced that dinner was ready so they all trooped to the kitchen and took their places.

"So, how's work?" he asked as he served the steaming casserole.

"Painfully slow. Three victims and numerous suspects."

"Still don't think my cult idea is viable?"

Oliver and Wednesday glared at Scarlett for mentioning the subject that so clearly had Joan on edge. Scarlett was oblivious to their reproaches and Joan began repeatedly tapping the knife on the edge of the plate.

"Are you going to start painting again, Mum?" Wednesday enquired, passing a plate to Scarlett.

Joan shook her head and stuck her fork into a chunk of beef, which she then moved around in the syrupy gravy. Her breathing sounded laboured as she pushed the air out through her nose.

"I'm making more bowls and vases ready for Christmas," piped up

Oliver, trying to fill the void in the room.

People around the table nodded in silent approval.

The meal was eaten amidst unasked questions. Joan and Scarlett were both drinking too much wine, and although they all knew Joan should not drink at all, they avoided confrontation.

"I still think an underground cult has infiltrated Markham Hall and is picking off the students, one by one. Why are the police resisting such a plausible suggestion? Perhaps you're all afraid of delving into that murky world?" whispered Scarlett.

"We're not afraid of any such thing. You have no evidence to substantiate your claim. You went to London to find tenuous connections, but this is Cambridgeshire, not an inner city suburb in the capital."

Wednesday pushed her plate away, leaving some casserole, and took out her packet of cigarettes. Scarlett frequently cut her appetite by her words or behaviour. Wednesday scraped back her chair and walked over to the back door to light her cigarette.

Joan was reaching out for the wine bottle, when Oliver's hand rested gently on her wrist. Without saying a word, he pushed the bottle out of her reach and then took her hand and placed it on his lap, giving it a reassuring squeeze.

"Perhaps they'll come for me and relieve you all of the madness I inflict upon you." Joan's gaze travelled around the room touching each face and seeking their response.

"Mum, we want you to be around us, don't we?" replied Wednesday.

As Wednesday was the designated driver, Scarlett allowed herself to drink several large glasses of wine, which had done nothing but accentuate her elevated mood.

Wednesday stubbed out her cigarette in a flower pot by the back door, and announced they were going as she had an early start in the morning. In truth, she believed a monster was lurking in the room and she wanted to get out before it sank its teeth into her.

"Is Jacob working with you tomorrow?" Scarlett asked.

"Yes. Why?"

"Just wondered if he'd be free tonight?"

Wednesday rolled her eyes then kissed Joan and Oliver before jangling her car keys at Scarlett and walking into the hallway.

"She can be so boring and controlling at times," uttered Scarlett as she flounced around the table offering hugs and kisses to her parents.

"She has a tough job, love," said Oliver, holding her head between his cupped hands.

Scarlett shrugged her shoulders and waved theatrically as she caught up with Wednesday.

"Come on, trouble, let's get you home."

In the car, both women were thinking about Lennox, and both wondered whether he was thinking about them.

# Chapter Twenty-Four

Scarlett descended to the kitchen half wrapped in her dressing gown, with her mane trailing in knotted tangles over her shoulders. Wednesday pushed a mug of coffee across the table and announced she was off to work.

"Send my regards to Jacob," she said as she raised her mug in the air.

Lennox was already at the coffee machine when Wednesday walked in. He looked his usual dapper self, wearing the appropriate attire for a funeral. She wanted to ask him about his evening, but something in his demeanour recommended that she did not.

Arlow walked over to join them with a report in his hand.

"Forensics found a hair belonging to Colin Pollock on the travel blanket, which would have been a lead had he not been the one to bring it in."

"We could bring him in on that," said Damlish, who had arrived just behind.

"It would be inadmissible in court as we don't know when the hair got there. He's still worth watching, I suppose," replied Lennox.

Arlow and Damlish dispersed to their desks as Lennox watched Wednesday getting a coffee. Rubbing his hands together, he waited for her to take her first sip before addressing her.

"I got talking to a parent of a student at Markham Hall, and apparently, Colin Pollock had put himself forward as a candidate for the deputy head post several months ago, but went out in the first round due to non-acceptance by the parents on grounds of not being of the right class."

"And you think he's killing the kids for revenge?" replied Wednesday, screwing up her nose at the bitterness of the coffee.

"Not exactly, it's a flimsy motive. Nevertheless, that was never brought up in any of the interviews."

"There may be no significance in it. Did your evening go as planned?" She added.

"Just about. What about you?"

"Family evenings can be a tornado of emotions."

"More like a cauldron where mine are concerned," he mused.

It was time to leave for the funeral, and Lennox offered to drive. The weather was appropriately dull with a soupcon of drizzle in the air.

They parked a distance away from the church due to the number of cars already there. It looked like the entire community had come out to say their farewells to Claudia; a much larger turn out than for Tom Dolby. They saw Arlow and Damlish parking a little way behind them.

Wednesday and Lennox followed the chain of people filing into the cold stone church. Through the countless heads before them, they caught sight of the coffin on which rested an opulent wreath of white peace lilies and shiny evergreen foliage.

The wooden pews were full, so the detectives stood next to a pillar at the back, positioning themselves so they could see the last mourners arriving. Hushed mutterings were heard over the church organ as fellow students from the school filed in, lead by Colin Pollock. People shuffled and jostled around to get a space, rubbing shoulders and bumping elbows. The reverend looked pensive as he stood next to the coffin, clasping his hands together in a prayer-like position.

People looked towards Greg and Lucinda Edwards but avoided eye contact.

Scarlett entered and positioned herself at the other side of the church, with her notebook in hand. Wednesday saw her.

Her train of thought was interrupted by the reverend welcoming everyone. He faulted through the motions of expressing the sorrow felt in the community, not only for Claudia, but for her family and friends, too.

Everyone they had interviewed was there, excluding Stewart Cleveland, who was either late—or not coming at all. Even the Dolbys were there, putting themselves through the intense sentiments once more; each scene and Bible reading reminiscent of Tom's funeral. There were unrecognisable faces, which were no doubt contacts and friends of the Edwards from London.

The hymn "Abide with Me" was sung in harmony, thanks to the few remaining choir members led by Vera Olong. However, the tuneless drone from the students was loud enough to dispel the serenity of any hymn.

The congregation were sitting down when the peace was disturbed by the sound of Stewart Cleveland pushing through the crowd.

Everyone turned around to see what the commotion was all about, and when Lucinda Edwards saw him, she let out an ear piercing squeal echoing around the stark, stone walls. Greg Edwards held onto his wife's arm and tried to calm her.

"You should have protected my daughter. It's your school, you're to blame."

Lucinda was animated and in the domain of the church, she looked like a ghost revisiting her pile of decaying bones festering in the crypt.

Cleveland's face shone with droplets of sweat. He was clearly rankled by her outburst. Nevertheless he had the audacity to maintain his head high, and remain in the church. People shuffled away from him and began looking at him with contempt.

He remained mute and Lucinda was finally soothed by her husband, in time to follow her daughter's coffin back down the aisle towards the cemetery.

Mourners lined the abyss that was ready for the coffin, heads bowed and hands clasped together. Wednesday and Lennox stood back from the scene, surveying the ensemble and waiting for the coffin to be finally laid to rest.

Clusters of people began drifting away, including Stewart Cleveland, who had the decency not to stand centre stage. He briefly caught Wednesday's eye before looking down towards the gravel path. In that instant, Wednesday sensed a tinge of remorse in his eyes.

Oliver paced up and down while he listened to Joan babble on incessantly about any subject that entered her mind. He could not face eating yet more sandwiches, he longed for some hot food—specifically fish and chips. The fish shop was a ten minute walk each way, plus waiting time. He wondered whether Joan would hold out that long, without causing damage to herself or the environment.

He was so preoccupied that it took him several moments to realise someone was at the door. Eagerly, he dashed to the door and found a stranger standing there.

"Hello, I'm Reverend George Olong, I wonder if I could come in?"

Oliver and religion did not normally mix, but desperation made him waver from his usual route. He allowed him in and led him to the kitchen, where Joan was sitting and still talking.

"I heard about your plight from a parishioner, Nina Prince, who has a large collection of your pottery. Anyway, I thought I'd drop by and see if I could offer some support in one way or another."

Oliver hesitated, looking to his wife for some advice, knowing that she was incapable of delivering. Impulsively, he grabbed his coat and announced that he was off to buy their lunch. Joan stopped talking and watched her husband leave. She looked towards the reverend and then back at the front door closing.

"Now why don't I make us a nice cup of tea," he said as he looked for the kettle.

Forty minutes later, Oliver returned to find the front door ajar. Sure that he had shut it when he left, he stepped inside and called out to Joan. Embarrassingly, he could not remember the reverend's name.

The silence unsettled him. Dropping the bag of fish and chips on the floor, he hurried towards the kitchen, only to find it deserted. Two mugs, half full of cold tea, stood on the table. He wondered whether they were in the garden, even though he knew it was too cold for Joan, especially without her daffodil-yellow duffle coat which he saw hanging on a peg in the hallway.

Oliver's vision began to blur as he rushed from room to room, calling out to his wife. After running up then back down the stairs, he sped into the garden, out of desperation, to see if they were there. Joan was nowhere to be seen and neither was the reverend.

He trembled as he dialled Wednesday's mobile number, feeling light-headed waiting for her to pick up.

# Chapter Twenty-Five

The Edwards' home was filled with family and friends after the funeral. Although Lucinda had used caterers to supply a buffet, no one touched the food.

Greg circulated the room thanking people for their support. Lucinda was upstairs in Claudia's bedroom, staring out at the garden that was also in mourning. She did not want a house full of people; she wanted to be on her own to feel the presence of her daughter by her side.

The faint smell of patchouli clung to the air and the sight of Claudia's jewellery and hair accessories made Lucinda's heart lurch towards the pit of her stomach. She allowed her fingertips to brush over the dressing table that was spilling over with makeup and perfume bottles. There was so much hope for Claudia's future, and now it had faded away along with Lucinda's marriage.

She found herself thinking about the grandchild she could have had—another part of Claudia that had been so tantalisingly close. Why had she allowed it to be discarded like an unwanted piece of clothing?

"I thought I'd find you in here," Greg said from the bedroom doorway. "Some of the guests want to leave, but they wish to see you before they go."

Lucinda turned around and realised that the man standing there could no longer offer her the comfort, or the strength she needed to plough on with her pointless life. Nevertheless, she followed him downstairs to exhibit her grieving heart for all to see.

Back at the station, Wednesday and Lennox were mulling through the various possible motives for the three deaths.

"I don't buy the homophobic attack on Tom Dolby. There's no evidence he was gay, and there are no reports of a homophobic element within the community," Lennox said as he balanced on the back two chair legs.

"Okay, but what about Claudia's pregnancy? There's a motive straight away," replied Wednesday as she doodled on a scrap of paper.

"Right, but she'd had a termination, so what was the point in killing her, and in such a brutal manner?"

"Perhaps the father wanted her to keep the baby? We're almost certain the same person murdered the two boys—right? But we're unclear about the girl . . ."

"Different method—I know," interrupted Lennox. "Are we looking at two murderers that are working together? I understand that with couples who kill, the violence intensifies as they progress. Perhaps that's the path we should be taking?"

As Wednesday spun the thoughts around her mind, her mobile rang. She answered it and listened to the stream of words which flowed so hard, it took her a few seconds to compute what Oliver was saying.

"Maybe they've gone for a walk?"

Wednesday could hear in his voice that he was not satisfied with her answers but she did not want to convey her concerns about the reverend.

"Why don't you phone the vicarage and see if they are there. Let me know all is well, yes?"

Oliver reluctantly agreed to take her advice, but what he really wanted was for Wednesday to assist him.

"Trouble?" enquired Lennox.

"Mum has gone somewhere with the reverend, and Oliver is going spare. I'm not happy about it myself, but now is the wrong time."

Alex Green tapped on Wednesday's office door.

"Results have come in from the coated fabric found on Darren Giles's body. Its shower curtain material."

He waited for Wednesday to respond—he was barely aware of Lennox. Wednesday was slow off the mark, so he continued.

"It would suggest that the body was wrapped and transported in a shower curtain."

Wednesday thanked Alex and waited for him to leave, which after hovering and going slightly red, he finally did.

"I think he idolises you," said Lennox.

Wednesday chose to ignore him.

Once upon a time, they could have canvassed local shops to see if someone had recently bought a shower curtain; but with the internet, it had become a much harder task.

"We could visit all our possible suspects and check their showers. No sign of mildew could mean it's a new purchase," Lennox said.

Racing out of the office, she checked her mobile and hoped that Oliver had found her mother.


Oliver decided to search for Joan himself as it was his fault she had gone missing. The smell of fish and vinegar in the hallway turned his stomach, so he kicked the bag to one side, scattering chips as he left the house.

He wanted to call Wednesday again and he thought about calling Scarlett for a brief moment. He did neither.

Whilst walking towards the common, he tried the vicarage again, hoping someone would answer this time. He let it ring until finally someone picked up.

"Thank God . . . sorry . . . this is Oliver Willow, is my wife Joan there?"

"I'm so sorry; my husband had to rush to the bedside of a dying parishioner. I drove over to your house to look after your wife, but when I arrived, I couldn't find her. I thought perhaps you had got back and had taken her out," replied Vera.

Oliver hung up and scanned the expanse of land stretching out before him. Wisps of low cloud skirted the horizon, but the only person he could see was a lone dog walker. He ran up to them and asked if they had seen a woman walking about, but the walker just shook his head.

Guilt flooded his senses and nausea washed over his stomach. He knew he had not always been a good husband, but now he felt he had truly let her down.

# Chapter Twenty-Six

Wednesday and Lennox decided to visit each person involved in the cases in one way or another. They did not phone in advance, preferring the element of surprise to hopefully assist them in catching someone out.

They called in on the Dolbys first. Mrs Dolby answered the door, but she had long since stopped looking hopeful of closure. She let them in quietly, advising them that her husband was resting upstairs; she did not appear phased when they asked to see the bathroom. She remained at the bottom of the stairs as they located the room and found that the Dolbys had a shower unit with plastic sides—no curtain.

The black shadows under Emily Dolby's eyes looked like sooty thumb smudges. The strain of recent events was etched onto her face, with furrowed lines marking each tearful day.

"It's funny," she said as she turned towards Wednesday. "I struggled with being a mother, and now that I no longer am I miss it. I wish I'd known that before."

They apologised for the intrusion, and slipped out without disturbing her husband and without being able to turn back the time for Emily.

Their next stop was the Edwards residence. Lucinda answered the door and explained that her husband was staying in London for the time being. Her diminutive figure was dressed in a black silk shift dress and black patent court shoes. Her fingers were void of all rings, and around her neck hung a delicate, gold crucifix.

"Why do you wish to see the bathroom?"

"We're looking for something that will match with one of the crime scenes," replied Wednesday, keen to get in and get out as soon as they could.

The Edwards' bathroom turned out to be a wet room designed in black marble, with no curtain in sight. Lucinda showed them the en suite, but that only contained an ornate free-standing bath, a toilet, and a sink.

"Will you still catch the person who killed my daughter?"

Wednesday smiled wanly. "Are you coping on your own, Mrs Edwards? Is your husband back soon?"

"He'll be away for a while, but I'm coping thanks." She closed the front door softly behind them as they left.

"I didn't expect to find anything in either of the houses," said Wednesday as she reached into the glove compartment and pulled out a packet of cigarettes.

"We've still got four more places to visit. Shall we do the Wright's next?"

With her cigarette pinched between her lips, Wednesday climbed into the car and headed for the other end of Lavendly village. The village was split in half by a cricket green and a whitewashed cricket pavilion, which was used for village fetes and charity cricket matches. But now, the once chocolate-box village felt tainted by the deaths of the children, and it felt like the serenity could only be reformed once the perpetrator had been castigated from their *environ*.

They hoped they would be lucky to find only the wife at home. Lennox knocked on the door several times before it was opened by Des Wright.

He said nothing and let them in. Judith staggered to the kitchen door and asked them what they were doing.

"We need to see your bathroom, Mrs Wright."

With a wild flourish, Judith waved them upstairs. They pounded up the stairs two at a time like panthers and found the bathroom. It smelt damp thanks to the wet towels thrown in a heap on the floor by the bath. An overhead shower hung over the taps, dripping incessantly, leaving a lime scale mark on the bottom of the bath. A shower curtain was hanging on a rail over the bath. On inspection, there was so much soap scum and grim on the curtain, it looked much older than a couple of weeks.

They heard footsteps bumbling up the stairs before the smell of alcohol arrived at the door.

"Find what you wanted?" asked Judith.

"Is this the only bathroom in the house?"

Judith's head lolled backwards as she let out a throaty laugh. "Of course it is. It's not bloody Buckingham Palace."

As Wednesday continued inspecting the shower curtain she spotted tiny flecks of what looked like blood. Moving closer, she felt Judith move closer, too, until they were both tight up against the bath. Wednesday signalled to Lennox.

"We're going to need to take this with us," she said as she began unhooking the curtain.

"Whatever for?"

When Wednesday pointed out the flecks of blood, Judith told her that Des shaved in the shower, frequently cutting himself.

"That may be the case, but we'll let forensics clarify that."

"Whatever," replied Judith before bumbling downstairs.

The detectives left the house with Judith calling out a derogatory farewell to them.

Lennox slung the bagged evidence in the boot before getting in the passenger side.

Since losing his job at Markham Hall School, they expected to find Stewart Cleveland at home, and they were not disappointed.

After buzzing them in, he waited for them at his front door. His usual well-groomed appearance had been replaced by a shabby look that aged him. His cheeks had hollowed out and his eyes were set deeper in their sockets.

"Can't leave me alone?"

"We're checking out a lead that requires us to search the bathroom," replied Lennox.

Cleveland tilted his head and stepped back to let the pair in. Books had been taken off shelves and strewn around the lounge. He noticed the detectives eyeing the disorder and advised them that he was spending his free time revisiting the literary classics.

In the bathroom, they found a bath with a shower attachment on the taps; there was a shower rail, but no curtain.

"I hate shower curtains; they stick to the wet body and irritate the crap out of me. The floor gets wet though; see that damp patch in the corner?"

"When did you last have a curtain?" asked Lennox as he peered at the mould.

"I don't know, maybe a year ago. Why the interest?"

The detectives declined to respond and continued looking around the compact space. Cleveland stood in the doorway waiting to see their next move.

"Are you going to tell me what this is about or are you searching around aimlessly?"

"How's the fraud investigation going?" replied Lennox, eager to wipe the grin from Cleveland's face.

"Touché," he uttered.

Their next stop was the vicarage, and Vera Olong looked incensed when she opened the door to find them standing there. The request to see the bathroom was received with resigned irritation. She took them upstairs and showed them her bathroom.

"I hope you find all in order," she quipped.

They found a roll-top Victorian bath in the centre of the room but no shower in sight. She then showed them her husband's bathroom which was less elegant and rather more functional. However, it looked like a new shower curtain hanging on the rail over the bath. Just then, George Olong emerged behind them and enquired about their visit.

"New shower curtain, Reverend?" Wednesday asked.

"I have absolutely no idea. Perhaps the housekeeper put a new one up. Vera may know." He looked towards his wife with expectant eyes.

"I know nothing about it," she said, turning towards the detectives.

"Do you still have the old one?" Wednesday asked.

"I doubt it. I imagine it's been thrown out, and the dustbin men have already been this week. Is it important?" Vera asked. "Possibly," replied Lennox, brushing past the reverend and heading downstairs. "Are the bins out the back?" he called.

Once located, he was disappointed to find that the bin was indeed empty. He slammed the lid down and waited for Wednesday to reappear.

"Reverend, have you heard if my mother got home safely?"

"No I'm afraid I haven't. I'm sorry . . ."

"I feel it's my fault," Vera interrupted. "If I'd got there sooner, perhaps she wouldn't have wandered off." Vera's face glowed and she twisted her wedding band around and around her finger. "Perhaps George should have waited until I got there . . . Hind sight I suppose."

"Well, hopefully Oliver has found her by now," replied Wednesday, checking her mobile to see if she had a message.

Lennox hooted the horn as he sat in the car, impatient to move on to the next place.

"So we have two missing curtains and one blood splattered one," said Lennox, slipping a cigarette between his lips. "Any thoughts?"

"We still have to check out Dick Pennymore's residence before I formulate a theory. Nothing's conclusive as far as I can see. Perhaps forensics will come up with something on the blood."

"Gives you an opportunity to see Alex again."

"I think you're on the wrong track there, Alex only sees me as a work colleague, as I do him. Besides, I'm older than him."

Wednesday dialled Oliver's number and waited for him to pick up.

"Have you found Mum?"

"No, and I'm getting frantic, it'll be getting dark soon. You know how she hates the dark . . ."

"Look Oliver, stay at home in case she returns. Leave all the lights on for her to see."

"I think the police should be involved. I know you want to keep her illness a secret, but I can't think what else to do."

Wednesday knew he was right, and assured him that after the next visit she would get onto it.

Dick Pennymore was busy receiving barrels of beer at the back of the pub, and was unaware of the detectives' arrival. They watched him for a few minutes before grabbing his attention.

"And what can I do for you two?"

"We'd like to see your bathroom, please," said Wednesday.

"Strange request. Up the stairs, second on your left, I haven't time to show you. Knock yourselves out."

The living quarters above the pub was decorated in the same russet brown as downstairs. Plaster cornices were painted in gaudy gold, and an old jukebox stood in the corner of the lounge area. The air was scented by a couple of overflowing ashtrays on the coffee table, next to a pile of tabloid newspapers and used betting slips.

They walked down the dimly lit corridor and found the bathroom. It looked like it had not been cleaned since his wife died three years ago. The toilet seat remained in the upright position, and the mirror was marked with splashes of shaving foam and toothpaste. An avocado coloured bath fitted down one side of the room, and a matching toilet and sink occupied the other side. There was no shower or curtain to be seen.

"Waste of time," Lennox said as he headed downstairs, buttoning up his coat.

Lennox drove as Wednesday called the station and spoke with Maria Jones.

"Could you organise a few patrols to look for my mother, I'll send you a photo from my mobile. And call Oliver to discuss location."

Wednesday knew she could trust Jones to be discreet for the time being, but she knew the family elements she wished to keep secret could soon be divulged. Hunter could soon be privy to the madness that lay within her bloodline.

Wednesday watched the countryside flash by as she stared out the window. The bare branches on the trees extended their witch-like fingers towards the inhospitable sky. Thoughts turned to how frightened and cold Joan must be, and guilt swelled in her chest.

"Can we go back to the vicarage?" she asked.

"We can, but what for?"

"I want to take another look at the reverend's bathroom. I just want to check something that didn't seem quite right."

# Chapter Twenty-Seven

Scarlett put the phone down with her father's words still ringing in her ears. Her mother was out on her own and emotionally unstable. He had not the time for her to unfurl her own emotional distress on to him— Joan came first.

She had phoned in sick at work and had remained in bed until Oliver's phone call. She padded down to the kitchen and pulled a banana from the bunch. After two mouthfuls, she put the rest of the banana on the worktop and returned to bed, where she pulled the quilt over her head and hummed to herself.

Lucinda Edwards was surprised when her husband's car pulled onto the drive. He had not said he was returning so soon. She was unsure whether she should greet him at the door for old time's sake, or whether she should act out the new role life had thrust upon her. Her thoughts took so long to process that Greg was already in the door by the time she had decided what to do.

"I need some more clothes," he said without giving her eye contact.

He ran up the stairs, two by two, and filled the empty suitcase he had brought with him. She knew she was being selfish, but she could not stop herself from climbing the stairs and entering the bedroom.

"I'm not asking for us to try and keep the marriage going, but I detect that you are extremely angry with me over something, and I thought we should clear the air before solicitors get involved."

Greg folded some trousers and placed them neatly in the suitcase whilst he mulled over thoughts he found so difficult to put into words.

"I can't stop myself from blaming you for Claudia's death. You led me to believe she was purely studious, not an inkling about boys orbiting around her. Why did you do that?"

Lucinda sat on the edge of the king size bed. "You refused to acknowledge that she was growing up, that you would no longer be the only man in her life. You saw any boy as competition for her love. It wasn't right. Your love crossed boundaries it shouldn't have."

Greg turned towards her, red faced and fists clenched. "Don't you dare tell me what I can and can't think. You know me very little, very little indeed."

"I don't see how I can be blamed for her death. We were her parents . . ."

"But you kept secrets from me about her life. What else have you kept from me?"

He twisted the polo top he was holding so tightly, that it looked like an elongated sausage. Lucinda traced the cornrow patterns in the plush carpet with her eyes as she toyed with telling him everything. Perhaps he already knew?

"Perhaps some things are better left unsaid. No need to sully your memories," she whispered.

"My memories are already tainted thanks to you and your incompetent parenting skills. My mother always said you were style over substance."

Lucinda prickled with anger at being made to feel inferior to the Edwards' standards. She could fell him with one swoop, or she could protect her dead daughter's innocence, but as Greg headed towards the bedroom door to leave her forever, she chose to speak.

"She had a termination."

Greg stopped in the doorway and dropped the suitcase from his hand.

"It occurred to me that the baby was perhaps yours," she continued.

He walked up to her and struck her across her face before collecting his suitcase, running downstairs and slamming the front door. She knew she would never see him again, and that she would never know the answer to her question.

The reverend's car was no longer in front of the vicarage when Wednesday and Lennox arrived, but undeterred they rang on the bell hoping to find Vera in.

After awhile, they heard footsteps and then saw Vera peering through the window. She looked flustered and initially refused to open the door.

"He's not here, he's seeing parishioners," she called from behind the door.

"Never mind, we just need access to his bathroom again," replied Wednesday, anxious to get in.

"I'm not really sure if I should let you in. You seem to have it in for my husband. He's a man of God, a good man."

"I'm not passing judgement on him, Mrs Olong, I just want to see the bathroom again."

Vera opened the door with her head held high. "Should my husband get a solicitor?"

"Not unless you think he'll need one," replied Wednesday before darting upstairs.

"What are we looking for exactly?" asked Lennox.

"The curtain wasn't sitting right somehow. Looked like it was put up in a hurry."

She was right. Some rings had been missed so the curtain was hanging unevenly. As she studied the rings carefully, she found tiny fragments snagged underneath the new shower curtain.

"Look at these, Lennox. I wonder if these would match up with the fragments found by forensics. Pass me an evidence bag, will you."

Vera stood in the doorway, silently watching the proceedings with her hands clasped together. Tears began to creep into her eyes.

"Is he in trouble?"

"I don't know right now, but I would appreciate him remaining in the local vicinity for the time being."

"I hear the Edwards are getting a divorce," said Emily Dolby to her husband as he passed her a cup of tea.

"I don't take too much heed of local gossip, and neither should you."

"The death of a child has many repercussions on a family, that's all I'm saying."

James stood by the fireplace with his hands in his pockets, staring at the school photo of Tom on the mantelpiece. "Do you regret that Tom was our only child?" he asked her.

Emily sipped her tea, hoping the silence would be a substitute for an answer.

"Maybe you're glad we only had the one, seeing as you found parenting hard work sometimes." He turned to look at her as he spoke.

"This is a pointless conversation, James. We can neither change nor hope for a different past or future. We have what we have, and that's it."

As Emily rose up to leave the room, James followed her with his eyes, unsure of whom his wife had become or ever was. He missed Tom very much.

As soon as they reached the station, Lennox took the evidence down to forensics, whilst Wednesday sought out Jones to get an update regarding her mother.

"No news I'm afraid. If you're really worried I suggest you talk to Hunter, get some more officers out there."

Wednesday thanked her before seeking refuge in her office. She dialled Oliver's number and he answered after a couple of rings.

"Mum not back then?" she said as she slumped in her chair.

"No, and now it's dark. Where the hell is she, Eva?"

"I have no idea. Have you checked her friends, or the hospital?"

"I've checked everywhere and everyone."

"I've got a few things to get finished here; then I'll come over to you."

Lennox knocked at her door and entered. "I thought you could do with this," he said, putting a mug of coffee on her desk. "Any news on your mum?"

Wednesday shook her head, nursing the mug of hot liquid between her hands. "Everything is guiding us to the reverend, but I can't help thinking it's being done on purpose."

"You don't think he's guilty?"

"I'm not convinced, but I'm not sure who's doing the guiding. Everything is whirring around in my head."

"I think you should get off to Oliver, you two could work better together to find her. I'll cover you."

Wednesday thanked him and left the office before Hunter could see. Lennox had quite a big heart under his big ego, she thought to herself.

Oliver rushed to the front door when he heard it open, only to stop in his tracks when he saw Wednesday walk in alone.

"Sorry, it's only me."

"Don't be sorry love. I'm just glad you're here."

When her mobile rang, their hearts bounced into their mouths. It was Alex Green.

"I've matched the fragments of shower curtain from the vicarage to the ones found on Darren Giles's body," he began, "but there's more, excuse me . . ."

Wednesday pulled her ear away from the phone as Alex sneezed.

"Sorry. Anyway, I found some partial prints on both the fragments around the body, and they belong to a Colin Pollock."

Wednesday hung up before dialling Lennox's number.

"I was just about to call you," he said, "Colin Pollock's up a tree threatening to hang himself."

They agreed to meet in the woodland by the cemetery. She was about to apologise to Oliver, but he shook his head and waved her off.

# Chapter Twenty-Eight

Wednesday and Lennox found Colin Pollock easily, thanks to the blue lights flashing through the bare trees. As they approached the huge tree in the centre of a clearing, they saw Pollock sitting on a thick branch with a noose around his neck and the other end of the rope tied around the branch.

A fire officer approached the detectives. "As soon as he jumps, the squad car will drive under him then we'll get up and cut the rope. That's the plan, so it's over to you to try and get him down without the noose."

"Mr Pollock," she called up, "can we talk things through before you take an irreversible drop."

"I have nothing to say. Just leave me alone," he shouted back. Although it was cold, his face sparkled as the tiny beads of sweat caught the flashing lights.

"You know we can't do that. I'm sure nothing is this bad."

"You know nothing of my problems; I'm too far gone to be saved."

"Admission of guilt can go some way to appease your mental anguish."

Pollock laughed at her for saying something so trite. He knew that his mental anguish would never subside, and that if hell existed, that was where he was heading.

"You have no idea. Things happen right under your noses and still you haven't switched on to what it all means."

"Why don't you fill us in?"

He laughed again and shuffled forward on the thick arm of the tree. Officers around him came alive to his movements, hearts pulsating faster, muscles flexing.

"You only see what you want to see. The thought that behind the banal and so-called normal lives hides something sinister and ugly, is too unpalatable for society."

"Show us the ugly then," coaxed Lennox, stepping closer to the tree.

"Stay right where you are, I don't trust you," shouted Pollock as he rocked on the branch.

"Why don't you talk to us, and we'll stand right here and listen," Wednesday called up.

"Some women think having children will bring them happiness and fulfilment, and then they find out their babies become teenagers and it's no longer fun."

"Are you talking about specific mothers?" asked Wednesday.

"Stop interviewing me and let me talk," he retorted.

Wednesday and Lennox stood side by side in full view of Pollock, and waited for him to continue.

"I would hear mothers complain to me on parents' evenings, at choir practice, and in the street. They said they admired me for working with teenagers; they wanted my support and help. They wanted their children to behave."

"Is that what Tom and Darren were? Unruly teenagers who needed controlling?"

"Something like that, but it was never meant to happen that way."

"Tell us how it was supposed to happen."

Pollock rubbed his hairless head and then beat his fist on his scalp. "I was guided, through a spirit. I messed it up and now I must die."

"You don't have to die, it won't bring them back. We know you were involved as we've found your DNA on the cocktail stick in the hut and fingerprints on the fragments of shower curtain. The right thing to do now is tell the parents what happened so it brings them some form of closure."

Wednesday could feel beads of sweat slithering down her back even though her face and fingers were freezing. The dusk had brought drizzle in the air, and she could sense miniscule droplets clinging to her eyelashes.

"What happened to Claudia? Why was her death so different?" Wednesday persisted.

"She *was* different. She had taken a life and so she had to be punished."

Wednesday wondered how he knew about the termination when Claudia's own father did not know. "That was a violent way to die. Did you act alone?"

"She was numbed by drugs; she wouldn't have suffered as much as she should have."

"You didn't answer my question. Did you act alone?"

"You should look closer to home, DI Wednesday, and just let me die."

Wednesday looked at Lennox, who shrugged his shoulders at first, and then suddenly said, "Your mother, Wednesday, where's your mother?"

Wednesday stepped closer to the tree, disregarding his orders to stay back. "What have you done with my mother?" she said, with her heartbeat pounding in her temples.

"We have all been used in one way or another, and nothing can stop it from moving forward."

She called to him that he was not making sense. She stepped closer again until she was an arm's length away from the sturdy trunk.

"Your mother is having new life breathed into her. Her mental infliction will be expelled from her body, and then the work begins—but not with me—I am to be left behind, I'm no longer needed."

Wednesday's face grew red, how did he know about Joan's illness. She wanted him to jump, but not before telling her where Joan was. She had to play it cool.

"Who no longer needs you? What are you talking about?"

"She now has her own child within. My soul will live as it lives."

Who was pregnant, thought Wednesday. She mulled over the past few hours and remembered the faint smell of vomit in one of the bathrooms they visited. Then she remembered.

"Are you telling me that Vera Olong is having your baby?"

"Bravo, Detective. I'm a castigated father to be."

Lennox moved towards Wednesday and whispered in her ear that he thought they should get to the vicarage.

"Arlow and Damlish can look after this burke," he said, nodding in Pollock's direction.

They jumped into Lennox's car and sped off. Wednesday radioed the station to advise Hunter of their movements, and to request back-up.

Vera's car was parked outside the vicarage, so unless she had gone on foot, they presumed she was in. All the windows were closed and the place was in darkness. Wednesday rang the bell a few times then tried the handle, only to find it locked.

They decided to check the perimeter to see if they could gain access another way. Walking around the back, a beam of light hit the ragged lawn, making them look up towards the source. Squinting in the brightness of the light, they could just make out a shadowy figure appearing from the window in the attic.

"Is that Vera?" asked Wednesday.

"I can't tell. We need to get up there."

"Let us in, we need to talk," called Lennox through his cupped hands.

"I have nothing to say. You won't get me alive."

They recognised Vera's voice.

"Have you got Joan Willow?" called Wednesday.

"I couldn't save your mother's sanity, her madness runs too deep. You should've come to me much sooner."

"Where is she?"

"Up here with me."

A cold sweat encased Wednesday's body, but her mind focused on the task in hand. She had to show she could cope.

Lennox remembered the French windows that could easily be broken into, so he suggested Wednesday keep Vera talking whilst he broke in.

She grabbed him by the arm. "I have to go in. If my mum is up there, only I will be able to reassure her."

Reluctantly, Lennox let her go, on the proviso that she did not put herself in danger.

Wednesday wrapped her scarf around her fist and smashed the pane of glass adjacent to the handle. Slipping in through the French doors she felt her way around in the shadows, almost knocking over a vase in the process. She could hear Lennox talking.

She inched her way along the dark corridor and found her way to the staircase. She crept up as quickly as she could, anxious for Vera not to be warned of her arrival.

Listening to Vera's voice, she mounted the tiny wooden staircase and groped her way to the entrance of the attic. Although the door was closed, chinks of light shone through the cracks in the wooden door. Wednesday strained to see if she could hear her mother's voice, but all was quiet apart from Vera's periodic responses to Lennox.

Wednesday put her ear to the door. Vera had stopped talking and Wednesday could not detect any sounds of movement. Wrapping her hand around the handle, Wednesday gently turned the white ceramic knob and opened the door until she could peer through the gap.

Her eyes had to adjust to the intense light in the room. Gradually she saw Vera standing by the full-length window. In the corner furthest away from her, she spotted a crumpled figure huddled under a blanket.

Wednesday took a deep breath and entered the attic. She looked towards Vera and called out her name. Vera swiftly turned her head then glanced in the direction of the far corner. The bright lights glinted off the butcher's knife she was holding, and cast deep shadows allowing the evil in the room to multiply.

Vera glared at Wednesday then rushed towards the huddled figure. "I couldn't save her," she said, pointing the knife in the direction of Joan.

"How did you try and save her?" asked Wednesday, shuffling forward almost imperceptibly.

"Re-birthing of course. That's the way for people to be cleansed and purified to move forward."

Wednesday's puzzled look made Vera smile. With one hand on the knife and the other on her abdomen, she tilted her head and stared at Wednesday. "You have questions, I can tell."

"What does re-birthing involve?"

"It involves wrapping someone up tightly in a blanket, then lying on top of them to mimic being in the womb. They have to fight their way out of the birth canal to be re-born, without the remnants of trauma from the first birth to cloud their character."

The blanket shifted and both Wednesday and Vera looked towards it. Wednesday bit her lip; it was too soon to make a move.

"Who is present when you do this?"

"I think you already know one person. But he is weak and no longer worthy of my affection."

"You mean Colin Pollock." Wednesday inched forward slowly. "I'd feel happier talking to you if I could come closer."

"Stay where you are. I'm in charge here," Vera hissed as she brandished the knife's thick blade in her direction. "You asked who else was there. Would it surprise you to know that the mothers were there? Mothers are essential at a birth after all."

"Emily Dolby and Judith Wright were there?" Wednesday replied incredulously.

"Emily was a lot more functional than Judith, but they're all the same. They watched as their child struggled in the womb—reliving that fateful day that would change their lives forever."

"Was killing the boys an accident then?"

"I'm not sure. I hate the people around here with their perfect lives as parents. I wanted to be a parent, but my husband was too focused on caring for God's children to have one with me."

"Is that why you set him up, led us to believe he was guilty."

Vera laughed and said he deserved it. The blanket moved again, and Wednesday could no longer resist.

"Let my mother go. You don't need her in here."

"What do I get in return?"

"What are you asking for?"

"I want to keep my baby. I want to finally be the mother I'm supposed to be."

"You won't be able to keep your baby in prison, if that's what you're angling for."

Vera's legs stopped supporting her for a few seconds. Her head dropped so she could see her burgeoning belly which she rubbed in a circular motion. The light caught a silver globe hanging around her neck.

"My husband and his god have made me be this way. If the deaths were accidents I'd get to keep my baby, right?"

"What about Claudia's death. How was that an accident?"

"She deserved it. She was blessed with a baby, and she flushed it out, caring not for the life of the unborn. She had to be punished."

Vera recounted how Colin Pollock knew Claudia's parents would be away, and so he faked his car breaking down and requested to use the phone. "He drugged her and took her to the rambling hut, where I was waiting. He thought we were going to cleanse her through re-birthing." At that moment, she chose to let out a long sigh. She recounted how she found beating Claudia very therapeutic and soothing.

Feeling the moment was right Wednesday moved towards her mother as Vera backed away towards the balcony. Joan stirred on Wednesday's touch. She felt clammy and appeared drowsy, unaware of her surroundings. Wednesday helped her mother to her feet and guided her to the attic door where an officer was waiting to take her to the attending ambulance.

Wednesday found she was able to move closer to Vera, close enough to smell the hint of vomit that followed her around.

"You know there's no way out for you, you've killed three children. You won't be allowed to keep yours."

Wednesday held her hand out which only made Vera move a leg over the balcony rail, so she was perched precariously on the rail.

"Where's George?" she asked.

"I'm here." His voice came from the doorway.

"See what you've done to me," she said, turning to look at him. "I'm going to take you down with me. It's your fault these things happened and there's evidence all over the vicarage linking you to the crimes. Your name will be blackened." The bitterness in her voice was palpable.

"I have a solid alibi for the nights of the murders, Vera," he said as he leant against the door frame, wringing his hands. He was dressed in casual clothes, and smelt of soap.

"Is God your alibi, you miserable excuse for a man?"

"No, my partner and child are. I have a three-year-old son whom I visit regularly. Nancy has always known about you and has been understanding about the situation. I didn't know how to leave you, but you've helped me with that conundrum. I'm also leaving the Church to be with my family. I will serve God another way."

Vera gasped for air as the reverend's words sunk in. She held a hand to her throat, so the sapphire in her engagement ring glinted in the harsh light. "You . . . You have a family?" Vera's high-pitched voice grated the air, and the pain of what she had heard seized her chest so hard she struggled for breath.

"I do, but I'm suffering with the guilt of suspecting you of doing something nefarious and not saying anything to the police. All the rumours in my last parish were because of you. It was never to do with me. I should have spoken up and now these deaths are a heavy burden I'll have to carry in my heart forever."

Wednesday watched as Vera's grip on the rail got tighter, and her hips shifted further over the rail. The reverend's contribution was literally sending her over the edge. Wednesday needed to re-focus Vera's attention on her.

"Was it you who left Scarlett Willow cryptic messages?"

Vera gave a short, mirthless laugh. "I thought I'd have more fun with your sister, but she holds madness within her that translates her fear into nothing but smoke. I thought I could unbalance her mind, but I failed."

Wednesday refrained from answering back and signalled to the reverend to back away.

"I hate the very air you people breathe. The ungrateful and selfish mothers deserved to lose their kids. They couldn't cope with teenage tantrums. I gave them their freedom back and this is how I get thanked—hunted like a witch."

Vera hoisted her other leg over the rail. "I won't let you take this child from me."

Wednesday lurched towards her, arm outstretched, but she was too late.

# Chapter Twenty-Nine

Maria Jones knocked on Wednesday's office door.

"A call has come in, a suspected suicide. Here's the address. Hunter wants Lennox to go with you."

It was another day of constant drizzle, and the ambulance was still outside the house when they arrived. Curtains twitched as they walked up the path to the already open front door.

They found James Dolby standing in the hallway with one hand twisting the hair on top of his head, his eyes red rimmed. He registered their presence after a few minutes.

"I can't believe this. I feel like my life is spiralling towards an abyss."

"Could you tell us what happened?"

He stretched out his arm and handed Wednesday the suicide note left by Emily. In it, she explained her rationale for seeking help from Vera Olong, who seemed to empathise with her difficulties raising a difficult teenager. Vera's suggestion seemed harmless enough, rather like acupuncture. She was so convincing, leading her to believe the re-birthing session would cleanse Tom's soul.

Emily went on to describe the harrowing session, where she witnessed her son struggle under the blanket until ultimately, she and Vera had crushed the very breath out of him. She wanted to stop the process, but she got swept along with it all, and then it was too late.

The letter went on to ask James to forgive her for never wanting to be a mother, and for being a deficient one when Tom finally arrived. For being only half a wife for him, and for bowing out of life in such a way that God would shun her forever.

Wednesday asked to keep the letter as evidence, until her death was confirmed as suicide.

Wednesday and Lennox left as Emily's body was taken away, leaving

James Dolby standing in the middle of the lounge, staring out the window.

"So much misery," said Lennox, climbing into the car and reaching for the packet of cigarettes. "Hunter offered you a few days leave to be with your mother, why don't you take it?"

"Because that would be admitting I'm flawed and couldn't hack it. Hunter would never forget it."

Lennox lit his cigarette.

"Don't you think we smoke too much?" she asked before lighting hers.

# Chapter Thirty

Like every year, an opulent Christmas tree stood at the entrance to the church. Everything looked the same except for the new reverend who was greeting his new parishioners on Christmas Eve. He had been warned of dwindling numbers, but he hoped his blemish-free career would encourage people to return.

A man in a dark grey suit wandered up to the church door and hesitated before accepting the reverend's outstretched hand.

"James Dolby," he said before quietly stepping inside and sitting in a pew at the back. He bowed his head and said a prayer for his son but not for his wife.

People around him shuffled in their pews, averting their eyes.

The reverend watched as a couple moved towards him, swaying as they walked. As they reached him, the smell of alcohol made him flinch backwards before extending his arm to greet them.

Judith Wright paused to speak to him, ignoring his hand. "I hear there's free wine on offer." She sniggered before pushing Des forward.

At the other end of the town, The Crow was crammed with people. Dick Pennymore was happily filling his cash register with money. Rowdy Christmas songs played in the background, and the sound of an occasional party popper pierced through the thick wall of sound. A fire roared and crackled, and groups of young people wearing silly hats and tinsel, giggled and flirted with one another.

In a grey prison cell, Stewart Cleveland sat on the edge of his bunk, with his head in his hands. He contemplated how he had gone from being a headmaster, to a prisoner for fraudulent theft, all thanks to his addiction to gambling. The judge had given him plenty of time to reflect on his actions, and to consider what he could do when he got out.

His cellmate coughed a smoker's hack and turned over in his bunk, making the whole frame rock. Cleveland wrinkled up his nose at the man's rank body odour which sat heavily in the air.

He missed being with his parents for the festive season. They had sent him a meaningless Christmas card, seemingly unable to surmount the deep disapproval they now had for him. He knew his relationship with them had been irrevocably damaged.

Jacob Lennox's parents had gone to a party without him, so he sat in their lounge watching mindless festive drivel on the television and drinking his father's single malt whisky.

Although they had not mentioned it, he knew his parents were desperately missing their grandsons and disappointed in his failure. He feared they may spend some of the holiday analysing his behaviour. He threw another glass of malt down his throat and waited for the feeling of tender warmth to rise up from his stomach to dull the anguish in his heart.

Oliver and Joan's house was filled with the spicy aroma of mulled wine and pork crackling. The large round table was littered with dirty plates, crumpled up napkins, and discarded coloured paper crowns.

The Christmas tree was decorated with remnants of Christmases past. A traditional eclectic mess of vibrant and faded colours tumbled down the branches, ending with an oversized red bow wrapped around the pot.

Joan looked tired and strained; a tremor twitched her head almost constantly. By her side sat Oliver, who had accumulated more grey hair over the past few months. He held her hand, giving it an occasional squeeze.

"Has Jacob mentioned me lately?" Scarlett whispered in Wednesday's ear.

"You're wasting your time with him; he has family issues and a stressful career . . ."

"I know, I know, but I still think we could make a go of it, if only he'd call. Maybe the new year will see us getting closer. Yes, I'm sure of it."

Wednesday sighed and poured herself another mulled wine. Reaching into her bag to retrieve her packet of cigarettes, she found an envelope addressed to her. It was a Christmas card from Alex Green. He wrote that he hoped they would have the opportunity to see more of one another in the new year, and not just over dead bodies and microscopes. She smiled. Perhaps that was why he looked crestfallen when she said she was not attending the Christmas party.

She knew the female contingency of the station were disappointed that Jacob Lennox would also be absent. Undeterred, Jones organised a night at the local curry house in the new year.

She lit the cigarette that was trapped between her pursed lips. Blowing out the smoke, she found herself thinking about her mother and Scarlett, and wondered how long it might be before the monster crept insidiously into her sanitized life.

The Christmas card slipped from her lap turning her thoughts to work and inevitably Lennox. He had turned out to be a reliable colleague. Her only source of concern was his dalliance with Scarlett and where that might lead.

She stubbed out her cigarette and moved to sit by her mother. Nestling into her she allowed herself to be encapsulated by her mother's unconditional love. The only type of love she was capable of accepting. For now.

# Acknowledgements

To James Logan and Jessica Kristie for being continually supportive and encouraging. I treasure you both.

# About the Author

Hemmie Martin spent most of her professional life as a Community Nurse for people with learning disabilities, a Family Planning Nurse, and a Forensic Nurse working with young offenders. She spent six years living in the south of France, and currently lives in Essex with her husband, one teenage daughter, Rosie, one house rabbit, and two guinea pigs. Her eldest daughter, Jessica, is studying veterinary medicine.

Lightning Source UK Ltd.
Milton Keynes UK
UKOW03f0633271213

223628UK00023B/1664/P